EFFORTLESS

A LEGACY NOVEL

BETHANY-KRIS

Published by Bethany-Kris

www.bethanykris.com

eISBN 13: 978-1-988197-50-0

Print ISBN 13: 978-1-988197-49-4

Cover Art © Jay Aheer

Editor: Elizabeth Peters

For the wild-hearted girl who inspired Camilla, and who taught me to love myself when I didn't even know that was possible. Those were some of the best years of my life. Thank you, J.

CONTENTS

CHAPTER ONE

"HOW'S THE Skip's pet doing today?"

"Did the big boss send the little boss to work in the slums with the rest of us today?"

"Oh, too good to look at us, Tom?"

"Sure he is, Randy. Little underboss-in-waiting hates getting his hands dirty, ain't that so, Tom?"

Tommaso Rossi's greatest enemies had always been boredom, and a severe lack of patience when it came to other people. He was easily distracted, but as quickly as his attention could be caught, it was lost. Add that into the fact he didn't like to wait for anything, and it could be a bad combination for a man like him.

He blamed these characteristics of his on his father, Tommas Rossi. The man had given Tom both his name and his restless nature.

It helped that Tom's father had also given him a decent drive to get shit done when it needed to be done. His father, an Italian crime boss for the Chicago Outfit, handed down the wisdom that blunt honesty was a better gift than lies. Deceit would do nothing for his end-game except make him untrustworthy in the eyes of others. A man in the mafia wouldn't benefit from having a stain like being a liar on his back.

Tom worked hard. Constantly. Another lesson from his dad. His last name afforded him a certain amount of respect for some situations in their criminal organization, but it also meant fuck all if he hadn't earned it.

That's why when Adriano Conti's crew members tossed insults and ribbed him with their comments as he strolled through the warehouse, Tom didn't even look at the young guys. Stupid, useless fuckers. Replaceable foot soldiers.

He knew it.

They knew it.

Their words meant less than shit beneath his thousand dollar Italian leather shoes. They weren't going anywhere at the end of the day.

Except maybe jail.

Tom didn't have much issue with letting the comments roll off his shoulders on any other day. He was a secondary Capo working under Adriano—his uncle. Adriano had been Tom's mentor—one of many—for longer than he cared to remember. Before he knew how to drive. Years before he'd ever gotten his dick wet properly. Men like Adriano had been the ones to teach Tom the business—the family.

A long time.

It was Adriano's warnings and reminders from years gone by that Tom heard in the back of his head when the comments and ribbing started. The foot soldiers for Adriano's crew had been coming for Tom on this level since before he was a teen.

It's your rite of passage, Tommaso. We all dealt with that nonsense, too. There'll come a time when they won't even be able to look you in the eye.

Fact was, Tom got the insults worse than anyone else ever had, and he didn't need Adriano or his father to tell him the truth. To the foot soldiers in the crew, Tom was nothing more than a spoiled, secondary Capo, underboss-in-training, and the son of a boss. That was it.

He couldn't be like them. They couldn't be like him.

"You can't say hi today, Tom?"

Out of all the voices following him, Tom did care to acknowledge that one. One of his oldest friends—Lou.

Over his shoulder, Tom waved a hand in response. For now, that was the best he could do for his friend. It was better they didn't seem too friendly while the other foot soldiers were around. No need for Tom to go causing Lou any problems on his side of things.

They all had fucking masks to wear, after all.

Lou was one of the only soldiers in Adriano Conti's crew that didn't treat Tom like shit whenever he had to be in the same vicinity. He was the only one that didn't try to push every single one of Tom's buttons just to see if he could get him to react.

He swore it was a game for them.

Tom let Adriano's office door slam shut harder than he intended to. The space was empty. The Conti Capo hadn't even showed up yet, but he made damn sure to tell Tom to roll his ass out of bed before eight.

Sinking into a torn leather chair, Tom scrubbed a hand down his face.

Once it doesn't bother you anymore, they'll back off. Don't let them see it gets on your nerves, Tom, his father used to say.

Tom didn't know how much more unaffected he could seem than avoiding all eye contact, refusing to speak, and demanding respect when he was in charge. He no longer engaged the insults and teasing unless he absolutely had to, and never with violence.

It wasn't his place as only a secondary Capo.

He'd fucking hoped that by twenty-one years old—essentially the same

or close to the same age as those guys out on the main warehouse floor—
they would have at least tried to make room for him. They didn't have to
like him. He didn't ask for anything except a little bit of respect and peace
to himself.

Tom let out a heavy sigh, and scrubbed a hand down his unshaved
jaw. Mostly, he made a conscious effort to rid his mind of the useless
feelings. They wouldn't do him any good.

A few minutes later, Adriano strolled into the office. The older man—
and father of three girls—barely acknowledged Tom at all as he ended a
phone call.

"Yeah, Lissa, I'll grab you some Chinese tonight ... yeah, that, too.
Bye."

Alessa—or Lissa, to only a select few in Adriano's family—was Tom's
aunt. His mother's only sister. Actually, Alessa was his mother's only living
family besides her kids and in-laws.

They didn't talk a lot about it. Nobody did.

Everybody that grew up in the Chicago Outfit had come to a silent
understand over the years that The Chicago War between the four families
within the organization had done enough damage. It had taken enough
people. There was no reason to pay it lip service, too.

"You look like shit," Adriano said.

The guy didn't even look at Tom when he said it. Tall, broad-
shouldered, and built in a way that spoke of his football years, Adriano
Conti was not a man to be messed with. He also didn't indulge whine-fests
from any-fucking-body.

Tom included.

"It's nothing," Tom said.

"You sure?"

"You wanted me to handle something today, didn't you? Here I am.
Let's get to that, Adriano."

"No uncle for me today?"

Tom scoffed "Like that would help my fucking case, right."

Adriano lifted a brow, and then his gaze drifted to the closed door.
"The guys were quiet when I came in."

"As they should be for their Capo."

"But not for you."

Tom clenched his teeth in an effort to stay quiet. All it did was make
his jaw tight, and his uncle didn't miss it.

"Just ... don't bother," Tom told him with a subtle shake of his head.
"It's like high school with those idiots out there. People all say the same
things to me about it. *Ignore them. Don't let them bother you.* If somebody says
something to them, it only makes it worse."

"You're usually better at brushing them off, Tom."

9

He didn't need Adriano pointing that out to him. He was quite aware that his irritation levels were climbing higher by the day.

It brought him back to his biggest enemies.

Boredom.

Patience.

Tom didn't know what he was bored with—work, Chicago, the same old shit every day, or what. He didn't know what would fix his boredom. It should have been simple. If he wanted something, he went out and got it. He just didn't know what it was he wanted.

His lack of give-a-damn was seriously starting to mess with his patience, though. It showed every single time he had to force himself not to put his fist through one of those idiots' heads.

Tom's father had the patience of a saint.

His mother? An angel.

Tom?

Less than zero at the moment.

"You know what," Adriano said, "I can handle this myself today, Tom. Take the day off. Go do something else for a while."

"I can do what—"

"It's not your choice to make. I don't need you here in a bad mood, and halfway to kicking somebody's ass. Two boosted trucks are supposed to keep those fools busy. I'll put Lou in charge of watching them."

"Lou's good," Tom said with a nod.

"Yeah, I know. One fool, I might not mind letting get somewhere in this business of ours." Adriano flicked his hand toward the door. "Get. Don't make me tell you again."

Tom pushed up from the chair and exited the office without a goodbye. Adriano wouldn't want one, anyway. He made it halfway across the warehouse, nearly to the front entrance doors, when another insult came hurling his way.

He didn't even know what the guy said.

He barely heard it well enough.

Tommaso *should* have let it go.

It took a single spin of his shoes against the cement floor, and five long strides before his fist crashed into the guy's face. Jake, or some equally generic name that could be forgotten. The crunch of bone smashed against Tom's knuckles.

Something akin to relief settled through Tom. The teasing feeling skimmed along his now bruised and bloody knuckles, but it didn't reach where he needed it the most. It still wasn't enough. He reared back and punched the guy again.

All the while, Tom never said a word. He didn't even blink. He didn't have shit to say, just a damn point to make.

They thought he was some weak-ass rich fuck who couldn't go toe-to-toe with them on anything, certainly not on the streets.

Tom had news for them.

He fixed his jacket as he walked away, but a form caught his eye in the office doorway. Adriano leaned against the doorjamb, and shook his head once.

"Go see the boss," he heard his uncle say. "A day off will not be enough, Tom."

What in the hell was that supposed to mean?

"Where's Sara and Rebeka?" Tom asked.

Tommas, his father, worked on lighting the cigar in his mouth as he spoke. "At school, Tom. It's the middle of September."

Ah, yeah, shit.

Usually his little sisters would be tearing up a storm in the house. Sara was almost a decade younger than him, and Rebeka, twelve years younger. He tried to make time for them, when he could, but work kept him away from the Trentini mansion far more often than he was inside.

"Are you going to stand in the doorway and draw attention all day, or sit down?" his father asked.

Tom took a seat in one of the bucket chairs across from his father's desk. For a long while, the two sat in silence. Tom, lost in his thoughts and irritation. And Tommas, puffing on a cigar that would likely have his wife barking at him later.

Some shit just never changed.

Tom liked it when it was just him and his dad like this, though. His mother used to call them twins, as their behaviors, habits, and features mirrored back at one another more often than not. By the time Tom was seventeen, he stood eye-level with his father at six-foot-two. He shared his father's chiseled jaw and sharp cheekbones. The squared chin, strong nose, and blue-gray eyes. He had once worn his dark brown hair a bit longer, but now opted to have it cut short, while his father's was peppered with a bit of gray at the temples. Their smiles were more smirks or grins than anything else.

"Adriano called," his father said.

"What, like a little tattletale? Am I going to get punished by my dad now because I got pissed off, and let it show?"

A chuckle echoed from across the way.

"No," his father murmured. "I'm surprised you went this long without knocking somebody out, honestly. What was it today that got to you?"

Tom shrugged under the weight of his Armani suit. "Nothing in particular. I've heard it all before. I just had enough, maybe."

"Maybe?"

"I'm bored out of my damn mind, Dad. I work with those same idiots every day. As long as they think they can get away with it, they don't leave me the fuck alone. I'm starting to think there isn't much point to keeping my cool when breaking their faces gets me better results."

Tommas let out a thick cloud of gray smoke, and set the cigar on the edge of a crystal ashtray. "You know, nobody ever told you that the way we handled our business as young, made men is the same way you have to handle it, Tom."

He eyed his father, considering the words.

"Kind of seems like it."

"Why, because nobody's jumping in for you when it's happening?"

"I mean—"

"You know that won't do anything for you at the end of the day, don't you? It's you who is responsible for making your name and position with those men clear, Tom. Nobody else can do that for you, son. If the way you want to do that is with fear and brute force, then so be it, but do so and be fucking consistent about it."

Tom laughed under his breath. "You think?"

"We all have to do what we have to do."

Yeah, he knew that, too.

"I am, though. Bored. Tired."

Tommas sucked air through his teeth, and nodded like he could see all of those things. "Frustrated. Restless. Irritated. Why, though?"

"I don't know. I'm not …"

"What? Tell me, and then maybe I can help."

"I'm twenty-one, Dad. Isn't it time for me to figure out my own shit?"

Tommas cracked a smirk—the closest thing he ever got to a smile when Tom's mother wasn't involved. "Still my boy, no matter your age."

"And my boss."

His father's grin faded fast. "And that, too, yes."

"I don't know what I want, Dad. That's half the problem."

"I don't understand."

Tom scratched at the underside of his jaw—a nervous tic, and one of his only tells. "Have you ever felt like you wanted something, or were missing something, but you just didn't know what in the hell it was?"

Tommas lifted a single brow high. "No, I can't say that I have. I always knew what I wanted—she was simply out of my reach for a while."

Abriella, his father meant. Tom's mother.

"I don't think it's a woman," Tom said. "I've just been at a point lately where nothing is doing it for me. I'm bored."

"You said that already."

Tom lifted an empty palm and tipped it over as if to say, *That's what I got.*

Nothing.

He had nothing.

"Is this about the gunrunning thing again?"

Tom scowled.

He didn't even try to hide it.

His father didn't miss it.

"So it is," Tommas said.

"No."

"You can't run guns, Tom," his father said. "I made my decision on that. I've told you this a hundred times already. It puts too much attention on you, and as it is, our organization already has enough attention. You want to move up in the family—gunrunning and other business will force too much of your attention away from where it should be."

"Dad—"

"We've had this chat, Tom."

They had.

A lot.

"Then why let me do it before?" he asked.

Tommas leaned back in his chair, and stared hard at his son. "Theo needed an extra pair of hands. You have a liking for guns. It worked. You made a friend with that Cross Donati while you were doing it. It's not like you didn't get something out of that, Tom."

"I was *good* at it, Dad."

"And you're good at this, too." Tommas shrugged, adding, "Here's the thing, son. I intend to move you up in the Outfit, and you know this has always been our plan."

"Yeah, I know."

"I will not have your attention split between responsibilities, or worse, have men in the organization thinking you're the weak link because the top is not where you want to be. My motives for keeping you where you are happen to be well intended."

"I'm not one for the politics of the mafia."

"And yet, you still need to be, Tommaso."

Tom knew he was going to get nowhere fast with this conversation. His father wouldn't budge. He hadn't budged an inch since Cross—the gunrunner for the Chicago Outfit—headed back to New York a couple of months back. Tom thought maybe his father would let him pick up a bit of Cross's slack in some areas, but that was a fucking pipe dream if there ever was one.

Tom and his father were close—he loved Tommas fiercely. Just like his mother.

They had *one* issue.

This was it.

Tommas let out a quiet exhale, and picked up his still-burning cigar. "I think what you really need is a break, Tom. All good made men need one occasionally. Besides, it'll give you some time to reflect on things. Issues here. How to handle them. Whatever else. You've earned the break, son."

"Oh?"

"That's what I said."

"And where should I go for this *break*?"

His father flashed his white teeth in a grin. "That's for you to figure out. Say hello to your mother on the way out. Also, don't even think of heading out of the city without doing something with your sisters first."

That was that.

Tom found his mother in her library. A massive, bookshelves from floor to vaulted ceiling, room in the mansion that Abriella hid in more often than not. Family portraits—young and old—covered one far wall. A wall of bay of windows overlooked the estate grounds, showcasing colorful leaves littering the ground.

His mother smiled over at him from her white chaise as he entered the space. She rested her book beside her, and waved him further in.

Old paper, leather, and ink wafted through the air. Vanilla and lavender followed right behind. His mother loved her candles and oils. Teas and sweets.

This was Abriella Trentini Rossi's space.

Her room.

No one else's.

Here, Tom knew his mother worried about nothing. She shed no tears. Other worlds sucked her in, and she only came out when called.

Like now.

"Hey, baby," Abriella said.

Tom bent down to kiss his mother on the top of her dark-haired head. "Hey, Ma."

"You look … stressed."

"That obvious?"

His mother smiled a little. "Always, to me."

"Dad said I need to take a break."

"I bet he's right, Tom."

"I bet we won't tell him that, will we?"

Abriella's smile bloomed wider. "Never."

Her hand patted his cheek with a soft touch, but she said nothing to push him on what was wrong, or how he planned to fix it beyond what he already offered. It was one of the many reasons why he loved his mother.

"Sit for a while," she told him. "I'll read to you."

"What, like when I was a boy?"

"Reading is good for the soul, Tom."

"Depends on what you're reading, Ma."

"A thriller."

Tom could do that. He grabbed one of the leather chairs, and pulled it closer. Sinking into the seat, his mother started to read. Between the silence of the library, the familiar scents clinging to his every breath, and the comfort of his mother's presence, he could almost sleep. He was relaxed.

Problem was, as soon as he left the mansion, it would all be gone.

That's when Tom got it.

He was looking for something like his home. Or he needed something like it. He just didn't know what in the hell that even was.

Tom unceremoniously dumped a black duffle bag on the foot of his bed as he dialed a familiar number on the phone, and put it to his ear. His two-level house just outside of the city limits wasn't anything to scoff at, but it didn't feel like home to him, either. He'd bought it on a whim, as his trust fund afforded him the ability to do so before he had been making decent money himself. He had wanted to be closer to business and family and not right in the heart of Chicago in a cramped apartment.

He hadn't even bothered to really decorate the place.

In his ear, he heard the call click.

"Donati here," a familiar voice answered.

Tom balanced the phone between his shoulder and ear as he grabbed a couple of things from the closet. "Cross, man, what's up?"

"Not much, Tom. Something come up with the next run, or what?"

"Nope."

Tom wasn't surprised the first thing Cross thought at his phone call was business. It was just who Cross Donati was at the end of the day. Business first, and everything else was secondary. Cross came from a New York Cosa Nostra family—another boss's son, like Tom. The two had made fast friends when Cross and Tom got put together as partners when the Outfit started trafficking guns. It helped that Cross was only a couple of years older than Tom, but didn't treat him like a kid, or as though he was where he was because of his last name.

Their friendship lasted.

A couple of months back, Cross headed home to New York after living in Chicago for almost three years. He hadn't been back, but a gun run was coming up soon. Tom figured he would see his friend then.

Fate had different plans.

"You busy?" Tom asked.

Cross chuckled dryly. "Man, I am always busy. Not more than usual, though. Heading over to my parents' place today to see them."

"No, I mean for the next week or so. Maybe more."

"What?"

"I thought I might visit," Tom said.

"Door's always open for you, Tom."

New York was a sufficient distance from Chicago to make it worth the cramped flight. A familiar face made it welcoming enough, too.

"My flight leaves tomorrow in the morning," Tom said.

"Let me know when you land."

Friends like Cross were hard to come by.

CHAPTER TWO

"***THIS IS*** *your wakeup call, Cam!*"

Brothers—but especially older brothers—were things made by the Devil. Camilla Donati would fight anybody who tried to tell her differently. Her brother in particular was the very worst when it came to making her life a special kind of hell.

She still loved him.

He was one of her very best friends.

Soft thumps hit the wall as her brother came closer to the bedroom.

"Come on, Cam. Get up. Right now."

"Fuck off," Camilla grumbled from beneath the mound of blankets. "It's Saturday *morning*, Cross. Go away."

His voice came louder and clearer then. "Nope."

"Oh, my God. He's hot, but he's so fucking annoying that it makes me want to kill him."

"I *did* hear that," Cross deadpanned.

Cool air hit Camilla's skin a second before the blankets fell to the floor. Both Camilla, and her friend who had opted to sleep over instead of catching a cab home, glared up at Cross. August hadn't lied—Cross was handsome, dark-eyed, black hair, and strong features. He didn't lack in female attention, as far as that went.

Her brother just didn't entertain the attention.

August groaned again and rolled over in the bed. "I hate your stupid, pretty face, Cross."

"Pretty is kind of insulting. I'm not a boy."

"Want me to call it ugly?"

"Yeah, but it's not," Cross replied. "Cam, get out of bed. You're late for breakfast. Ma and Cal sent me over to yank your ass up."

Camilla grabbed the blanket from the floor, and tossed it over herself once more. "Tell them I'll be around."

"You partied last night, didn't you?"

"New club in Coney," August answered. "It was the *shit*."

"Cam, you're not even legal age to drink," her brother muttered. "And

17

August is two years younger—"

"*Almost* two years younger," August jumped in. "I turned eighteen in August, thanks."

"Nice to know you're legal for something else, now, but that's not the point."

Camilla peeked over at her friend to see August's dark chestnut skin had flushed with a heated crimson hue at the surface of her cheeks. August took after her Nigerian mother in her features, while her Italian, lawyer father had taught his daughter to take no shit.

August had something akin to a crush on Camilla's older brother since the two girls met in high school. Cross treated August with the same annoying affection he gave to Camilla—like a little sister he was paid to bother. Besides, Camilla figured her brother was still too caught up on somebody from his past to notice anyone else.

"Get out of my room," Camilla told her brother. "Better yet, get out of my apartment."

"Can't. Promised Ma and Cal, I would bring you to breakfast."

At the thought of food, Camilla's stomach threatened to revolt. She should not have taken those extra three Jell-O shots the night before.

"August can come, too."

Her brother said it as though he was dangling an offer Camilla couldn't refuse. She knew better.

"Internship starts today with the Bared Brands," August said as she climbed over Camilla in the bed. "I'm … Shit, get up, Cam. I'm going to be late."

"Why does that mean *I* have to get up?"

"Because your stupid cotton pillowcases are a bitch on my hair when it's not in a protective style, and I like the way you fixed it up the last time."

Camilla grumbled, but forced her way out of the bed.

Cross headed for the door with a wave over his shoulder. "Thirty minutes, Cam."

"Make me coffee, Cross!"

"I'll think about it," her brother shot back.

He would make her coffee.

She knew it.

Camilla had two best friends in the world.

One was August—the Brooklyn native with the crazy curls. The other had always been her big brother.

August passed over the conditioning pomade she kept at Camilla's place—considering the two might as well be roommates a lot of the time—and took a seat in front of the vanity. Camilla gathered August's thick, coarse hair with a practiced hand.

"Just like last time?" Camilla asked her friend.

In the mirror, August nodded. "Big pom, but tease it out like a faux-hawk down the top and middle. I need to get my braids in before winter comes."

Camilla had spent a lot of time with August and her mom over the years of their friendship. Some of that time had been sitting in salons because her friend's hair needed to be maintained no matter if she wore it natural, in braids, or with a weave. If anything, Camilla figured that's where she had picked up some of her talent for fixing August's wild hair, not to mention, her own …

Right now, Camilla's hair was a platinum blonde mess with a purple fade of curls that needed a good soak in hot oils. August's mom—Ada—had taught Camilla how to take care of her hair to an extreme given the abuse she put it through monthly.

Next week, it might be red, or back to brown. Maybe Camilla would put colorful streaks through it, or cut it all off.

She never kept one style for long.

"You know you're going to be amazing today, right?" Camilla asked.

August's russet gaze met Cam's dark brown eyes in the mirror. "Kind of nervous. I feel like Dad got me this, and not you know, *me*."

"First, maybe your dad put in a good word, but who cares? Graphic design, marketing, and branding—that's your focus for college. This one-year internship with Bared Brands is going to be fucking awesome for that."

Plus, August was smart as hell. Skipped a grade in middle school, got a scholarship into the prestigious private school Camilla attended, *and* a full ride for college. Her friend could and would do whatever she put her mind to.

"Maybe."

"Keep me updated through the day."

August cocked a brow. "Girl, did you think I would do anything different?"

Not at all.

"About the club thing—"

Camilla held up a single finger to shush her brother without saying a word. She took a long sip from the coffee he'd handed over in a to-go mug from her cupboards. The creamy, sweet drink perked her up just enough to be agreeable.

"Never talk to me before coffee, Cross. You know this."

Her brother's familiar brown gaze rolled upward. He navigated the city streets to head east. Breakfast at a Newport restaurant on Saturdays was a new thing their parents wanted to do ever since Cross came home from Chicago a couple of months earlier.

"How'd you get into the club?" her brother asked.

Camilla smiled slyly. "Wouldn't you like to know?"

"Do you know the security at the door, or did someone get you a fake ID?"

"Both?"

"Cam."

She shrugged. "Guess we're going to pretend like you weren't the biggest trouble making shit on the planet from the time you were thirteen, huh?"

Cross cleared his throat. "This is not about me. It's about you. I'm … looking out for you. Yeah, that works."

"Bullshit. I paid Zeke."

"I knew that bastard got you a fake ID," Cross bitched under his breath.

Her brother's best friend was way off-limits for Camilla in *any* kind of way—though he was cute, and probably a good time—because the guy treated her like a little sister. A side effect of having grown up around the guy since she was born.

"Be nice. He was looking out for me since you were in Chicago and all."

Cross nodded. "Right, by getting you into *clubs*."

"Like you never used to go into clubs with Catherine Marcello when she wasn't legal age?"

Her brother stiffened in the driver's seat of his Porsche at the mention of his ex. Camilla half-smiled to herself, but hid it by taking another drink of coffee. The best way to get Cross off a topic of conversation was to put his ex into it.

"At least it was just August in your bed this morning."

Camilla snorted. "I apologized for the guy, Cross."

"He had *nothing on*, Camilla."

"And the girl," she added. "I apologized for her, too."

That was the first time her brother found out Camilla didn't have a preference when it came to hooking up with somebody. As long as the guy or girl was going to be a good time, she was all for it. They had to be gone by morning, or soon after—that was her deal.

Camilla didn't do relationships. She was too young, and having too much fun being nineteen, in college, and out on her own to settle down with somebody. Any relationship she did dabble in was done almost as soon as it started.

She found boys to be like toys. Fun to look at, cool to play with, but then she quickly lost interest. Although, she had never gotten into a relationship beyond sex with a woman, she figured it would probably end up being the same.

Camilla's interest just couldn't be kept for longer than it took to have an orgasm … or five.

That didn't stop people from trying, though.

"I mean," Cross said, glancing over at his sister, "the girl definitely wasn't too bad to look at other than the fact she tried to kill me with one of your crystals. You know, when she threw it at my fucking *head*."

Camilla laughed.

So she had an active sex life. Her brother liked to pick on her about it sometimes, but he never made her feel like she was doing something wrong. He never shamed her for the choices she made, and instead, only asked if she was safe and okay.

She loved her brother for that, really.

"She thought you were breaking into my place or something," Camilla said.

"Because we don't look like siblings at all," Cross replied wryly.

He was right. The two shared the dominate Donati features, but where Cross took a stronger, more masculine version, Camilla was the lighter, feminine side. He was sharp lines, and she was soft curves. She barely reached five-foot-six in heels, while he towered over six feet. Her brother smiled, and showed off cut-from-stone cheekbones, and she carried her mother's delicate nose and petite figure.

A person couldn't miss how much the two looked similar, though.

"Maybe she thought you were going to try to join in or something," Camilla said. "Some people are freaky like that—the whole sibling get up, you know."

Cross made a gagging noise in the back of his throat. "That's enough of that. Jesus Christ."

A dinging bell took Camilla's attention away from her brother for the moment. A notification on her cell phone let her know that the paper she needed to have in on Monday was now pushed back until Friday. Apparently, the professor for the class had come down with some kind of wicked bug and would not be back in classes until Friday.

School was the one and only thing Camilla did not mess around with. Her social and personal life did not get in the way of her schooling. From Monday to Friday, she was ass-in-chair at every class, lecture, and whatever else she needed to do.

Her goal to become a NICU nurse—to take care of premature babies like she had been once—would not be screwed up by any-fucking-thing. Camilla would make sure of it. No matter what she had to do.

"Yes."

She did a little happy dance in the passenger seat.

"What's going on now?" Cross asked.

"The rest of my weekend just opened up, big brother."

Cross smirked. "Oh, how so?"

"Nothing due for school. Nothing to do. August is going to be busy, busy. *Free weekend.*"

"Zeke is having a house party tonight."

Camilla *did* like the sound of that. "Who's going?"

"Our people," her brother said. "Some you know, and some you don't. Better than a club."

"That's debatable. Besides, it'll be awesome because I'm going. Anywhere I go is fucking awesome, thank you very much."

"Yes, Camilla, because you vomit glitter and piss fabulous. I don't need the lecture again."

"Is it a lecture if it's true?"

She grinned at him.

He just shook his head.

"You love me," she said.

"Just enough not to hate you, sure," Cross replied. "I don't know how you manage to have a hangover and still be this annoying first thing in the morning."

"Or is it that you don't like how I turn conversations around on you."

"You know what, it's both."

Camilla smiled sweetly at him, but said nothing.

She didn't need to.

Her point was made.

It was another forty-five minutes of Cross and Camilla seeing who could annoy the other the most before her brother pulled into the parking lot of a familiar restaurant. Inside the cozy, homey decorated Newport bistro, they found their parents already waiting at a table close to the windows, and with a spread of food on the table.

Camilla's hangover was all but gone.

Her stomach growled instead.

She put the thoughts of food aside for the moment to deal with greeting her waiting parents. They always came first when the two were in the room. She loved Calisto and Emma beyond measure because they never forgot to love her—*ever.*

Her dad, always her hero and supporter, stood to give Camilla a tight, one-armed hug that still reminded her of the man who used to have pretend tea parties and let her paint his fingernails. Only once, though.

Once her father let her go, Camilla bent down to kiss the apple of her mother's cheek with a smile. Emma was another cornerstone for Camilla—

never failing, always holding strong, and loving her through the rest.

"Figured we better send Cross over to get you when you didn't pick up my call," Calisto said as he took his seat.

Camilla sat beside her father.

Cross took the chair beside their mom.

"I was out late," Camilla said. "Didn't hear anything until Cross bulled his way into my place."

Her brother shot her a look.

Camilla shrugged.

Her parents didn't ask a thing about where she had been, or what she had been doing the night before. They never did. At nineteen, almost twenty, Camilla didn't have a lot of rules enforced down upon her by her parents. Really, they had never strapped her or Cross down with rules or demands.

She knew that she was lucky. Other *principessas*—girls like her with an Italian, Cosa Nostra boss for a father—were not as fortunate. Their life did not allow for very much freedom. Yet, her father made sure she had as much semblance of freedom as he could allow without being unsafe.

A good example was the enforcer she knew was on her watch. Or rather, the couple of men who rotated to keep an eye on her. Her father made her aware of the men, but also made it clear they did not report back on Camilla's whereabouts or anything else she did. They were just there—in the background of her life—to keep her safe should something happen. They kept a healthy distance, and otherwise, gave her privacy.

So far, those enforcers had never needed to step in for Camilla. Other than the few times the men had taken her to a safe house when issues came up with other organizations her father dealt with, she didn't see them. She hadn't even known their names until a couple of years ago when she first moved out of her parents' home.

Sure, being a woman meant Camilla wasn't supposed to know details about the criminal organization her father ran, and her brother participated in. She was far from dumb.

Observant.

Quiet when needed.

Not, however, stupid.

"Make sure you're not late for classes on Monday," her mother said.

"I won't."

Like they even had to worry at all about that.

Camilla emptied the last bit of Pinot Noir from her glass while waving for her brother's friend—Zeke—to grab her another. Cross had always been clear on the rules when Camilla partied. Be safe. Never drink from a glass you didn't pour or see poured, or a drink taken from someone she couldn't explicitly trust.

She trusted Zeke.

Turning her back to the loud music pumping through the Odessa beach house, Camilla tried to focus on her phone call.

"Give me all the details," she demanded.

"Damn, I can't even hear you very well."

Camilla cursed under her breath, but headed out the back exit of the house where a few people had gathered to drink, and smoke. The heady scent of weed clung in the air, but she focused on her conversation with August.

"Details," Camilla said when the music was all but a deep murmur at her back. "Give me them."

"It went good. Basically a what's what, and the stuff I'll be doing."

"That's good, right?"

"I got the impression my main job is to keep Brock Darling's specialty coffee full all day."

Camilla barked out a laugh. "You're kidding."

"Not really."

"Ugh."

"We'll see how it goes. It's a high energy environment. They started the magazine a few months ago, too, so there are some opportunities for me to learn there. Everybody made it seem like Brock isn't hard to work for."

"That's a plus."

The music blasted louder behind Camilla as someone came out of the house.

"Where are you?" August asked.

"Zeke's place."

"Your brother there, too?"

"Not yet. You wanna come and party?"

August made a sad noise. "Can't. Someone's going to need their coffee at eight sharp tomorrow morning."

"He doesn't do church?"

"Apparently not, but hey, it gets me out of it, too. I don't need an excuse on Sundays, now."

"Nice."

"Right? So hey, text me tomorrow sometime. We can try to meet up."

"Will do," Camilla said. "Love you."

"Love you, girly."

By the time Camilla got back inside the house, and found Zeke waiting with her *safe* glass of wine, she caught sight of her brother coming through the front door.

Cross, and someone else.

She only figured the guy had come with her brother because Cross chatted with him as the two navigated the people together.

Camilla didn't have a clue who he was, but the guy was *gorgeous*.

Tall. Lean. Blue-eyed. Dark-haired. Strong features. Sharp lines.

Physically, he wasn't anything to scoff at. She didn't care how bold it seemed of her to look him over while she had the chance. If the guy didn't want to be looked at like he was something she wouldn't mind taking a bite out of, he shouldn't look that fucking good walking across a goddamn floor.

Who was he?

Long fingers like he played an instrument, maybe. Or maybe like his fingers were built to play something a little more sinful. Built like he could run a ten-k without losing a breath. A half-smile that spoke of an easy nature, but could probably melt panties when he turned it on a woman.

There was nothing boyish about him.

Not a damn thing.

Dressed in black slacks, black silk shirt, and black leather shoes, he looked damn good. The guy walked with a confidence she knew was probably learned. Yet, his disinterested gaze swept over the faces of the people like he didn't give a shit who they were.

He looked like all kinds of trouble.

And a whole lot of fun.

A little cocky. A touch of arrogance. Nothing innocent about him.

Exactly Camilla's type.

The fact the guy was Cross's friend didn't bother Camilla at all. That didn't make him off-limits to her. As long as it didn't interfere with his business, her brother didn't give a shit. Not to mention, he never told her who she could or couldn't sleep with, date, or otherwise.

Cross was good like that.

"Who is that?" she asked Zeke while she still had the time. Soon, her brother and his friend would be too close to ask. "With Cross, I mean."

"Oh, that's Tom. He's spending some time in the city, I guess."

"Tom?"

"Tommaso Rossi—Chicago."

Oh.

Oh.

Camilla caught Tommaso's gaze with her own the closer he came. His straight eyebrow cocked high as his gaze drifted over her face. He then looked over the silver, bodycon dress she had slipped on earlier.

He was a lot like her, it seemed.

Bold.

Unashamed.

Down his gaze went to her bare legs, and the Valentino rockstud black and silver heels she wore. Then his striking gray-blue gaze jumped back up to meet hers once more.

Camilla grinned, and took a sip of her wine. Her night just got *way* better.

CHAPTER THREE

"AT LEAST wait until I'm not looking to eye-fuck my sister," Cross said under his breath. "That's the respectful thing to do, Tommaso."

Tom heard Cross's warning loud and clear, but it still took him a couple of extra seconds to tear his gaze away from the platinum and purple-headed blonde across the room. He knew Cross had a younger sister—nineteen or twenty, somewhere around there—Camilla. Although, he had never met the girl.

No, not a *girl*.

Definitely a young woman.

Very much woman.

All woman.

Tom's gaze darted back to the woman in question as Cross stopped to chat with somebody. He figured his friend's attention was distracted enough that he wouldn't notice or mind Tom sneaking one more peek at Camilla Donati.

Petite in stature, she would barely reach his chin, and that was with her heels on. And speaking of the heels ... Those damn things had spikes all the way around the straps, and they looked made for some kind of fun and sin.

There were at least another thirty women in the room. All dressed in some variance of skirts, dresses, or jeans that hugged their asses tight enough to make Tom wonder how the fuck they could even breathe.

Yet, something about Camilla kept his gaze drifting in her direction.

Edgy makeup, with crystals placed along the cut line of her eyebrows. Red lipstick so dark it was bordering on a black crimson. Round, large brown eyes that someone else might have mistaken as innocence staring back from them.

He didn't see innocence at all.

Not the way she was looking at him.

Pretty wasn't the right word for her delicate features and naturally pouty lips. Pretty made him think of fragile lace and inexperience.

Alluring was more like it, with just a touch of sex to color her up.

Like a rose.

Attractive, silky smooth, interesting and beautiful. Just enough sexy to make it impossible to resist touching it. Hidden dangers in the form of thorns ready to injure and scar.

"She single?" Tom asked when Cross finished with his conversation with the stranger. He couldn't even help it. The words came out before he could stop them. "Your sister, I mean. Is she?"

"Kind of makes you look like a lovesick fucker when you keep staring, Tom."

"Your point?"

Cross sighed, and scrubbed a hand down his jaw. "Cam doesn't know what a relationship is, so yeah, she's ... available."

"What's that mean?"

"Not my business, that's what."

Tom didn't press for more. "Why aren't you pounding me into the ground right now for even looking at her? She's what, nineteen, or—"

"She'll be twenty soon."

"Didn't answer my question."

Cross shrugged. "Cam does Cam, man. She does whatever the hell she wants to do, and nothing anyone else says has much effect on her. As long as she's having fun, nobody's bothering her, and she doesn't need me to step in, then I step way the fuck back. She's my sister, not my property."

"So you wouldn't mind—"

"Literally not talking anymore about it because I don't care, and I don't want to know."

Good enough for Tom.

"I mean," Cross added quickly, "she doesn't usually mess with my friends, so good luck with that, huh?"

Tom chuckled.

He didn't need fucking luck.

She was still looking at him, too.

"Zeke!"

Cross's holler gained the attention of the man standing beside Camilla. A single wave of Cross's hand sent Zeke heading in their direction.

"What, you're not even going to introduce me to her?" Tom asked.

His friend laughed at him, and hit him hard on the back.

"Fuck no," Cross said. "I'm not helping you. I just won't stop you. See the difference?"

"You're a shit."

"Not news, man."

"A real shit."

"I said what I said," Cross replied.

Well, if Camilla was anything like her brother ... Tom didn't plan on going very far with her, anyway. One could only take so much Donati attitude before it drove them up the fucking wall.

Zeke nodded to Tom as he joined Cross. "Tommaso. Haven't seen you in what, a couple of years?"

"Something like that. How's your father?"

"Wolf is … Wolf."

"So, riding your ass, right?"

Zeke laughed. "Every damn day."

Out of the corner of his eye, Tom watched Camilla tip her crystal wine glass up for another sip. He saw just the tip of her tongue peek out to edge along the rim of the glass. His throat and slacks tightened to an almost painful point.

She knew what she did.

She was looking right at him.

Camilla cocked an eyebrow, and watched him through long, dark lashes. Like she was fucking challenging him or something.

The woman didn't know who she was playing with.

Not at all.

"We'll catch up tomorrow or something, all right?" Tom asked.

He wasn't even looking at Cross or Zeke now.

"That girl is like a Venus Fly Trap," Zeke muttered. "All she's got to do is sit still, look pretty, and the next stupid fucker falls right into her snare. Watch yourself, Tommaso. Before you know it, Camilla will have you falling in all kinds of love with her, and then she'll smile when she waves you goodbye. That's her deal—she doesn't know how to do anything different."

Was that supposed to be a bad thing?

Tom didn't think so.

"Okay, that's enough of this," Cross said. "Let's get me a drink."

Tom took one more look at Camilla to consider his next move. She decided for him with a little tilt of her head as if to ask him to come over.

"Later," Tom said over his shoulder.

Neither of his friends answered him back. That, or he just didn't hear their response.

Tom slid in beside Camilla, with their backs turned to the entrance of the kitchen, as she took another sip from her wine.

"So it's *Tommaso*, right?" Camilla asked.

She peered up at him, sly and sweet at the same time. How did she even manage that?

"Most people call me Tom, but Tommaso passes when I'm not in Chicago, or if it's my mother using my name."

"Why's that?"

"My father is the Tommas of the family."

Camilla nodded. "Ah, I see. I'm—"

"Camilla," Tom interjected. "I know."

Her gaze drifted to where her brother was snagging a new bottle of unopened bourbon from the top shelf of Zeke's liquor cabinet.

"I bet you do," she finally said. "You know, everything they said about me is true."

"How do you know they said anything at all?"

"Because everybody deserves a warning when it comes to me." Camilla grinned wickedly, gave him a wink, and took another drink of her wine. "My mother likes to say I'm a free spirit. Wild-hearted. Everyone else has a compass, and it points them north to keep them settled. My compass is broken, but that doesn't stop people from thinking they can fix it."

"Not all broken things need to be fixed. Sometimes, the interesting and beautiful parts are the broken ones. It's the story, not the ending, that tells the tale."

Camilla laughed a sexy, musical note. "You just took my easiest pick up line, and turned it into something beautiful."

"Let's call it a talent of mine."

"One of many?"

Her crimson lips curved sinfully, baring her straight, white teeth. He didn't miss the suggestive undertone in her question at all.

His cock perked to life all over again.

Quick-witted. Unashamed. Tempting. Beautiful.

Probably dangerous.

For a heart.

For a soul.

For any man in her path.

Right then, Tom was the one standing right in front of her oncoming destruction. Camilla Donati was a bombshell. One hell of a combination when it came to a woman. He either wasn't smart enough to get out of the way, or he just didn't care.

Tom understood all too well what Zeke had meant earlier with his warning.

It would be far too easy to fall in love with a woman like Camilla. All she needed to do was just speak to a man. She spoke, and he was caught.

Just like that.

Who the hell was this girl?

How had he missed meeting her for this long?

"What brought you to New York, Tom? Chicago not keeping you entertained, or what?"

"A break," he said. "A much needed break, Camilla."

"You can call me Cam."

He smirked. "Is that all I can call you?"

Camilla's brown eyes darted up to his, and that teasing tongue of hers came out to wet her bottom lip. "If you're funding, feeding, or fucking me, then I guess you can call me whatever the hell you want, Tom, but only *when* you're doing those things."

Yeah, love.

It would be easy, he knew.

He'd marry a woman like Camilla in a heartbeat. She was one of a kind. There wasn't another woman in her vicinity who could keep his attention like she just had, or match her fire.

"Just remember, it ends when I say it does," Camilla added with a shrug.

"Got it."

"Have you been drinking tonight?"

"No, why?" he asked.

Camilla handed over a small clutch. "I've had two glasses—enough to be over the limit on a test, not that I can even feel it. Sucks being short when it means you can't absorb alcohol as fast. You drive; I'll give you directions."

"Your place or a hotel?"

"I like waking up in my own bed. Plus, I've got a weapon that can kill you hidden within reach in every single room, so …"

"I sincerely hope you're not joking."

Because that would be the perfect topper on the sexy, fan-fucking-tastic creation that was Camilla Donati.

"There's a reason why my brother never worries about me, Tom. He's taught me well." She beamed at him. "And no, I'm not joking about the weapon bit, either, in case you want to test my limits."

Camilla's teeth sunk into her bottom lip after she added, "And I don't have very many of those—limits, I mean."

God, he loved that, too.

"Let's go." She ticked a finger over her shoulder, and set the wine glass to a small end table against the wall. "We'll see if I can make your break from Chicago worth it, Tom."

Hell yeah.

Camilla headed for the front door. Tom was right behind her. He wanted to see that ass and those hips of hers sway as she walked, after all. The show she put on was damn good. He wasn't disappointed.

Tom used the key Camilla had given him for her apartment to unlock the door. He barely got one foot inside the open concept space before Camilla had tossed her bag and jacket aside. In a blink, she was on him.

On fucking him.

She stood on tiptoes in her heels, fisted his shirt, and yanked him down for a bruising kiss. His arm snaked around her small waist to drag her closer—he wanted to feel more of her tight little body against his.

There was not one goddamn thing about her kiss that was innocent. Not a thing about it was sweet. She didn't wait for him to deepen it. Instead, her tongue darted into his mouth to war with his, and then she pulled back just enough to bite his bottom lip.

Hard.

He let out a rush of air, and his cock hardened.

Camilla just laughed as she pushed a hand against his chest, and stepped away from him. She tossed a sexy wink over her shoulder as she headed for the back of the apartment. "Bedroom is this way, Tom."

"So we're just gonna get right to it, huh?"

"Did you come to play or fuck, Chicago?"

"It's *Tom*, Cam."

"Better make sure I don't forget it then."

Sweet Jesus, save me.

Tom didn't know how to back down from a challenge. It wasn't in his nature. The Rossi genes were full of stubborn, arrogant men who all liked to rise to the occasion. Him, included.

He darted after her, and discarded his shoes and jacket to the couch as he passed. He tugged his shirt up over his head as he stood in the doorway of her bedroom. Earthy tones colored the walls. Crystals sat along the dresser and window ledge. A deep red and black bedspread covered a four poster California king-size bed.

Camilla was already pulling down the zipper at the front of her silver bodycon dress. She grinned at him, leaning forward just enough to tease him as she pulled that damn zipper lower. Like she enjoyed taking her time, and making him guess what she looked like in nothing but skin and heels.

"Heels on or off?" she asked.

"I'm an ass and legs man, and they make yours look hot as hell. Definitely on, Cam."

Her grin turned sexier, somehow.

"Thought so."

With that, she pulled the zipper down to where it stopped at her navel. All he could see was the olive-tone of her skin, and the black silk covering her breasts. His mouth went dry as she pulled the shoulders of the dress down her arms, and her body shimmied back and forth. With each sway, the dress went lower, and Tom's dick got harder.

Camilla licked her lips as she pushed the dress down over her hips, and let it drop to the floor. She stepped out of the discarded pile, and looked like an angel gracing his life.

Fuck, she was beautiful.

Collarbones that showed.

Unmarked skin.

Red lips that he'd like to bite, fuck, and *more*.

So much more.

"The longer you stare, Tom, the less we get to do. You should probably know, my pussy's been wet since you walked into that party. Try not to make me wait. My patience is thin, and my attention is erratic."

He didn't need to be told again. It took three strides for him to reach her, and she already had an arm outstretched for him.

Cam grabbed the back of his neck, and dragged him in for another kiss that left him wishing he already had her on her knees or back. That black silk bra of hers came off easily under his skilled hand, and the surprise he found beneath it made him groan.

"Holy fuck, Cam."

Her perky tits fit perfectly in his palms, and his thumbs drove over the two barbell piercings in each one. Tiny little diamonds that glinted under the light. She sank into his touch with a soft sigh.

"Bite, kiss, or suck on them, but don't *ever* fucking pull on them," she told him. "I will cut your dick off while you sleep. Got it?"

Tom laughed. "Understood."

His hands skimmed up to her throat—pretty and delicate. His thumbs stroked her pulse point while she swallowed thickly, and stared at him through those dark lashes of hers. He couldn't stop himself from letting his hands wander higher, and roving over her full lips.

"This mouth of yours is something else."

"Fuck me damn good, and I'll make sure to clean all of me off with my mouth after."

"You look far too beautiful to have a mind, and a mouth that dirty, Camilla."

She smiled as though she took that as a challenge.

"If you can spank my ass, choke me, call me your slut, and still make me come while you do it, then you might just see how much dirtier I can get, Tom."

"You don't think that's dirty enough?"

Camilla pressed a kiss to his chin, and then nipped his jawline. "I think you need to stop talking."

"Done."

His hand slipped back down to her throat and grabbed tight. Her muscles jumped against his palm, while his other hand slipped beneath her

33

panties. He found wet, hot flesh there. A silky smooth, waxed cunt that warmed and slicked his hand. She took two of his fingers deep into her pussy, and then grinded into his thumb when he stroked the hood of her clit.

She came closer, until her body was pressed against his, and her mouth drifted over his throat. Ragged breaths danced over his skin as he fucked her harder with his hand, and added a third finger just before he started curling into her G-spot.

"Fuck, yeah," Camilla whispered. "Right there ..."

"You know this cunt's all mine tonight, Cam. All fucking mine. I'll eat it, fuck it, and whatever else I want to do with it for the night."

"*You better.*"

Not *please.*

Not *yes.*

No, *another fucking challenge.*

God, he could love this girl.

She would make it damn easy.

Camilla came with a high cry that only made Tom's cock painfully harder. He was starting to think he could feel his heartbeat in his dick. It was that bad. He pulled his hand out of her panties, yanked the silk down her legs, and shoved her back to the bed.

She fell with a laugh, and widened her legs while her back arched off the red sheets. Her fingers tweaked at the piercings in her nipples. He couldn't get the condom out of his pants fast enough; never mind getting the damn pants off altogether.

He blamed his distraction entirely on the sweet sliver of her wet pussy practically begging him to bury his face between her thighs.

"You want to taste this, or fuck this, Tom?" she asked.

"Both, babe. It's fucking both."

Camilla rolled over on the bed, pushed to her knees, and raised her ass higher. Her hips did that swaying thing again. Teased him, and challenged him without her saying a thing.

"Make me see stars with your cock, and I'll think about giving you a taste."

"Don't you test me, *donna.*"

Camilla's hand slipped between her thighs, and she spanked her pussy once, then twice. "Games are the fun part, Tom."

He finally got his cock sheathed in latex, and decided fucking her first was the way he wanted to go after her little show. He'd get her sitting on his face later.

Or another time.

Yes, he fucking would.

Tom's hand slid up Camilla's arching spine as he fitted in behind her.

She ground her pert ass and wet pussy along his length. She only pushed harder into him when he fisted her hair, and tugged hard enough that he knew it would sting.

"What do you want, Cam?"

"I want you to *fuck me*."

He slid his cock through the lips of her pussy, but only let the tip slide in just enough to give her a taste. She wasn't the only one who could tease.

"Now?" he asked.

"*Tom*."

"Hard, Camilla?"

"So fucking hard, Tom."

She barely finished her sentence, and he thrust in. Her wet cunt ate him up, and took in his length with the first flex. All the way to his balls. By the time he was done, she would probably have his balls soaked with her honey.

She did say she would clean it off, though.

Christ.

She felt good.

Hot, tight, and slick.

He dragged her up closer to let his next words whisper in her ear. "What was that you wanted me to call you, babe?"

Camilla shivered. "Your *slut*."

"My pretty little slut?"

Her hot skin trembled under his weight. He could taste sex on his tongue.

"All yours, Tom," Camilla said.

"Love this pussy of yours. It's all mine tonight."

At his words, her sex squeezed him hard enough to make his next breath catch. "Feel that, Cam? That's your cunt wanting more, babe."

"God, *yes*."

He pulled out, and then dived right back in. Over and over. A brutal pace that he felt in his damn bones. He felt her hand slid between her legs. Her fingers made a V shape around his cock, feeling every time he split her open again. Her pussy was a greedy thing—the wet sound of his cock filling her up faded into the noise of her moans. He slapped her ass every time he withdrew, leaving her skin pink and hot against his palm.

"More," he thought he heard her say.

"Fuck, is that what you like, Cam? What do you want, huh, my fingers stuffed up your ass, too?"

She glanced over her shoulder—all lust-hazed brown eyes, and smeared lipstick.

Yeah.

That's exactly what she wanted, he found. He gave it to her. She came on her knees, and rolled over to let him eat her cunt until she came again. And then she sucked his dick while he made her a coffee.

Every part of Camilla was wicked. Right down to her core. She could take sin, and make it feel inferior next to her.

Tom liked all of it.

Tom balanced a bagged bagel and a to-go coffee in one hand, and said goodbye to his father on the call while Cross waved him inside the club's office. "Yeah, I'll give Ma a call."

"Don't forget, Tommaso," his father said.

"Later, Dad."

Tom shoved the cell phone into his pocket as he stepped into the office. Cross sat behind a desk, Zeke rested on the edge, and an unknown guy was in the corner fucking with a game on a tablet. The paperwork spread out on the desk told Tom his friend was working—probably something for the club, but he couldn't be sure.

"Doesn't Zeke own this place?" Tom asked.

He tore into the bagel, needing food in his stomach after the night before. Who needed a gym four times a week when fucking a woman like Camilla was a goddamn marathon? Not that he was complaining.

"Cross is better with paperwork," Zeke said.

"How's my sister?" Cross asked, never looking up from the desk.

Tom swallowed the bite of bagel before he spoke. "You want to get into that, or …?"

"The only reason I haven't called to check up on her is because I knew you were coming over here this morning."

He had the slightest feeling that Camilla and Cross were more like best friends than siblings that couldn't stand to be near one another. Oddly, Tom was okay with that. He figured Camilla needed someone like Cross to keep an eye on her, and look out for her wellbeing. There were enough assholes out in the world as it was.

"She's good," Tom said. "Said she was going to call her friend— August, or something?—before she headed out somewhere."

Cross nodded as he scribbled something on the paper. "Good."

"What, were you the lucky pick of the night for Cam?" The guy in the corner smirked, and lifted a brow in heavy suggestion. "That girl's got no self-control. Girls, guys—whatever. As long as it'll make her scream, she's down for it."

"Sounds like somebody's got a hard nut for Cam but can't get further than having his limp dick in his hand," Zeke said. "Jealous that it takes her a quarter of the effort to pick up guys—or shit, *girls*—than it does when you pay for somebody to fuck you, Dane?"

The guy scoffed. "She's a hit it and quit it, type, but at least she knows it. Girls like her are what they are, and it's worth a good time but not much more."

Cross lifted his attention away from the work. Tom saw a promise of violence coated with hatred in Cross's dark eyes, but the guy in the corner seemed oblivious to the threat. On the corner of the desk, Zeke had stiffened into stone as he looked to Cross with a frown.

"Say that again, Dane," Cross said quietly.

It wasn't even a question.

It was a challenge.

Any smart man would have heard that, and backed the hell off as fast as he possibly could. Apparently, the guy was not a smart man.

"Come on, Cross. You know how your sister is. Everybody knows the girl's got just enough slut to make her interesting, but not enough wife to keep her around."

The night before—and the quick fuck he'd had with Camilla that morning—flashed into Tom's mind. All the things he'd said, and the words he'd used. She hadn't minded at all when he called her his pretty little slut. She'd only goaded him on and asked for more.

Yet, hearing someone else call her that outside of bedroom, without her approval, and as though it was meant to shame her ... well, fuck, it really pissed him off. He could guarantee none of the men in that room were saints. Every single one of them enjoyed sex, and had more than their fair share of women. Like fuck was some stupid prick going to insult Camilla just because she enjoyed the same thing he did, except she had a pussy instead of a cock.

Tom didn't even think about it; the magnum he'd picked up from Cross's home collection to have on him while he was in the city was in his hand. Before Dane knew what happened, Tom pulled the trigger and put a single bullet right above the guy's head.

Silence coated the room with a thick, bitter warning.

"Say it again," Tom urged. "Make my fucking day."

"Who the fuck do you think you are, Chicago? You can't—"

"My club," Zeke said.

"My sister," Cross added. "Pretty sure you know better than to put Camilla's name in your mouth with that kind of garbage, Dane."

"And since I don't know who the fuck you are," Tom put in, "I can safely guess you're not a made man, you don't mean shit, and you can be replaced."

"Yes, he can," Cross said.

Tom heard the permission in his friend's words. He took it. A slight adjustment to his aim, and he took a second shot. This time, the bullet plugged into Dane's forehead, and made the back of his skull crack morbidly against the wall.

Blood splattered.

Papers shuffled.

Zeke sighed at the mess.

"I was looking for a reason to get rid of that cocksucker," Cross mused as he peered over the dead man. "Made it easy on me, really."

"He deserved it." Tom went back to his bagel because it was starting to cool, and he liked it hot. A little bit of blood didn't bother him. "Want me to clean that up?"

"Well … I got somebody who'll do it," Zeke muttered. "I guess."

"Does your sister get that kind of shit from guys often?"

Cross sucked air through his teeth. "What do you think?"

"I think my father always told me to remember that anything a man can do, a woman can do it better, and only a weak man would insult her for it. Because weak men don't know how to deal with women who are not looking for a man's approval or opinion."

"Yeah, well, there's a lot of weak men in this city, Tommaso."

He understood what his friend was saying well enough.

"Good thing there's a few of the good ones left to look out for her, I suppose." He took a sip of the coffee. "Where's your father going to be today?"

"Why?"

"Thought I should pay him a visit, maybe."

Cross arched a brow, repeating, "*Why?*"

"Camilla."

His friend finally seemed to understand.

"One of his restaurants, likely. There's one in particular he likes to work out of." Cross rattled off the address before adding, "I already know what he's going to tell you, but it's not him you need to worry about."

"What?"

"My sister, Tom. She doesn't usually do second dates, that's all."

Tom shrugged. "I have a feeling I'd really fucking regret it if I didn't at least try."

"Your heart, I guess," Cross replied.

He didn't even need to ask what his friend meant; he already knew.

Camilla loved 'em, and left 'em. Or rather, she made a guy love her, and then walked away with a smile.

Tom was willing to risk it.

Besides, he was already in too deep now. Why back out?

"Oh," Cross added after a minute as he waved to the corpse in the corner, "and don't mention this whole thing here to my father. He doesn't need the stress at the moment, you know? He's got enough to deal with. I'll let him know when the time is right."

"Deal."

Tom stared at the open door of the restaurant's office, and realized the reason he wanted to stuff his hands as deep as he could into his pockets was because he was nervous. Fucking nervous. Like a *kid*.

Sure, it wasn't often he approached a girl's father for permission to date her, but this wasn't exactly the same. Camilla wasn't just *any* woman. She was the daughter of a Cosa Nostra boss, and if this life had taught Tom anything, it was that respect happened to be king of every room.

Even in New York.

He shook the nerves off, stepped up, and knocked on the open door with two knuckles. "Hey, uh, boss. Could I chat with you for a minute?"

Calisto Donati look up from the work on his desk. The similarities between the Don and his daughter were obvious, but subtle. The same shaped eyes, and color. Warm, yet also cold in a blink.

Behind the large desk, Calisto's eyes widened and his brow raised as he realized it was Tom knocking on his door. "Tommaso. I heard you were in town."

"Dad thought I needed a break."

"We all do occasionally. How is your father?"

"He's Tommas Rossi. How do you think?"

Calisto laughed in a knowing way.

Because fuck yeah, everybody knew what Tommas Rossi could be like. "As thick-headed and stubborn as ever, then."

"He can be," Tom said, smiling. "So do you have that minute, or ...?"

"Come on in. Close the door."

Tom did as he was told. The last time he had spoken to Calisto had been two years earlier during his nineteenth birthday. The Donati boss had been in Chicago for business, or something. Noting the curiosity burning in Calisto's gaze, and how he leaned forward to rest his hands on the desk, Tom figured he should explain why he was there.

"Cross told me where I could find you today." Tom tried not to get too comfortable in the chair. Just in case he had to bolt ...

"I wondered how you found me. Now, I'm more curious as to *why*."

Tom smiled, shifted again in the chair, and stuffed his hands deep in his pockets. Calisto didn't seem to miss the nervous actions.

Christ.

He really needed to knock that off.

"Shit," Calisto said. "Please don't tell me you killed one of my guys, or some nonsense like that."

Tom laughed, but he knew better than to mention the guy at the club that morning. Cross warned him not to, after all. He sobered and straightened in the chair. "No, nothing like that. But you know, depending on how this goes, make sure to tell my mother that I love her, and all that good shit."

Calisto's brow furrowed, and Tom stayed silent while the man cleared off his desk. When the man was done, and his attention was back on the conversation, Tom reminded himself that this wasn't a big fucking deal. He didn't need to be so damn nervous.

"All right," Calisto said, "give me the bad news. Whatever it is."

"Not that, either." Tom sighed, and cracked another smile. "It's just … I'm not used to needing to approach a girl's father, you know? I don't normally have to do that being who I am, and who my father is. Except you're not like other men, you're like my father, but here, in New York. And if someone approached my sisters before they went to Tommas—"

"Back the fuck up," Calisto interrupted.

Tom's gaze darted to Calisto. "Huh?"

"This is about Camilla? You're here about my daughter?"

"Uh, yeah?"

"Well, don't fucking pose it as a question, now. Either you are, or you are not. Which one is it?"

Calisto reminded Tom of his no-nonsense father's demeanor in that moment. *Don't fucking beat around the bush, Tommaso,* his father liked to say.

Clearing his throat, Tom said, "I am."

Calisto's shocked expression was the complete opposite of his next words. "Sorry, but you just came here for nothing, Tommaso."

"Pardon?"

"You wasted your time," Calisto clarified, "especially coming to me."

"That has got to be the fastest rejection—"

"No." Calisto rubbed at his forehead like he had a headache coming on. "I mean, I take it you're here to ask me if you can take my daughter out, and you don't need to ask *me* at all. I don't make those choices for Cam, I never have. Neither does her mother. She's nineteen, smart as fuck, too; so she is more than capable of saying whether or not she's interested in someone."

Tommaso rested back in his chair. "But you're …"

"For Camilla? I'm just her dad." Calisto chuckled, but then added,

"And I love her very much. So, should something happen between the two of you that displeases me because it displeases her, then you can safely assume we will revisit this conversation. But until then, Tommaso, the rest is up to, and has always been up to, my daughter."

"Okay."

Calisto waved at his office door.

Just like that, Tom was dismissed.

Just like that, he was good to take another shot at Camilla Donati.

Huh.

"So, have a nice day, and enjoy your visit. If it helps with Cam, she likes action movies, pretty cars, and dancing."

Tom didn't know if it *would* help, but fuck, it couldn't hurt.

CHAPTER FOUR

"SO ..."

Camilla made an effort to keep her attention on the steaks she was rubbing down with one of Emma's special sauces, and not the gossipy tone her mother used. Across the kitchen, her mother sat reading a book, while also keeping one eagle-eye on Camilla at the same time. She had learned to cook alongside her mother, yet Emma didn't trust Camilla to cook everything exactly the same way she did.

She partly blamed it on her mother being Italian. Another part of it was probably Emma's need to make sure her kids could handle themselves out in the Wild, Wild West that was the world. Her mom always had one of her kids coming and going from the house with the promise of some new thing to do. Usually cooking, but sometimes she changed it up.

"How's Daddy feeling today?" Camilla asked.

Maybe if Camilla asked a different question, she could keep her mother's attention away from whatever Emma was going to ask. Sometimes it worked; sometimes it didn't.

"He's feeling okay. The headache passed yesterday."

Camilla looked up from the steaks to find her mother was avoiding her daughter's gaze. She wasn't surprised. Her father's—Calisto—health was a sore subject. Something was wrong with her dad. Between the headaches, the episodes that threw him into his past, and the tests the doctors had him running to every other week, Camilla just knew ...

Something bad was going on inside her father's brain.

It scared her to death.

Emma and Calisto just didn't talk about it. At least, not to her. Camilla knew that her brother didn't give their parents much of a choice, especially as Cross was often the one to come and help when their dad slipped into one of his episodes. Emma had made it very clear that Camilla was not to step in during Calisto's episodes—he was always confused, and rarely cooperative. Sure, he had yet to get violent, but it was a possibility given he didn't know what the hell was going on, or even who they were sometimes.

It was rough.

Damn rough.

"You know, you can tell me if—"

Emma put on a blinding smile, and stopped her daughter from saying more with, "Everything is fine, Cam. Don't you worry about that, baby."

"If you say so."

"I do."

Camilla wouldn't get more out of her mother. That much was obvious. It seemed Emma had not forgotten about her little desire to get more info on Camilla's personal life, either.

"August stopped by to chat yesterday."

"Mmhmm."

"Brought me those bath oils she knows I like from the market."

"Oh?" Camilla asked.

She was not making this easy on her mother. Emma would have to drag it out of her daughter like she always did.

Camilla's personal life and business was rarely up for discussion with her parents. It wasn't that they put rules or expectations onto her because they didn't. Not at all. They didn't judge her for bouncing between one physical encounter to the next. They never said a thing about the fact she had yet to settle down, or even bring someone around to meet them. Both her parents were aware of the fact her sexuality was quite fluid, even though she hadn't dated women beyond the bedroom. They never batted an eye at that aspect of her life, either.

All her parents ever did was love, support, and encourage Camilla. They left the rest for her to figure out. She appreciated it.

But her mother?

Emma was *nosy*. She loved to know everything and anything she could. Sometimes, Camilla would indulge her mother just enough to satisfy the woman's curiosity. At least for a little while. This would probably be one of those times.

"What did August gossip to you about this time?" Camilla asked.

Emma fake gasped. "We do *not* gossip, Cam."

"Lies. That's a lie. It's the biggest lie you've ever told me. Lies, Ma. Try again."

"Now—"

"Lies. August comes here, and the first thing you two do is gossip about me. She's where you get all your info, Ma. I know it."

"Sometimes your father, too."

"See! I knew it. You're all the same. Gossips."

She loved her best friend dearly, but the girl could not help herself where Emma was concerned. Like Camilla had spent a lot of time with August's parents as a teenager, her friend had spent a lot of time with Emma and Calisto, too.

They were all close.

August's father was even one of Calisto's lawyers for the legal side of his businesses.

Some people mistook the closeness between August and Camilla for something else, as though they weren't *just* friends. That was nothing more than bullshit, and neither of them bothered to pay it any mind. August was so straight, she could be a fucking arrow.

And even if she wasn't, Camilla wouldn't be interested.

Sex ruined friendships.

It always did.

"Anyway," Emma drawled, setting her book down to the table. "She mentioned you met somebody at a party."

Camilla cocked a brow. "I'm not telling her anything ever again."

"Lies. You will."

Well, it was obvious where Camilla got her nonsense from.

"Probably," she muttered. "So I met somebody at a party, had some fun, and sent him on his way. Same business, different day, Ma."

"Tom, right?"

Camilla made a noise under her breath. "Seriously, does she tell you *everything*?"

"Sometimes."

"Jesus, August."

"So, you won't tell me anything about this *Tom*, then?" her mother asked.

"There's nothing to tell, Ma."

"Am I to assume it's the same Tom that approached your father about you?"

Camilla hesitated in grabbing the next steak to rub it down, too. "What?"

Across the kitchen, a slow smile grew on her mother's face. "Oh, you didn't know about that?"

"Tommaso approached Dad?"

"I guess," Emma said with a shrug. "But as you said, there's nothing to tell. Right?"

Well, there wasn't supposed to be. It was mid-week, now. Camilla hadn't heard from Tommaso since ... well, Sunday morning when he left her place smelling like sex and grinning in that way of his that made her wet.

She *had* given him her number. It broke about ten of her rules when it came to not doing second dates, or whatever, but he asked. She didn't refuse because she probably wouldn't turn away a second round with Tommaso Rossi.

Camilla didn't know what it was about him—maybe the way he looked at her when he thought she didn't know—but he made her curious.

That was a dangerous game to play for a woman like Camilla who was hell bent on living her best, and most unrestricted life for as long as she could. Fun was her thing—freedom to have it was her deal.

"So, he approached Dad, huh?" Camilla asked.

Emma laughed quietly. "You said it was nothing, Cam."

"It kind of still is nothing, Ma."

"Could that change?"

Camilla went back to work on the next steak. "Even *if* I were to hang out with him again, it'll never go further than that, Ma."

"Never say never, baby."

She didn't respond.

Everybody needed to have their dreams, after all. Emma's dream was for Camilla to find someone—anyone she could love who would love her back—and settle into forever with them.

Camilla wasn't ready to burn that dream for her mother.

Not yet.

On the island, Camilla's phone dinged with an incoming text. She discarded her work to wash her hands, and check the message.

Speak of the devil, and he shall appear.

Tommaso's contact rolled across the home screen with an accompanying text. *You busy?* That was the only thing he asked.

Camilla considered ignoring it, but a part of her didn't want to. *At the moment, yeah. Dinner with my parents.*

Later, then? His reply was damn near instant.

She couldn't help but grin.

A couple of hours and I'll be free, she messaged back.

I'll pick you up, came the reply.

Camilla almost asked how he knew where her parents lived, but didn't bother. He was friends with Cross, so maybe that was how. Plus, she recognized Tommaso's last name, and knew of the father he had mentioned to her. He was likely connected to the criminal organization in Chicago—the Outfit, people called it.

That was his business, though.

He didn't share.

She didn't ask.

See you then, Tom.

"Who was that?" Emma asked when Camilla put the phone back down.

"Don't worry, Ma. The next time August comes to visit, I am sure she'll fill you in on all the dirty details. You don't need me to."

Emma smirked. "Nope, I sure don't."

"You've really never been to Luna Park?" Camilla asked.

Tommaso held out a piece of cotton candy for her to take. She bit the sweet candy straight from his fingers, and sucked on the tips to clean them off. Her wink only made him laugh, and grin in a way that had her stomach clenching.

"Never. Been to New York lots of times, but I never came down this way."

"Coney Island and the amusement park is like … a rite of passage for tourists."

He raised an eyebrow. "Can't say I'm really a tourist, though."

"Might as well be."

"New York is a lot like Chicago—less windy, maybe."

"Chicago is *not* like New York. At all. New York is far better, thanks."

Tom glanced over at her with a wicked glint in his eye. "Do you really want to get into it with a Chicago native over which city is better?"

"We have proper pizza."

"Define proper, Cam. You can get a good pizza on every block in Chicago. But we've got killer hot dogs that you can't beat. It's a damn art form. Try again."

"Yankees. Mets."

Tom scoffed. "So we're going to pretend like the Cubs don't have the best fans in the fucking world, huh?"

Camilla pressed her lips together to keep from smiling. "Lower crime rate here."

"Dirtier politicians here, too."

Goddamn him.

Then, Tommaso added, "We get to be The City by the Lake. You get to be The City by *New Jersey.*"

Camilla fake glared. "A *polluted* lake, thank you."

Tom shrugged. "Didn't say I swam in it, did I? I just said we have a better view."

"You're such an ass."

"You started this," he shot back.

Camilla stopped their walk by moving in front of him, and putting a finger to his chest. "New Yorkers stay up all night, and this is where all the big players come to have fun. We've got Fifth Avenue, historic churches, and—"

"Cheaper to live in Chicago," Tom interrupted, never budging, "people know how to put garbage in the trash, our rats aren't the size of cats, and people might actually say hello to you in our city. Don't even try to have this fight with me, *donna*. You will lose all over this park."

"You're ... *impossible*."

"Bet you like it, though."

Camilla couldn't help but laugh. "And arrogant, apparently."

"I mean, if it works, let it work, babe." He flashed her a sinful smile. "But hey, you got the biggest mob family here, so take that as a win."

She knew he didn't mean her family, particularly, but ...

"I'll take it," Camilla said, huffing as she spun around on her suede heeled boots.

Tom didn't let her take a single step. He caught her wrist with his hand, and then yanked her back around fast enough to make her vision swim.

Camilla barely got the chance to catch her breath before Tom was kissing her. His kiss was still new enough to her that it made her heart race as she fisted his jacket, and dragged him closer. Yet, somehow, it felt familiar enough that all she wanted to do was sink into him, and slow down the world for a minute.

That was kind of terrifying ...

And wonderful.

People blew past them in the park; headed for rides, games, or food. Camilla suddenly didn't care because she was far more interested in the way Tommaso's tongue flicked against hers as though he wanted to tease her.

Or promise something ...

She wondered if she could get him to put that tongue of his to use again. She liked the way his facial hair scratched and tickled her skin, and she bet it would feel really good somewhere else, too.

Like between my fucking thighs.

Far too soon for her liking, Tommaso pulled away. His hand skimmed over her throat and jaw before his thumb stroked along her sensitive lips. "Just say it, Cam."

Dazed, and damn near ready to drop to her knees right then and there for him, Camilla peered up at Tommaso. "Say what?"

"Chicago is *better*."

"Blasphemy, Tom. All lies."

"It can't be a lie when it's the truth. Just say it, babe."

"We've got the accent, Tom."

"Okay, I did not want to pull this one out of my pocket, Cam."

She tried to glare again, but she could still feel the graze of his lips against hers as he talked, and that made it *hard*. "Pull what out?"

"Chicago-style deep dish pi—"

"Don't you *dare*."

"Pizza," he finished. "I know it's your favorite because you had a box of leftovers in your fridge, and one in the trash."

"August ordered them!"

"Liar. Someone's cheating on New York, and it isn't fucking me, Cam."

"I hate you," she hissed.

"No you don't."

He looked so damn smug.

His grin was enough to melt her panties off.

"Trying really hard to keep hating you right now, Tom, but mostly I just want to fuck you."

"We could probably make it back to the car in like ..." He glanced down at his watch. "Ten minutes or—"

Camilla was already darting behind him, and back the way they had come. He chased after her with a laugh.

Camilla was still stretched full with nine inches of Tommaso Rossi. She could taste her own cum from when he'd kissed her after having his head between her thighs, and she wasn't through the aftershocks of her third orgasm. He had two of his fingers buried deep in her ass, while his fingers grabbed hard enough to her hip to leave bruises.

She loved it.

Being well into September, it sure as hell wasn't cold, but it wasn't really warm, either. The car was still hot enough from their fucking that she didn't even care about the cool air starting to whisper along her skin.

His teeth dug into her jaw as he yanked her down harder onto his cock. It ached in the best possible way. So deep, and right to her very bones. She'd already rode him to her second and third release, but he was working her body now. Pulling her onto his cock, and letting her work her clit with the tips of her fingers all the while.

When his lips grazed hers again, she could taste the salt from her skin on his tongue. She liked the way she tasted on him.

She could come again.

If he just kept fucking her like he was, it would happen.

"Christ, Cam, you're so goddamn wet."

Yes.

"And hot, babe."

All over.

She was thanking car manufactures for dark tinted windows, New York weather for the blast of rain that sent people scattering from the lot to find shelter, and this man under her because she was about to come again.

"I want that cunt of yours to give me what's mine, Cam. Don't you want to come on my cock again?"

In her ear, his voice was husky. Gravelly, and thick. Her name crossed his lips, and she was a goner.

So blissed.

So high.

Camilla barely got through her next release—with her cries high and broken—when he pulled her down on his cock twice more. Progressively harder until he held her there, and she felt his muscles tense.

"Fuck, *yeah*," he grunted.

Her laughter filled the car.

Breathless.

Spun.

"You're making me break my rules," she told him.

Tommaso chuckled, and leaned back to rest his head on the window. "What are those?"

"Mostly, you're making me like you—I keep coming back."

He grinned.

She almost hated how the sight of it made her want to get them going for another ride.

"Well, you won't have to worry about that for much longer, Cam."

"What, why?"

"New York is a break, remember? I have to head back to Chicago in a couple of weeks."

An icy cold draft slipped down her spine.

Just like that, Camilla's high was gone.

"I blame *you*."

Cross hesitated at the front door of Camilla's apartment. He hadn't even gotten the chance to close the door before she hissed at him. His gaze darted between his sister on the couch, and August reading a book in the living room nook.

"What the fuck did I do now?"

"Now, right," Camilla tossed him, "because you're always doing something."

"Well, I get blamed for a lot of shit, sure."

She pointed at him, unfazed. "You know what you did."

"Not really," Cross said.

Camilla glowered at her brother.

August sighed in the nook. "Just ignore her. She's in a mood today."

"I'm not in a—"

"Been in a mood since Wednesday, actually. I've been regretting my choice to come over today ever since I got here."

"Is that why you didn't go to church yesterday?" Cross asked.

Camilla ignored him.

August answered instead. "That's exactly why."

"First, I had a big test today, a class discussion on the impact of workplace accidents, and a lab due. I needed to get the lab done, and I wanted to make sure it was perfect," Camilla said. "And you know, everything else, too."

"Liar," August said under her breath.

"Okay, well, I brought you Chinese food like you demanded when you sent me a text this afternoon. But hey, if you're going to bark at me about shit I don't even understand, then I'll just drop it and go."

Camilla eyed Cross from the side. "Close the fucking door. I give my neighbors enough of a show as it is."

August snorted. "Right, I bet."

"Shut up."

"You said it!"

"Nobody else gets to, though," Camilla replied.

August glared.

Camilla looked away.

So maybe she was in a mood.

Maybe she had been in a mood for a while.

She neither wanted to talk about it, or admit why it was still lingering in the back of her mind like a sickness she couldn't kick. This was stupid. This was not what she did—it was not her deal.

Camilla Emma Donati did not get heartsick over a fucking *guy*.

Wordlessly, her brother crossed the room, and took a seat beside her on the couch. He passed over the bag of Chinese. She dug through it to find what she wanted, and then handed the bag over to her friend for August to do the same.

Camilla was half way through the rice and chicken before she spoke again. "He's leaving in two weeks."

Cross glanced over at her. "Tommaso, you mean?"

"Yep."

"You didn't know that, or what? He was only here to visit, Cam."

"I ignored it."

"I don't get—"

"He made me *like* him, Cross."

Her brother sighed. "Huh."

"And now he's leaving."

"That makes you …"

"Pissed off, Cross. It pisses me off!"

"Saying it lightly," August put in.

Cross ignored the other girl, and Camilla knew she had all of his attention. Her brother was good like that. Her second best friend—her very first best friend.

"Not sure what the problem is, Cam."

"The problem is that now I might like to see Tom again. Not *see him* like a relationship, but he's going. So I can't do that at all."

"Liar," August mumbled through a mouth full of noodles and beef. "You treat boys like toys, Cam, and you know it. You could have another Tom tonight if you wanted."

Cross pointed at August, saying, "Truth."

"I blame you," Camilla repeated.

Her brother only leaned back on the couch.

"Want me to kill him?"

Kind of.

Not really.

She loved her brother more for asking.

"I'm sad," Camilla admitted.

"Maybe you'll figure it out," Cross said. "Or maybe it won't matter by the time he heads out of the city. Who knows?"

"You're really not helping."

"I brought you food. It's the best I can do. Look at it this way, Cam. Once he's out of this state, you won't have to worry about icky feelings crawling into your heart, and you'll be good to go again."

Maybe.

"I still blame you."

"I didn't bring him here."

"Keep thinking that, brother."

CHAPTER FIVE

"WHY IS your sister ignoring me?"

Cross groaned as he fell back on the couch. He used a gray throw pillow to hold over his face for longer than Tom thought was probably healthy. Then, his friend mumbled something Tom couldn't understand.

"What was that?"

Cross whipped the pillow to the side, and glared. The pillow crashed against the flat screen television—making it sway dangerously—and then fell to the floor.

"I said," Cross grumbled, "why can't this pillow just fucking *kill me*? That'd be awesome."

"You're dramatic."

"I told you not to get into it with Camilla, Tom."

Fair enough.

"So this is her deal, now? She just drops somebody with no warning and that's it?"

Cross sighed, and stared at the ceiling as though he wished it would swallow him whole. "Usually, yeah, that's exactly what she does. Mostly after a first date, though. So, maybe feel special because you got two."

Then, his friend's gaze darted to him. "It was twice, right?"

"Fuck off, Cross."

Cross shrugged. "Listen, I don't like to get into my sister's personal business. As a rule, I let her do whatever the fuck she wants. She brings me into her shit enough as it is, and I don't like that, but I deal with it."

"Does that mean you know why she won't answer a text from me?"

"You're making it really difficult to like you, Tom."

"I like Cam, Cross."

"Well, that was your mistake to make. Camilla's feeling-phobic. She's got some kind of commitment issues burrowed so deep, nobody's digging them out. A guy looks at her too long, and she bolts as fast as she can before the feelings catch and spread. Get it?"

"I think you're being—"

"I'm really not overstating it," Cross interjected. "She's never had a boyfriend, Tom. Not once. Not in school. She took her best friend to prom. She's never taken someone home to meet our parents. The girl just doesn't *do* relationships. I told you that from the start—this is on you, really."

"You're an asshole."

"Still not news, Tom." Cross waved at the comfortable reclining chair beside the couch. "Take a seat, man."

He fell into the chair, but the tension in his muscles didn't relax. He felt like a bag of fucking rocks. Hard and uncomfortable. *Painful.*

Cross was right.

Tom had been warned.

It still kind of fucking stung that Camilla wouldn't even tell him to screw off somewhere. At least that was closure to everything. This was … something else entirely.

He didn't like it at all.

Cross sat up straight on the couch, and used the coffee table to hook his Doc Marten boots one over the other at the ankles. The two friends had a staring contest with the blank screen of the television before Cross spoke up first.

"What is it, man, lovesick or pussy whipped?"

Tom rolled his eyes upward. "It has to be one of those two? It can't be something else entirely?"

"Is it?"

"I don't really know her, Cross. I know enough to know I would like to know more."

"That's a lot of *know*s in one sentence, man."

He ignored Cross's joke, and considered his own words.

"Maybe it's a mixture of everything," he said after a stretch of silence.

Tom didn't even know himself, and he felt like a foolish fucker for even admitting it silently. Damn, though, there was something about Camilla that just got under his skin in the best way—the *right* way to make him take notice.

Females were females. Tom had never found one interesting enough to really make him want to get to know her beyond a physical or shallow relationship.

Camilla did that.

She did it with demure eyes, sex on her tongue, and a killer smile. She sealed it with quick wit, a filthy mind, and one of her winks.

She barely had to try.

This wasn't fucking fair.

"So you think you're love sick, pussy whipped, and confused?" Cross asked. "Because that mess makes me confused."

"I'm about to sound like a fool."

53

Cross cocked a brow. "Do I get the option of leaving before you do? I've never met a guy who went a round or two with my sister, and then suddenly grew a fucking vagina. Really not interested in meeting one now."

"No, you can't leave. I need advice. Who better than her brother?"

"You haven't met August, have you? I can introduce you two. It is August's only mission to get Camilla in a relationship. My sister just doesn't know it, yet."

"You said Camilla's got a thing for girls, too. Is August someone she—"

"No," Cross interrupted firmly.

All right.

Tom moved on. "You gonna let me talk this out, or not?"

"You have heard the whole saying about it being better to keep your mouth closed, and let people think you're a fool, than to open it and prove it, right?"

"Do you think you can love a person just by meeting them? Maybe it gets dirtied by distractions or whatever. It's just … fuck, like you *could* love them if you had the chance. That's lovesick for you."

"Yeah, I do think that's possible."

Cross said nothing else.

Tom looked over at him. "Why?"

"Just know it is, man. For some people, that's how it happens. You meet her, and there she is. No one else is ever going to be that girl for you. Some people meet theirs at fourteen years old, and fuck the rest of their life for anything that might come close after she's gone. So yeah, it's possible."

The tone Cross offered allowed no room for questioning. His friend was so private where women and relationships were concerned, that Tom knew better than to press for something more. Cross wouldn't answer, anyway. Just who he was.

"Cam likes you," Cross said.

"Likes something about me—usually without clothes on."

A disgusted grunt echoed from the couch.

"No, I mean, my sister likes you, Tom."

"How do you know that?"

"Here's the thing, man. I'm never going to betray my sister by talking about the things she tells me. Me and Cam … you have to understand, someday, we might be all we have left. That's the nature of being who we are, with a family like ours. She's never felt like she couldn't come to me— there is nothing she couldn't feel safe to bring to me, and I won't ruin that for her. Everybody needs somebody they can fall back on, and I'm one of those people for Cam."

Tom cleared his throat. "Yeah, I get that."

"I like you, though, and you're my friend. So, I'll let you in on something else where my sister is concerned. If you were any other stupid fucker with a hard nut for Cam, I'd laugh while my sister broke your heart all over New York. Actually, I'd probably help her get you out of the state."

"You're kind of horrible."

Cross shrugged, but agreed. "But hey, she does like you, and I think you have to understand Camilla, that's all."

"Understand her how?" Tom asked.

"Her, Tom. Just *her*. How she is, you know? Respect the walls she's put up, and how she chooses to do her thing. She's got enough people who keep trying to put their wants and opinions on her life, instead of letting her figure it out on her own."

Tom kind of understood what Cross was trying to tell him, but he wasn't sure where that left him with Camilla.

She didn't do relationships. She didn't do anything that might suggest a relationship. The littlest thing might send her bolting fast enough away from him that he wouldn't ever be able to catch her.

Tom didn't want to risk that happening. Not when something as wonderful as Camilla was the prize.

"So ... I go home, then," Tom said.

Cross looked over at him. "You kind of have to anyway, don't you?"

"No, I mean ... I go home because there, I'm not here. I'm not forcing her to keep a distance, or making her overthink. I'm not pushing anything on her there, or asking her for more than she is giving. We're not playing some cat and mouse game. She's got the idea of space, and I've got—"

"Not a whole hell of a lot."

A damn chance.

"A new friend," Tom said, grinning.

Cross chuckled. "Keep working that reverse psychology, man."

"Not working anything, but if that's what she wants, you know?"

"Always give them what they want, yeah."

Exactly.

"Tommaso."

"Hey, Ma."

"Pretty sure your plane was supposed to land this morning."

Tom kept half of his concentration on his mother, and the other half on the paperwork he was signing. "Something came up. I'll be home in a few days."

"In time for supper?"

"Depends on what you're cooking."

"I think I could pull out some pork chops for your spoiled self."

"You know me too well, Ma."

Abriella laughed. "You've been gone three weeks, Tommaso. I was looking forward to having you home again."

"I'm on my way, Ma. I promise."

"Better be." Then, his mother moved the phone away with a sigh. "Fine, Tommas. Take my only phone call with my son away."

"I'm not—"

"Oh, here."

Tom's father came on the line with a chuckle. "She's pissed at me, now."

"I bet."

"You should have called her more while you were away. She frets, and then I'm left dealing with it."

"I'm a grown man; I can handle myself, Dad."

"Mmhmm," Tommas hummed.

He didn't sound like he meant it at all.

Tom handed the paperwork for a rented Bugatti supercar over to the dealer. He had just shelled out far more money than he wanted to admit just to have the car for the day he would be leaving the city. They didn't have the car on hand at the moment, and would need to get it out of safe storage. That was going to take a couple of days.

It was worth it.

She'll like it.

Fast cars were a thing for Camilla, apparently. Tom had not forgotten what her father told him.

"Are you still there, son?"

"Yeah, just finishing up some business here." The final paperwork was handed over with a nod from the man behind the desk. "Thanks."

"Drive safe, sir."

Tom was already leaving the office with a wave over his shoulder.

"What business?" his father asked. "It sounded like a car deal."

"It's nothing. Spending money. That's all."

"You are coming home soon, aren't you?"

"Like I told Ma, I'll be there in a couple of days as something came up I want to do."

"Good. It's time for you to get back to life, Tom. *Here*, I mean. Adriano's been having nothing but problems with the crew since you took off, and he could really use your help to settle the guys again."

Tom scowled as he exited the business. His rented Mercedes was still waiting at the curb, and running. A man stood beside it, and waited for him to hand the car back over now that he was done inside. At the moment, he was more interested in the conversation with his father than the car.

"What problems?" Tom asked. "Because I've called Adriano every couple of days just to check in and make sure nothing came up that he needed me for. He didn't mention shit about issues with the crew, Dad."

"It wasn't anything he couldn't handle, Tom."

"And now he can't handle it, or what?"

"More like he doesn't want to. That's his right as the—"

"First Capo of the crew. Yeah, I know."

He didn't need that damn lecture again. He was all too aware that being the secondary Capo for the Conti crew of the Chicago Outfit left him doing the dirty work Adriano didn't want to do. It meant he got the difficult guys, the harder jobs, and the cleanup.

Most times, Tom didn't mind. He had learned over the years that this was his road to travel in order to get where he needed and wanted to be in the business. He intended to be a boss. His father was determined to make sure Tom worked every fucking level in the family business that he possibly could before he came anywhere near the top.

"How was your break, by the way?" his father asked.

"We're just dropping the crew conversation, then?"

"For now. Answer me."

"It was ... good."

"Good. That's all?"

"Interesting, Dad."

Tommas laughed quietly. "I will have to take your word for it. I never found New York to be particularly inviting to me—for your uncle, Damian, or his kids, sure. Never for me."

Sometimes, bad blood was impossible to wash out. Or, that's what his father always told him where the New York families were concerned. Well, one family in particular. The Marcellos. It wasn't really open for discussion between him and his father, but Tom knew the rules. For now, the Chicago Outfit bended to the demands of the Marcello family because they had control of New York, and the Commission made up of North American crime families.

"Did you find what you needed, or figure out how to deal with the issues back here?" Tommas asked his son.

"Figured out it feels a hell of a lot better to crush their face with my fist than it does to ignore them, and I get a better reaction out of it." Tom nodded to the man who held open the Mercedes's driver door, and slipped into the car. The engine purred under his handling. "But you always told me not to handle every disobedient man with violence because it only teaches fear, and—"

"Not respect."

"Yeah, so I guess no, I haven't gotten very much figured out. I'm more relaxed, though."

"Some men need a harsh hand, Tommaso, and some only need a harsh word. You will figure out which man is which. That is how you'll win this war."

"How do I figure out which is which, Dad?"

"By paying attention. Some men are like vicious dogs, and the only way to deal with them is to put them down. Others are just loud, disruptive, and intimidating, but they know how and when to step back with the right motivation. Figure out which men fall into which category, son. Also, I sincerely hope you've put this gunrunning nonsense to bed, Tommaso."

And just like that, Tom's irritation was back in a blink. "Not really, actually."

"Shame."

His father hung up the call without a goodbye.

Right then, Tom didn't mind.

His mind was on someone else …

Tom leaned against the hood of the Mercedes as people filtered through the parking lot. Beside the car, Camilla's Mustang GT sat parked and waiting for her. It was the only help Cross was willing to give Tom where Camilla was concerned. Her location, and when he could find her there.

So, here he was, at Rory Meyers College.

Waiting.

"Two questions."

Tom's head lifted at Camilla's sweet voice. He found her standing twenty feet away with a messenger bag slung over her arm, and wearing navy blue scrubs with the school's emblem on the right breast pocket. Even in scrubs and plain white shoes, with her hair pulled back into a neat ponytail, and her face free of makeup, the girl looked good.

Amazing, really.

He smiled. "What's your questions?"

"Is that Mercedes a rental or yours? I didn't see you driving something before."

"It's a rental. I just traded it in for something else, but I have to wait a couple of days for it."

"And that something else is …?"

"You only said two questions, Cam."

She pursed her lips and narrowed her eyes. "Okay, second question, then. Why are you at my college?"

"Just thought I should say goodbye before I head out of state in a couple of days, that's all."

He didn't miss the way her lips pouted or her shoulders dropped. She hid it quickly enough, sure, but it still happened.

"Well, have a good flight, I guess," Camilla said.

Tom tipped his head toward the car. "I'm not heading out of state for a couple of days. Just thought you would like to know when and all."

Camilla abused her bottom lip with her teeth, and fiddled with the strap on her bag before saying, "I figured not answering your last couple of texts after Luna Park would have given you the hint that I'm not interested in anything beyond what we already did, Tom. We hooked up a couple of times, that's it."

"Had you answered my messages, you would have figured out I just wanted to meet up before I headed out of state. Say goodbye. Like friends do."

Her gaze darted away from his. "Friends, huh?"

"Sure."

"I don't fuck my friends, Tom."

"Well, we're definitely not anything else, right?"

Camilla cleared her throat. "Friends, then."

He brought out a package from behind his back, and Camilla's smile grew at the sight of what he held in his hand.

A small cupcake with one single candle on the top.

"Someone might have let me know it's your birthday today, but you didn't want to do anything for it because—"

"I was in classes all day," she interjected with a wave at the school behind her.

"Understandable. You must be studying nursing, right?"

"The end goal is to be a NICU nurse," Camilla admitted.

"I didn't know that, but it seems like it would fit your personality."

"You think you know my personality?"

"You've given me some peeks at it despite the fact you tried to blow me off," he replied.

She shot him an apologetic look. "Except here you are."

Tom flashed a grin and held the cupcake out for her. "With cake. Happy birthday, Camilla."

She came close enough to take the cupcake, and looked it over. "I'm really not looking for a relationship, Tom. That's why I blew you off, okay? Not because you're just good for a fuck, or anything else. I don't want to get involved with someone like that."

"I'm not asking for a relationship, Cam."

"No?"

He shook his head.

"Just a friend."

She smiled. "A friend, then."

"Eat your cake. All queens should have their cake, Cam."

She did.

He took the whole day as a battle won.

CHAPTER SIX

"WHY IS Cami girl pouting in the corner like somebody took away her puppy or something?"

It was Camilla or Cam to anyone else in her life, but at the salon she used along with August, the ladies always called her Cami. At first, she had tried to correct them, but found it didn't make a difference. Honestly, she quickly learned that nicknames were the way these stylists showed they liked a person. It was when they didn't give a client a nickname that a person had to be concerned about a missed clip, or a fucked up fade.

August was currently half way through getting her micro braids put in—a protective style she would keep for likely the whole winter. They had already been at the salon for going on four hours, and would probably be there for another few.

Camilla didn't mind. The salon was one of her favorite places, and *Chilla's Styles* was the only business she allowed to touch her hair now. The ladies knew how to work any kind of hair, weren't afraid to tell Camilla she was going to lose all her hair if she didn't relax with the chemicals, and August had been going here for years.

"Seriously, look at her," Chilla said as she finished another micro braid on August's head. "She's all sad over there—she's got a new pink fade, a blow out, and she might as well be boohooing."

"I am not," Camilla said.

"Girl, don't you lie to Chilla. I've known you since you were sixteen, Cami. You're all smiles whenever you get your hair done up."

Camilla scowled, and looked out the window. She was not in the mood to talk. Well ... really, she just didn't want to talk about what was bothering her.

August snorted. "Her newest boy toy is heading back home today, I guess."

Chilla raised a brow, and took another look at Camilla. "That so? Got your heart turned up for a boy, huh?"

"No," Camilla said. "I'm not turned up for anybody."

"Then why did you say that like you're all pissed off or something?"

Laughter filled up the salon from the other stylists and clients. Chilla was too good at her job—both wielding the tools to style hair, and keeping her patrons entertained. Camilla was not usually the topic of conversation, though.

"It didn't go the way it usually does for her this time around," August filled in. "Somebody didn't break hearts this time. He seemed to be pretty cool with how she rolls."

"And she rolls right back out of their life, right?" Chilla asked.

August laughed lightly. "Exactly."

"So what's the problem, Cami girl? Isn't that your deal with people? You're just out for a good time, not a long time. There isn't anything wrong with saying you might have found somebody you don't want to roll on."

Camilla let out a long sigh, and knew there was no way she would be able to get out of this conversation now. "Actually, I thought he might say goodbye."

Silence echoed back.

She looked to August and Chilla. Neither woman moved. Chilla, already working on the next micro braid, had stopped working altogether. August stared at Camilla as though she had suddenly grown a second head.

"What?" Camilla asked. "Is there something on my face?"

August smirked. "Other than *love*?"

Camilla made a gagging noise in the back of her throat. "That nonsense doesn't exist, thanks."

"You're going to tell me that you don't believe for a second your father loves your mother to death?"

Fine.

"So for some people, it happens. For me, it's like a unicorn. It doesn't exist."

"Does too," August said in a sing-song fashion.

"Stop your moving, Aug," Chilla said, getting back to work on the braids. "Maybe the boy was just following your lead, Cami girl. Decided to roll on out like you always do."

A small piece of Camilla seriously hoped that was not the case. A larger part refused to let her admit it.

"Not a boy," August said quietly, "very much a *man*."

Chilla cocked a brow, all interest and a sly grin. "That so?"

"Tall, dark, and handsome. Blue-eyed. *Cute*."

"You didn't even meet Tom," Camilla said to her friend.

August shrugged in the chair. "She told me about him. He's also got a good nine—"

Chilla whistled loudly, stopping August from saying more. More laughter lit up the salon, but the stylist passed a glance at the preteen girl having her natural hair combed out in the next chair. "That's enough, Aug.

We're going for family appropriate here."

"Yeah, August, shut up," Camilla grumbled.

"Sorry," August said.

"But not really," Chilla finished for her.

August grinned, but stayed quiet.

The growl of an engine outside the Brooklyn salon took Camilla's attention away from the conversation. For the moment, she was grateful.

Then, the car with the sexy noise came into a view. A black and red Bugatti supercar with silver accents pulled up to the curb directly in front of the salon's bay windows. Camilla's gaze widened at the sight of the beautiful piece of machine.

Next to a good fuck, Camilla liked fast cars.

Liked them *a lot.*

Just the sleek lines and sharp body of the Bugatti was enough to make her wet between her thighs.

And then he stepped out of the driver's side.

Tommaso.

Camilla's heartbeat raced, and thumped hard in her throat. She hadn't even realized that she was standing from the chair until she was at the front door.

"Is that him?" she heard Chilla ask behind her.

"Fits the description," August said.

"My God, isn't he something to look at."

"Right? She needs to get a picture of that just to keep," someone else said.

"Cami girl's about to get happier, ain't she?" Chilla asked.

"Jesus, you have no idea how much I hope so," August said.

Camilla wasn't paying them any mind. She stepped out into the cool, late September air, and tightened the bomber jacket around her neck to keep the breeze out. Tommaso leaned against the passenger side of the Bugatti with the kind of grin that could melt her fucking panties off … if she didn't throw them at him first.

She realized in that moment she had not given Tommaso enough credit when she described him to August. His fit, lean form looked damn good wearing a black suit, and looking like he was ready for some black-tie event. His gaze lifted from the ground to her as she stepped out on the curb. All it took was him swiping his thumb along his bottom lip, and Camilla swore between him and the car, her panties were done for.

At least she had gotten the all man part about Tommaso right when she filled August in.

"Don't lean against that car," Camilla admonished him.

Tommaso chuckled. "What, why? Do you know how much money I paid to switch my rental for this? And all for one single day, too. Well, I only get to drive it for one day."

She didn't understand what he was talking about, but it didn't much matter, either.

He gestured at her hair. "The pink is new. I like it."

"I change it up often."

"How often?"

"Often enough that I don't know what my natural color is anymore."

Tommaso laughed loud and hard, and fuck him for looking that good while doing it, too.

"How did you know I was here?" Camilla asked.

His gaze darted to the salon behind her. "You do know there's like fifteen people in the window watching us, right?"

She looked over her shoulder.

He was right.

Camilla gave them a wink, but quickly went back to Tommaso. "Everybody likes soap operas, Tom."

His brow furrowed.

"What?"

"Nothing," she said. "Again, how did you know I was here?"

"Someone let me know."

"My brother?"

Tommaso tipped a hand over, saying, "Someone."

"You couldn't text me?"

"I thought a face to face might be better. Also," he said, as he stepped away from the car while gesturing toward it at the same time, "I thought you might like to drive me to the airport."

Camilla's heart skipped a damn beat. "Seriously?"

"Someone else mentioned you liked fast cars."

"That's why you traded your rental in for this?"

"I mean, are we playing twenty questions, or are we driving?"

Camilla waffled between Tommaso, or going back inside. "August is still getting her micro braids put in."

"August doesn't give a shit!" someone yelled out the open salon door.

Tommaso's laughter came out dark and heady. "Oh, I get it, now. Soap operas. Do you gossip in salons as much as they do on the television, too?"

"Yes," someone else shouted from inside the salon.

Camilla glanced up at the sky, and almost wished the heavens would open up to swallow her whole. Tommaso's voice brought her back to reality.

"You can drive, babe."

He dangled keys, and let them jingle.

Her gaze wavered between Tommaso, the keys, and the Bugatti that looked like it was made to race and sin all at the same time.

"God, I love that car."

"Good."

"Was it my dad that told you I liked fast cars?"

Tommaso's grin said it was her father. "Maybe. How did you know I talked to him?"

"My mom let it slip. You never mentioned it to me, though."

"You made it pretty clear you weren't up for anything other than some fun where I was concerned, Cam. I'm still good with that, babe. You know?"

"Is that why you went and did this?"

She waved at the car.

Tommaso didn't give away a thing. "Really, I just figured since I was heading back to Chicago today it might be fun to hang out for a bit. Had you given me a chance, I would have taken you out to see a movie or dance. Your father said you liked that kind of stuff, too, but I was left with using your one other weakness."

"Fast cars."

He laughed. "Fast cars, Cam."

"You're heading to the airport right now?"

"Yeah."

"And you want me to drive you?"

"Yep," he said. "Well, we need to stop at my hotel first to grab my bag."

"How am I supposed to get back?"

She assumed the car would need to be left there for pickup.

Tommaso smiled. "Have some faith in me, Camilla. Do you want to drive this beast, or not?"

He jingled the keys again.

"Yes, she does!"

This time, it was August who called out.

Tommaso looked far too smug for his own good.

Camilla snatched the damn keys. "Let's go."

Camilla pulled the Bugatti into the underground parking garage of the hotel Tommaso had been staying at during his time in New York. She assumed he had been staying with Cross, but apparently not.

"You coming up?" Tommaso asked.

"Was this in your plans, too?"

"Pardon?"

"Get me here for one last fuck before you go?"

"No, actually I was having breakfast with your brother when they called to say the Bugatti was ready to be picked up. I went from there to the salon, and I've got just enough time to get to the airport at the moment. So again, do you want to come up, or are you good here?"

Okay, so that was a little bitchy of her.

Tommaso didn't even call her out on it.

"Go get your bags," Camilla said. "I'm good here."

"Suit yourself, babe."

Camilla did get out of the car to get a second look at it after Tommaso had disappeared into the elevator at the other end of the garage. She traced the car's beautiful lines with her fingertips, but nothing more. Leaving smudges on its paint job would be a sin, really.

She had bent down to wipe a speck of dirt off the grill's emblem when Tommaso's voice came from behind her.

"Do you two want to be alone, or …?"

Camilla stood with a laugh. "That was fast."

"I was gone fifteen minutes, actually."

She wasn't even ashamed that she had gotten lost in the car. "It's one hell of a vehicle."

"I'll remember you like it, then."

"And what's what supposed to mean?"

Tommaso's lips quirked up at the corner. "Means nothing, Cam. You ready to head to the airport?"

For a long while, she simply stared at him. He stared back, unmoved.

"Don't make a big deal out of what I'm going to ask, okay?"

"Depends on what you ask," Tommaso countered.

Camilla rolled her eyes. "Just … we can keep in touch, right? While you're back in Chicago, I mean?"

"I was kind of hoping we would, yeah."

"But we'll still be—"

"Friends," Tommaso interjected, and arching a brow. "You're not very used to this, are you? The whole friends thing?"

"Not with benefits," she admitted.

"Why?"

"Someone might catch feelings, or something. Isn't that what always happens? Somebody catches feelings for the other person and ruins the whole thing."

Tommaso chuckled. "Camilla, don't be crazy."

Something akin to hurt stabbed at her chest. "What, like somebody *couldn't* feel anything for a girl like me?"

Instantly, Tommaso's grin faded. "That's not what I meant at all."

"Then what did you mean?"

"I meant, it's a little late for either of us to be worrying about that sort of nonsense, Cam. I walked out of your apartment the next morning thinking you were the girl of my fucking dreams."

"You don't even *know* me, Tom."

"Nope, I thought that before I knew you liked cotton candy, or that you want to become a NICU nurse. I thought you were pretty fucking spectacular when you picked me up at a party, and barely even had to try. I like the way you run your life like it's nobody else's business, and I like where you come from. I still don't know a whole hell of a lot about you, but I would like to on your terms. That's it, and that's all."

A knot formed in her throat at his admission, and her chest tightened. She *liked* it—liked that he felt something for her, and was willing to say it out loud even if it meant she might bolt like a scared little deer.

Still, Tommaso stared at her, and kept her pinned in place with the intensity of his blue-gray gaze. "But it's like this, Cam, you're just not up for that with me, or anybody. That's fine; it is, really. Besides, we can keep playing this little game you've got going on for as long as you need to, but it won't make a difference in the end."

"I don't ... understand."

"I'm not the only one who caught some kind of feelings here, Cam. Otherwise, you wouldn't give a shit if you ever talked to or saw me again after today."

His statement made, Tommaso moved past Camilla to get back in the passenger side of the car. She stopped him by grabbing onto his wrist, and pulling hard enough to spin him back around to face her.

"You think that's why I asked if we could keep in touch?" she asked, unable to hide the defensive tone coloring up her words.

Tommaso smirked, and came close enough to Camilla that he crowded every bit of her personal space. She was forced to look up at him, and every breath she took was saturated with the scent of his woodsy cologne.

"That's exactly why, Camilla," Tommaso said. "That's why you agreed to be *friends*. Why you let me break your rules. It's why you didn't tell me to fuck off when I came to your school, and why I'm here right now. But we'll play your game, babe, for as long as you need. You do you, and I'll be over here doing me."

"You're ... you are ..."

Tommaso's grin deepened. "Need an adjective?"

"Frustrating, Tom. You're incredibly arrogant and frustrating."

"All of that and more, yeah."

His smug smile was still firmly in place. She almost wanted to wipe it right off his face, but she didn't. It seemed like her mind and body were not in agreement at all. One part of her was as angry as she could ever be—indignant that he called her out like that—while another part was extremely turned on.

"This does not accurately reflect how I feel right now," she told him with narrowed eyes. "Just so you know, Tommaso."

"What's *this*?"

"This!"

She reached up and grabbed his jaw, letting her manicured fingernails dig into his olive-toned skin as she pulled him in for a kiss that burned straight through her body. Like a fucking forest fire that had just caught a breeze, the intensity kicked up in her blood stream, thickening the heat in her body with every strike of his tongue against hers. It burned out of control, and devastated every rule and line she had in those moments.

He had been right.

She *hated* it.

His kiss reminded her of the way he fucked—strong and brutal. Every inch unforgiving and demanding. All hot and not a taste of sweetness to be found. Enough to make her wet and weak at the same damn time.

Tommaso groaned a sexy rumble as one of his arms wrapped around her back. He dragged her even closer to his body, and then grabbed her ass. In one moment, Camilla had been standing on the ground. In the next, she was lifted and sat down on the hood of the Bugatti.

She was all too aware that they were in a public underground garage, but that didn't seem to matter to her overheating body at the moment. Unashamed, and needing some kind of friction to soothe the sudden ache between her thighs, she widened her legs to let Tommaso slip in between them and get closer.

His erection grinded against her jeans. Like a silly, horny teenager getting her first taste of what pleasure might feel like, she moved her hips to feel more—to get more. She fisted his blazer and kept him tight against her body. His fingers dug into her backside, pulling her into the hard ridge of his cock.

Rhythmic and constant.

Firm and persistent.

Tommaso's lips ghosted over her throat, and his teeth left bite marks on her collarbones. He sucked on her neck as she trembled, and probably left a nice mark behind there, too.

As his mouth drifted to her ear, Camilla felt ready to explode.

All his sinfulness came back in a blink.

A few quick words.

Pretty slut. And, *gonna come rubbing on me like this? Where's your self-control, Cam?*

With him, she had none.

Camilla couldn't find it in herself to be ashamed.

Not at all.

It was only when Tommaso's lips found hers again, and he kissed her hard enough to make her mouth go numb, did the pressure finally release. She orgasmed with nothing but the pressure of his dick rubbing against her clit through her jeans.

And somehow, Camilla wasn't even surprised.

"Holy fuck," she mumbled into Tommaso's neck.

His laughter rumbled all over her body in the best of ways. She was still rocking her hips against his groin, and trying to get the last bit of that feeling she could. Thankfully, the garage was still empty, and she considered getting down on the ground to her knees right then and there to repay the favor.

Tommaso's fingers gripped tightly onto her thighs, and stopped her from moving. "Christ, you have got to stop, Cam, before you make me come in my pants like a damn fool."

Breathless, she tossed her head back and giggled. "Like you just did for *me?*"

"Hey, that takes skill. It doesn't take anything at all to do it for a guy, thanks."

She shook her head, and he kissed her mouth softly. The sweetness in the action made her still.

Tommaso didn't miss it for a second. "Hey, what's that for? Why'd you go cold like that on me?"

"I … I can't take you to the airport," she said quietly.

Tommaso kissed her quivering chin, and then her frowning lips. "Why not, babe?"

"Because you were right about what you said earlier. I'm just not sure what I want to do about it. I haven't been sure since the day we went to Luna Park. That's why I avoided you."

"Already figured that out, Cam. That doesn't change anything."

"It does for me, Tom. So we've got this great physical attraction, like nothing else, and I don't want to get it confused for something else. You know? I need to figure out if it's something else, or just nothing playing games with my head."

"Camilla—"

"I can't figure it out when I'm still messing around with you on the physical side of things. That's all."

"All right."

That was all he said.

All right.

Not like he was pissed off, or even disappointed. Actually, he smiled at her, and then kissed the tip of her nose in the sweetest way. Camilla didn't even do sweet because she was far from it, but here Tommaso was … and shit, it only made him that much more attractive.

"I'll call a cab to take me back to the salon where August has my car," Camilla said. "You should go—don't want to miss your flight."

Tommaso pushed away from Camilla with a chuckle. "No worries on the cab. I'll call one for me. This car is rented for another week—they don't do these luxury brands by the day at that place. Shame to waste it, right?"

Camilla let out a laugh. "Seriously?"

"Someone said you liked fast cars, babe, and I couldn't pass it up."

Every single word he spoke was another fissure crack inside her walls. Every touch, smile, and move he made was another fist clenching around her heart.

Camilla was not ready for this kind of thing.

She didn't know how to *do* this kind of thing.

Tommaso was unfazed. "Drop the car off to your brother when you're done with it at the end of the week. He knows where it has to go."

"You're killing me here, Tommaso."

In ways you can't possibly know.

He only smiled again.

"Call me or something, Cam. Keep in touch. You know you want to."

She didn't say yes.

She didn't say no, either.

CHAPTER SEVEN

THE PINK *faded super quick, and the ends were dry, so it's a bob now*, Camilla's text read.

Tom laughed as he read over Camilla's latest message. It had only been two weeks since he left New York, and this was one of the few messages Camilla actually sent him. He didn't initiate contact because he figured she had shit to settle on her own. If she wanted to talk to him, she would.

And she did.

A bob, huh?

Her reply came instantly with, *No bangs, and wavy.*

Tom was heading into the warehouse where the Conti crew usually worked out of. Other than his friend, Lou, and Adriano, the warehouse should be empty of other foot soldiers. Some were working their usual places—dealing, stealing, or whatever else.

A couple of them had some kind of scheme planned for boosting a truck just outside of the city limits. They wouldn't be back until later—when the whole crew would gather to handle the stolen goods—and Tom was grateful.

He was in no mood to deal with their defiance and ignorance today. Their nonsense had lessened since he came back from his break, and the time away had given him back some patience to handle it better should it come up again.

For now.

Tom supposed it helped that Adriano had stepped back from the crew a bit. Now, Tom was no longer the secondary Capo answering to Adriano, but rather, the head of the crew giving orders and making business for them. He wasn't sure whose idea that had been, and all Adriano offered was that he had other things to handle for a while.

It was one thing for the men of the crew to disrespect a secondary Capo. A guy who had a title, but who also didn't have a whole lot of say or control to begin with where the crew was concerned. Well, it was something else entirely now that Tom had the run of the place.

Given his propensity to walk a thin line where patience was concerned,

Tom had a feeling the guys on the crew would likely be careful for a while. Test him out, maybe. See how far they could push before he snapped back.

Just how it was.

He lifted the bay door to the warehouse as he looked back down at his phone. His first inclination had been to ask Camilla for a picture of the new hairstyle, but he hesitated.

Fuck it, he told himself. She started this conversation, so he took that as a sign she must have wanted to chat.

Show me, his next text said.

Tom shoved the cell phone into his pocket as he crossed the warehouse floor. Lou worked at the other end moving boxes to the far wall out of the way for later. His friend forgot his task as he saw Tom coming in his direction.

"You're not done yet?" Tom joked.

Lou leaned on a metal table. "Hey, if you wanted fast, you should have got one of the other pricks to do the job."

"Do you want to be one step closer to getting arrested, or doing grunt work and staying out of trouble?"

"Point taken."

Tom had also delegated this particular task to Lou for another reason. It allowed him five minutes alone with his friend without anyone else from the crew standing there to listen in like a bunch of *cafones*. He didn't need Lou taking shit from the other guys because the two were friends.

In his pocket, his phone buzzed with an incoming text message. Likely Cam. Tom was already pulling the phone out when Lou spoke again.

"Shit, I haven't seen very much of you since you got back from New York. How was that, by the way?"

"Interesting," Tom said, his attention now distracted by the photo loading up on his phone. "Very interesting, man."

To say the least.

"Business, or …?"

Tom glanced up to find his friend watching him curiously. Lou was not like Tom, really. His friend hadn't been born into mafia royalty like he had. Lou was just another foot solider; a kid that had come from Nothing, Chicago, and found easy money on the streets. He got mixed up in some business with Adriano's crew when he was fourteen or so, and the rest was history where his career in the mafia was concerned.

The two had met when Tom was a teenager following his uncle around. They had made fast friends, and here they were years later.

"New York is New York," Tom said. "Anytime someone from Chicago goes there—unless it's the boss—we all defer to whatever family we're there to deal with, you know? We don't have much pull or say there. So, no, not business."

"Just personal, huh?"

Tom looked down at his phone, and a slow grin spread over his face. *Personal.* Damn right. Every bit of that trip had been personal in too many ways to count for Tom, and it seemed like it wasn't entirely over yet.

Not if the picture he was looking at was any indication.

Camilla had taken a shot from her painted red smile, and down her naked chest. She had pulled her black lace bralette down over her ribcage, and he could see the high-waist, skin-tight pencil skirt covering the crossed legs. Her tongue was peeking out through her grin, and the tip graced her upper lip.

Like a damn tease.

Pink, hard nipples with new studs in the barbells. A single diamond dangling from a thin chain around her delicate throat. A throat he really wished he was holding onto at the moment while he fucked her cunt, mouth … ass. Fuck, he didn't really care as long as his dick was wet and inside Camilla.

Shit.

Yeah, he had gone there to that filthy place in his mind quick, fast, and in a real damn hurry. To be fair, he blamed her and this picture.

She hadn't lied about the bob, either. Platinum blonde, still, but she had lost the pink fade. The bob ended an inch or so below her jaw line, and had a soft, beachy wave to it. The very tips of the strands still held a faded touch of pink, but it wasn't as vibrant as it had been just two weeks earlier.

It still looked damned good.

Tom had the distinct feeling that Camilla could make any hairstyle look like something out of a runway show. He couldn't help but ask, *What are you going to do next?*

Camilla's reply was instant. *That's what you ask when I send you a picture like that?*

Laughing under his breath, and entirely forgetting about his friend just a couple of feet away, Tom typed back, *I was thinking about choking you while I fucked you, but the new hair had me curious. I like the new studs, by the way. The pink balls matches the hair a bit.*

I was thinking of getting something else done—lower, you know?

Tom whistled, and typed back, *How low?*

Her reply came in fast again with, *I've heard sucking or biting on a clit piercing feels like—*

"What are you grinning about—whoa," Lou said as he tipped Tom's hand down and got a partial view of Camilla's picture—only her legs given how many texts had come after the picture—and the texts.

Tom hadn't been expecting that, as he'd been too lost in his conversation with Camilla to pay any mind to his friend. Instantly, he jerked his arm back and got the phone out of Lou's sight. "No way, man. Fuck off."

Lou's eyes flew wide, and he tossed his hands up in surrender. "Shit, sorry. You were grinning like some kind of fool, and I just thought—"

He pointed at Lou, saying, "Not your business, okay."

"I got it, Tom, no worries."

Tom's phone buzzed again, but he didn't take the message. Instead, he shoved the phone in his pocket and decided to wait for a bit when he didn't have somebody looking over his shoulder. Even if that somebody was a friend. Camilla hadn't sent that picture for anybody else to be looking at, and Tom wasn't going to break her confidence in that way.

He meant to say something else to his friend, but the raising of the warehouse's bay doors took his attention to the incoming crew members.

Actually, just two.

Two that should have been with one other guy for the heist of a truck full of high end goods. The shit sold well on the streets in markets, vendors, and other places. Like a black market right out in the open for stolen product.

"Where's Joshua?" Tom asked.

The two fools looked between each other with wary gazes. Tom didn't see an incoming truck, either.

"And where's the fucking shit you guys were supposed to have here already?"

"Something happened," one of the two—Dale—said.

"We had to hightail it out of there. Josh got left behind," the other one—Terry—put in.

"Behind," Tom echoed. "What's that fucking mean, huh?"

"The blue line came out in force, Skip."

"Damn," Lou muttered.

"He got picked up by the cops?" Tom asked, both pissed and concerned.

This could be attention they didn't need.

The two foot soldiers nodded. "Yeah. It wasn't an easy boost like we thought—guess the trucker thought something was up."

Or the three idiots weren't careful enough.

This was a problem Tom didn't need at the moment. Only two weeks into running this crew on his own, and already, his guys were getting picked up on the street like fucking thugs. He couldn't really afford to lose a guy, considering how much work they had, but the twenty-something-year-old would be replaced soon enough. They couldn't be seen with someone getting picked up by the cops—it was bad for business.

"Your contact with Joshua ends now," Tom said, heading for the office in the warehouse. "All of you. No contact at all. Pass the word around. If I find out any of you are hanging out with him after he gets released—if he even does—you're done. You'll be lucky if you get a proper fucking grave. Don't test me."

"Got it, Skip," came the collective reply.

Tom hadn't fully closed the door before the conversation started up. They likely thought he couldn't hear him.

"Little boss needs to relax," Dale said.

"You guys know how this works," Lou replied. "You get picked up, then you're dropped. That's all there is to it."

"What, sucking Tom's dick now, Lou?"

"Fuck off, Terry."

"That why you were doing the grunt work today instead of helping us, or what?"

"Keep pushing him," Lou warned, "and keep pushing me, asshole. See what happens."

Tom closed the door. Lou had his side of things handled, and there wasn't much more he could do without possibly causing his friend more issues with the guys. Nobody needed that shit.

Pulling out his phone, he saw the rest of Camilla's text he hadn't gotten the chance to read, plus her newest one.

I might get it done, she said.

Tom couldn't help himself, but that wasn't anything new where she was concerned. *Tell me more*, he typed back.

Tom handed over a stack of cash to Adriano, and the older man slid it into the machine on the desk. The bills slipped through the counter, and came out in a neat pile on the other side. A number lit up the screen.

"You're about ten thousand short," Adriano noted.

"Might have helped had those bunch of idiots not fucked up the heist last week, not to mention the fact I lost a guy altogether."

Adriano hummed under his breath. "Josh still in lockup?"

"Seems so. Can't afford the bail, I guess."

"You're keeping the rest of them far away from him, right?"

"Best I can."

Tom had gotten wind that one of the guys from the crew paid a visit to Joshua, but nothing more. He only let it slide because the guy was upfront about it, and his motives. Apparently, Joshua's girlfriend was skipping town, and dropped by to let the other guy know. After that, it was all radio silence.

"I get why the cash is short," Adriano said as he glanced up at Tom from his seat behind the desk, "but that doesn't excuse it, Tommaso. That's the thing about this business—your father expects his dues, regardless if you've hit your bottom line or not. Figure something out with the guys, or make up the difference owed on your own. That's how it works. Got it?"

He didn't like it, but he understood.

"Yeah, I got it," Tom said.

"Also, keep an eye on those idiots."

"What do you mean?"

"You might be short for another reason, if you get my drift."

"Sticky fingers?"

As in, *thieves*.

Adriano lifted one shoulder in silent agreement. "I was rotating payment pickups because I thought the cash coming in was a little low. Not every payment fluctuates, you see. So when each one does fluctuate, and it's the same guy every time doing the pickup for you or running the scheme, that tells you something. Keep an eye on that."

"Yeah, I will for sure."

Nobody needed a thief on their crew.

"How's the crew otherwise?" Adriano asked.

"Quiet."

Adriano cocked a brow like he didn't entirely believe Tom. "That so?"

"They're not giving me shit to my face anymore."

"Just to your back, huh?"

Tom chuckled. "How did you know?"

"I had the same shit pulled on me when I was a young Capo. To be fair, I was even younger than you. That probably didn't help my case, or anything, but yeah. I handled it. Theo handled it when he worked under his brother. Your father handed it when he worked under his father. Make them—"

"Respect me, I know."

"Easier said than done, right?"

Tom shrugged. "I come from a different place than them, Adriano. They know it, and I know it. There's no hiding from it. I sit where I do for an entirely different reason than why any of them are sitting where they are. None of them are willing to let me forget it."

Adriano smirked. "Perhaps you should remember not to let any of them forget that despite your last name and position, you've still earned your spot, Tommaso."

"Dad likes to tell me—"

"Fuck your father."

Tom stilled, and let out a cough. "Pardon?"

Adriano waved a hand. "Listen, sometimes I think the boss forgets what it was like to be a young Capo trying to gain some ground with ignorant fuckers in a crew. Especially a crew they didn't build themselves, or a crew that was just thrown at their feet. He forgets that at one time, the Rossi name didn't mean privilege, but a fucking stain he had to work twice as hard as everybody else to get rid of. A stain that far too many weren't willing to let him forget he had to wear even when he did work ten times as hard as them to prove his worth.

"So yeah," Adriano continued with a laugh, "Fuck your dad on this right here. You do what you have to do to get control of that crew, and make them get their shit together. Take a guess at what your father likes more than subservient men, Tommaso. Go on, guess."

"Good business?"

"*Money.*"

Tom nodded. "Fair enough."

"Make good money, and he's not going to give two flying fucks how you've got the crew to do what you want. They're foot soldiers, Tom. They're replaceable. Sure, you vet them, and that takes a bit of time to make sure they're not some Fed or cop weeding their way in, but still … a couple of foot soldiers is nothing at the end of the day in this business. Fodder to a bigger fire, that's all."

"There are some good ones in the crew."

Adriano agreed. "There always are. Be mindful of those. As for the others … well, don't let them cause you too much grief. Otherwise, like a pack of stray dogs, they'll gang up on you when you're not looking. You're not a weak or stupid man, *nipote*. Never let them believe you are. Ever."

Appreciation and gratitude filled Tom, but he shoved it down. Adriano was not the type of man who liked platitudes or other nonsense. When he gave advice, he simply intended for it to be put to use, and little else.

"And while we're on the topic of your father," Adriano said after a minute.

Tom relaxed in the chair. "What, now?"

"You need to go pay him a visit."

"I will."

He'd been over to see his mother and younger sisters since he got back from Chicago. His mother made him pork chops like promised. He had left the mansion before his father got home, though. He wasn't in the mood to chat with Tommas, yet.

Tom was still a little sore on the gunrunning thing, after all.

"He might have mentioned to me that you're avoiding him," Adriano said.

"So?"

"Why?"

"Why does it matter?"

"Because beyond business, he's also your father, Tom."

"Who doesn't seem to want me to do the kind of business I want to do, Adriano."

His uncle smiled faintly. "The gunrunning?"

"Did he tell you that, too?"

"No, I just know you. Let it go, Tommaso. You don't have the time to be running the Outfit's guns with Cross Donati, and handling this crew as the head Capo."

Tom sucked air through his teeth as an idea filled his mind—one he wasn't very pleased about. "Was that why the position was finally handed over to me when I got back from New York? Dad got the idea in his head I was going to come back heavy on the gunrunning thing, and figured out a way to keep me busy?"

Adriano just stared at him.

Tom didn't look away, either.

"Well?" he asked. "Is that why?"

"You can handle this, and you were ready for it."

"That doesn't answer my question, Adriano."

"I'm not required to," his uncle replied.

Because *yes*, that's exactly what his father had done. It only pissed Tom off even more, and made him want to keep avoiding his father, if possible.

"I've let you know your father wants to see you," Adriano said like he could read Tom's mind, "and you know how this business goes."

"Never shun a boss."

It was a rule.

Adriano grabbed the stack of cash still sitting in the machine and said, "No, you never shun a boss, Tom, even when he's your father."

Fuck.

It took Tom another week before he finally went to see his father. Sara and Rebeka were showing off their new shoes and dresses when Tom strolled into the living room. Instantly, his little sisters might as well have been crawling up his damn legs.

"What do you think, Tom?" Sara asked, doing a spin to show off the dress.

"What's it for?"

"Nothing special."

"Mine's got more sparkles!" Rebeka shouted.

Tommas laughed from the couch, and stood. "All right, girls. Go find Ma for a bit, and bug her to buy you something else."

"Yes!"

His sisters darted into the hallway, and their shouts echoed back as they went in search of Abriella. She was probably hiding in her library again

"There's leftovers in the kitchen," his father said.

Tom shook his head. "Already ate."

Tommas arched a brow. "Oh?"

"Stopped in to see Joe on the way over, and had dinner with him."

"That's why you were late?"

"Guess so."

"Not because you've been avoiding me ever since you got back from New York a month ago."

Tom smirked. "Do I have a reason to avoid you, Dad?"

"I don't know—you tell me."

Well, if his father wanted to go down that route …

"I know you had Adriano hand me over the crew to keep my attention busy, and off the gunrunning thing."

Tommas nodded, unashamed. "And it's worked, son."

"No, I'm *busy*, but not dissuaded. It's still on my to-do list."

"I bet, however, it's not an argument I want to have tonight."

With a wave, Tommas headed out of the living room. Tom followed behind his father as the two navigated the large halls of the Trentini mansion. Soon, the two were inside Tommas's office with the door shut behind them.

Once his father was seated behind his desk, Tom took a chair in front of it.

"How's the crew, by the way?" Tommas asked.

"Busy."

He knew that was the answer his father wanted, and he didn't mind admitting it.

"It'll be a good lesson for you, then."

"How so?"

"Learning to delegate tasks, manage your time, and more. Being a Capo is not all sitting behind desks, idle hands, and throwing orders. Especially with a crew as difficult as Adriano's seems to be."

"Mine," Tom said. "It's my crew now, isn't it?"

Tommas smiled. "My mistake. What about New York?"

"It was a good trip."

"That so?"

"Yeah."

He would much rather be back in New York at the moment, but that was a discussion for another day. Likely not one his father wanted to have, considering.

"So, nothing interesting happened while you were there?" his father asked.

Tom had the distinct feeling his father was reaching for information, but what, he didn't entirely know. "Do you have something you want to ask me, or what?"

"I got a call, actually."

"From who?"

"Calisto Donati."

Ah.

There it was.

Tom rested back in the chair, and crossed his ankle over his knee. "What did he have to say?"

"Nothing, really. Just wanted to thank me for raising a decent son. Seems you went to him about his daughter despite the fact he doesn't put constraints down on the young woman regarding dating."

"What do you want to know, Dad?"

Tommas laughed, and his features relaxed from the previous sternness. "What made you seek him out—who she is, or something else?"

"Both. I know who she is, and I was interested in seeing her again. It's the right thing to do. You taught me that."

"Sure. Again, you said. You went out with her before you approached him?"

"Not exactly."

His father's brow raised, but he didn't push Tom for more information. Not that he would have given it. The two kept business like that private.

"She's why I stayed a little longer than first expected, actually," Tom admitted. "She had a birthday, and I wasn't ready to go at that point. Figured nobody would mind me staying a few extra days."

"Except you did know I wanted you back home."

Tom shrugged. "I still stayed, though."

Across the desk, Tommas stilled in his chair, and pinned his son in place with knowing eyes. For a long while, his father said nothing, simply stared at him.

"What?" Tom asked when he'd finally had enough of the silence. "Just ask."

"Are you still in contact with her?"

"Sort of."

They texted, had a call or two, but nothing more. Camilla had yet to ask if Tom planned on coming back, and he didn't even broach a similar topic. He didn't know what she was doing on the dating side of things, and she didn't ask him if he was busy with somebody else here.

Not that he was busy with someone.

His interest was still firmly tied up in Camilla Donati.

"Well?" his father asked.

Tom blinked, and realized he hadn't heard a word his father said. "What?"

"That probably answers my question, then. I asked if you planned on seeing her again, or whatever."

"Likely," Tom said.

His father leaned back in the office chair, and steepled his fingers. "Would you consider it serious?"

Tom laughed darkly. "Not at all."

"Yet, you just implied you intend to see the young woman again, and you're still in contact."

"Isn't that what friends do?"

"Friends don't typically get romantically involved, Tommaso."

Fair enough.

"It's complicated."

His father chuckled. "Complicated women are usually not worth the effort, son."

"That's your opinion."

Tommas sobered, and eyed his son again. "Unless, of course, a man loves that woman. Do you? Is that what it is?"

"Do I what?"

"Love the woman. Camilla, I mean. Do you love her?"

"Kind of crazy to love someone when you barely know them, isn't it?"

His father waved that statement off. "I loved Abriella damn near instantly. Something about her just … called to something in me. Sounds strange, I know, but it's true. I didn't realize until later that I did love her, and I *had* loved her from the beginning. Nonetheless, it's possible, and it happens. In those cases, you usually learn the reasons why you love them as you go along. It's the souls that call the hearts together, Tommaso."

"You sound like a walking Hallmark card."

"I sound like a father talking to his son, thank you."

"I didn't really come to visit to talk about this."

Mostly, he just wanted to get onto a new conversation because the things his father said made a hell of a lot of sense. Tom just didn't know how to deal with it all at the moment.

How could he?

He was in Chicago.

Camilla was in New York.

"Would you rather argue about petty things I won't budge on?" his father asked.

Tom scowled. "Not particularly."

"Make sure you visit more often now that you're back home and settled in. I should not have to pass messages through my brother-in-law to get you over here, Tommaso. Do not let it happen again."

Damn.

His father was not messing around at all. Really, he didn't mind. His father's straightforward approach to almost everything was one of the things Tom appreciated the most about the man. That, and how he loved and cared for his family.

"Fine," Tom said.

"Tell me more about this … Camilla."

He shot his father a look. "Why?"

Tommas smiled softly. "I have a feeling I need to know. Not to mention, I'm curious. Go on, son, tell me."

"She's …"

"Hmm?"

"Different."

"Different," his father echoed.

"Amazing," Tom added. "Probably a little too wild for her own good. She's got this way about her. She's like nothing else I've ever come up against."

"Sounds like you consider her a challenge."

Tom fixed the cufflink on his suit, and laughed with a nod. "She is. Every bit of her is a challenge, Dad."

"And you don't know how to back down from one of those, do you?"

"You taught me not to."

"One of my best traits," his father replied. "What else can you tell me?"

Lots of things.

Nothing.

"I'm considering heading back to New York as soon as I can," Tom admitted. "But things are busy here—thanks for that—and I can't really afford to leave the crew to themselves when every other day, there's some kind of issue popping up. I'm the only one handling them."

"To see her, you mean?"

"Who else would I go back for?"

"You have friends there."

"Fine, then, yes. I would go back for Camilla."

Tommas nodded. "I see."

"That's it? You *see?*"

"Oh, son, the rest is not for me to figure out. That's *your* job, Tommaso."

Tom quieted for a long while before he said, "I like her."

"I can tell."

"Not sure what to do about it."

"Well … I suppose that's something else for you to figure out, too, Tommaso. That's life, son. It has a way of keeping things interesting for us all."

Wasn't that the fucking truth?

CHAPTER EIGHT

"TRY THIS one, Cam."

She took the second evening gown her mother handed over, and eyed the silk piece. "Kind of boring, isn't it? Jesus, Ma, it looks like something a good girl would wear to her Catholic prom while the nuns reminded everyone dancing to leave enough space for the Holy Ghost."

"Camilla." Emma stared at her daughter like she was talking to a small child who didn't understand big words. "Now, come on. Be serious."

Camilla looked at the dress again.

Hell, she *was* being serious.

"Well, it is, Ma. It doesn't even have a slit in the leg worth looking at."

She checked the tag, and rolled her eyes.

"For the price," Camilla added, "it should have *something* to make it worth putting on, for fuck's sake. I am not paying two thousand dollars for a dress that won't even turn heads."

"Could you not swear in this store?"

Camilla side-eyed the prim and proper ladies milling about the store, and being helped by other women. "Ma, we all say the same things when we're on our backs, right? You can't tell me none of these women haven't said something similar."

Emma's cheeks flooded with pink before she yanked the dress back out of Camilla's hands. "My God, you are *awful*."

She laughed.

Battle won.

Her mother was easy to play like that, honestly. She liked joking with her mother when Emma was least expecting it because it always made for a good laugh.

Like now.

"You love me," she told her mother.

"Good thing," Emma joked. "Seriously, though, find a dress. We can't be here all day, and there are other shops I want to go to."

"Yeah, yeah."

Camilla went back to looking through the racks of designer dresses while her mother headed for the front with the white chiffon and silk gown she had picked.

Camilla pulled a soft pink gown from the rack, and held it up to look the item over. It wasn't anything to scoff at. It was a sweetheart neckline with extra-large crystals decorating the bodice. The chiffon skirt wasn't poufy, and didn't give off the princess vibe, which she appreciated. The back was a simple zipper.

Nothing about it was inappropriate, as far as that went. It also didn't feel exactly prom-ish. Something Camilla hated about gowns. The front of the gown's skirt was slit up past the knees, and would likely show off a bit of leg.

Some nice heels, and it would do.

Camilla turned with the dress to find her mother standing there waiting. "What do you think?"

"Well, at least you found something that doesn't scream *club*."

"Or do you mean to say slut, Ma?"

Emma gave her daughter a look that shamed Camilla damn near instantly. "You know I would never use that word for you, Cam."

"I know. I'm just … Never mind."

"Touchy, I think. The word you're looking for is *touchy*."

Camilla moved a bit to the left as a woman passed her by. Once the lady was out of earshot, she turned back to her mother. "And what's that supposed to mean, Ma?"

"Just what I said. You're a little touchy lately on certain things. Not like you usually are."

"I am not."

"Camilla, I asked if you were seeing anybody lately, and you practically bit my head off."

"Because you talk to August all the time. You know I'm not seeing anybody. I never *see* anybody, anyway."

"Yes, but I didn't talk to *you*."

Camilla sighed. "Can we just get the dress and then go pick up August? She wanted to find a dress for tonight when we go out to the club. I promised she could look around with us today."

Emma frowned, but said nothing.

She knew her mother wouldn't push her for more.

It just wasn't Emma's style.

Right then, Camilla was grateful.

As it was, her phone happened to be burning a hole in her damn pocket. A single text earlier had sent her into a tailspin, and made her—as her mother put it—touchy.

Frankly, that was happening a lot lately.

Camilla could blame a lot of things to distract people when they pointed it out to her. She was getting damn good at brushing them all off when others asked about her mood. At the moment, the truth was scarier than she was willing to admit.

She was touchy.

Her emotions. Her interest. Her restlessness.

All touchy.

Tommaso Rossi was entirely to blame.

How did that presentation for your project go?

"Are you even listening to me, Cam?"

Camilla continued staring down at the screen of her phone despite how irritated August sounded. It was nothing, she thought. Nothing but a simple, stupid text from Tommaso that should not have sent her into an emotional tailspin.

Hell, it had now been *three whole months* since she last seen the guy face to face. Sure, they texted back and forth, and occasionally she called to actually hear him speak. That was about it, though. Their conversations were never too deep or involved.

They stuck to chatting about day to day things, and what the other was up to, if it was anything interesting. He never asked about personal shit— dating, guys, her family, or otherwise. She didn't ask him about those things, either.

One simple text from him should not make her world tilt on its entire axis. Like the world had slowed, tipped, and then started spinning in the opposite direction all of the sudden.

Yet, there the text was.

And here Camilla's world was.

Like a fucking Merry-Go-Round or something.

"Cam!"

Finally, Camilla looked up from her phone. "Yeah?"

August glared at her from across the bedroom. "What is up with you?"

"Nothing."

"Like you didn't just stare at your phone for ten whole minutes, and ignored me when I called your name over and over again?"

Camilla tossed the phone to the bedspread, and gave August all of her attention. "Sorry, August. That dress looks nice."

August pursed her lips, and gave Camilla a look that voiced her displeasure without ever saying a word out loud. Camilla swore her friend was too damn good at that shit, and it could make her feel like a child being scolded.

"Seriously, the dress is nice," Camilla said. "Actually, nice is kind of understating it."

"You think?"

"It's awesome, and you look great in it."

Camilla wasn't lying to placate her friend. The dress did look fantastic, and August pulled it off spectacularly. Despite wavering on buying the dress earlier because of the price tag, Camilla figured August would find the purchase more than worth it now.

With a little spin to face the mirror, August smoothed her palms over the maroon-colored club dress. The shiny beading on the low cut neckline sent sparkles casting a rainbow over her dark skin. She had pulled her micro braids into a high piled, wrapped bun at the top of her head, and used dark kohl to line her eyes, and red lipstick to emphasize her pout. The five inch heels topped the whole outfit and look off, really. It was just enough sex and sass mixed with sophistication.

Her friend might have only been eighteen, but she looked every inch of twenty-one in that dress and those shoes. Once Camilla was all dressed up, and they met their friends at the club, she had no doubt the group would have zero issue with getting past the bouncers at the front. Likely without even having to flash their fake IDs.

Besides, the majority of Camilla's friends were legal age to get inside the clubs and drink. She was edging closer to not even needing a fake ID at all, now that she was twenty. She wondered if partying in a club would still be as fun when she was no longer breaking the rules just to do so.

In her distraction, Camilla's gaze had wandered back to the bed, and the phone still sitting face down on the bed spread. All over again, her thoughts jumped right back to Tommaso Rossi, and his goddamn text.

He was like a habit she couldn't kick. Problem was, it had been a long while since she had gotten a fix of him.

Maybe that was the problem. Camilla just needed one more round with Tommaso, and she could get this lingering desire and confusion out of her system. She wasn't really sure it would work, though, all things considered.

Like the part of her that missed him. A part that wished they had been given just a little more time to ... well, to do anything together.

"Are you wearing the gold dress or the black jumper?" August asked.

Camilla glanced away from the phone. It wasn't like she needed to be caught staring at it again, or for August to think she was ignoring her. "Probably the gold dress."

"You're the only bitch I know that can pull it off."

She smirked. "Yeah, I try."

August spun back around to face Camilla. "Well, hurry up and get dressed. It's Jill's birthday tonight, and we still need to pick something up for her."

"Yeah, yeah. Chill."

She took her sweet time getting dressed, brushing her hair into a simple chignon, and then slipping on her heels. She took the most time with her makeup because unlike August, a splash here and there did nothing for Camilla. She liked the whole damn face to be done with some kind of edgy style to stand out in the crowd.

The two friends were just different in that way.

"You know," August said as she fixed a pair of Camilla's bangles onto her own wrist, "I thought you would be more excited about going out tonight."

"I'm excited."

"Really?"

Camilla shrugged, and dug through the closet to find a clutch and coat to match her outfit. "I mean, yeah, I guess. It's been a little while since I've been out."

She came out of the closet to find August staring at her in the oddest way.

"What?"

"A while?" her friend asked. "Cam, it's been like … three months since you were out and did anything like this."

Had it?

Camilla thought back, and realized August wasn't overstating it. Actually, she hadn't partied since that gathering at Zeke's where she met Tommaso for the first time. She could easily blame it on school as that had picked up, and kept her busy. Some test, a new project, lecture, or whatever else. Something for family usually kept coming up as well. Not to mention, just the day to day things for *life*.

Although, none of those things had ever made a difference for her in the past. If she wanted to go out and have a good time, then that's exactly what she did. If she wanted to go out and pick up some guy or girl to make her night a little better, then that's what she did when the desire arose.

Truth was, Camilla just hadn't been in the mood. Not for partying, or for random sex with a stranger.

"I guess it has been a while," Camilla said as she shrugged on a trench coat. The wide belt would cinch tight at her waist, and show it off beautifully. "All the more reason for me to enjoy it tonight, right?"

August smiled. "Right, babe. So hey, who was texting you earlier? Was that why you were acting like aliens had eaten your brain?"

Camilla laughed. "It was nothing, so let's go."

Not nothing, her heart whispered.

Tommaso had remembered a project presentation Camilla mentioned she had coming up. She randomly brought it up in a conversation to him almost two weeks earlier when she had to let him go to head out in order to work with a partner on the project.

Today, it had been due.

Camilla decided to go out to her friend's party at the club with August as a way to celebrate finally getting it done, and the great initial remarks from the professor.

But what really made her day? The thing that made her world tilt on its axis?

Tommaso remembering without prompting. Him *asking*.

She added it to the growing pile of things about Tommaso that kept making her like him more and more. Another thing to make her hesitate on deleting his number in an attempt to break the habit he was now becoming to her. Something else about him that made her think there was far more to Tommaso than she really knew.

More things she might want to learn.

Camilla wasn't supposed to be *that* girl. The girl that got heartsick over a guy she barely even knew.

But fuck …

Here she was.

Camilla sipped on the green Grasshopper martini at the bar as she mulled over the text on her phone. She should be out on the dance floor with August working off some of the calories from the sweet drinks, or upstairs in the VIP room with the rest of their friends celebrating Jill's twenty-second birthday.

But nope.

Instead of doing those *fun* things, Camilla was leaning against a bar, ignoring the dancing crowd behind her, and staring at a text. The same text Tommaso had sent her earlier, but she had yet to reply. She didn't give him a response to his message, but he also hadn't prompted her again, either.

Like he was the hunter, and she was the prey.

The guy was waiting on her.

Just like he said.

Sighing, Camilla set the phone down and emptied the rest of her glass without hesitation. Already, she was two drinks beyond the limit and wouldn't be driving home.

"Hey, are you going to come dance with us, or what?"

August's too-high voice told Camilla her friend was also feeling a little too tipsy to be driving them home. Camilla spun around just in time to see August winking and waving her fingers at a guy, gesturing for her to come back out on the dance floor.

Then, her friend's gaze was back on her in an instant. "Well?"

"I'm good. My feet are sore."

August looked down at the heels Camilla wore with a raised brow. "Really? Because you wear higher heels than those to workout, Cam."

Jesus.

Why did August have to know her so damn well?

"Also, that guy's friend has been checking you out for the last twenty minutes."

August pointed at the man sitting at a table a few feet away from the dance floor. Camilla found the guy was staring at her entirely unashamed at having been caught. He flashed her a cute grin which usually would have been something she took as a challenge.

Not tonight.

"Not interested," Camilla said, turning back to the bar. She waved at the bartender down the way to make her another drink. Not that she needed it. "Maybe another night, August."

"Seriously?"

Slowly, Camilla turned back around. "Yeah, why?"

"Camilla, that guy is topping six feet, and we both know you love tall. He's got blue eyes, dark hair, and a killer smile. He's *built* because guess what? They play hockey. All of that is entirely you're type, but you're *not interested*. Bullshit."

She passed the guy another look, and lingered on his handsome features a bit longer to take inventory. Nothing August said was a lie. The man was built, blue-eyed, tall, and entirely her type when it came to hooking up with somebody.

His height, eye color, and haircut also reminded her of Tommaso.

Just like that, Camilla wasn't interested. All it took was a single reminder of Tommaso, and she wanted the real thing much more than some one-night stand replacement.

"He's not him," Camilla said quietly, "and I'm just not interested, you know?"

August's brow furrowed, and for a second, Camilla wondered if her friend had heard her over the club's loud music. "Who?"

Apparently, she had heard.

Camilla shrugged. "Tom."

"Wait, so you mean to say if the guy was blond, and dark-eyed then you might have a different opinion?"

"Nope, not at all."

August lifted a single brow high. "Wow. Didn't think I would see the day."

"Shut up."

"Still not ready to face the music, huh?"

"*Shut up*," Camilla said, drawling the words out the second time. "Go dance with his friend, August, before another girl shakes her ass at him."

"Hey!"

"For what it's worth, you've got the best ass in here tonight."

Her friend smirked. "And don't you fucking forget it. Don't leave without me, huh? I'll go home with you. We can do breakfast tomorrow."

"Don't ruin whatever plans you were making with what's-his-face just for—"

"I'm going home with you."

Firm.

Absolute.

No room to argue.

Camilla nodded. "All right."

"And hey, text the guy back, Cam."

"How do you even know that's who was texting me earlier?"

"Lucky guess," August said, smiling wide. "Plus, I saw you over here staring at your phone like a zombie again. Figured it was probably about the same thing as earlier. We both know Tom is the only person making you act like that lately."

"Shut up."

August laughed. "Text him back."

Ugh.

"Fine."

"You don't have to make this whole thing so hard on yourself, Cam. Just ... welcome it."

"I don't even know what *it* is, August."

Her friend snorted, and then waved her off. "You're the most fucking impossible, clueless girl ever. I mean, I love you, but you really are that difficult, Cam."

"Lies."

"Mmm, nope. I'll go ditch the guy. We'll head out of here. Sound like a plan?"

Camilla nodded, but she was already looking down at her phone and typing back to Tommaso as August walked away.

Probably aced the project, Camilla typed.

Tommaso's reply came in thirty seconds later. *Congrats. Not even surprised. Smart girl.*

Camilla was a lot of things.

Filthy.

Loved.

Fun.

Restless.

Free.

Wild-hearted.

Smart.

Quick.

Out of all of those things, she wondered what it might be like to simply be *his*.

That scared her.

That made Camilla want to run.

What the fuck was wrong with her?

CHAPTER NINE

"LOOK AT your sorry ass sitting behind that desk, and doing fuck all."
Cross stood in the office doorway with his arms folded over his chest, and a
shit-eating grin plastered on his face. "This a new thing for you—sitting in
the Capo's chair—or what?"

Tom laughed as he stood from the chair. "It's a new development,
yeah."

"Since when? You weren't the one behind that desk the last time I was
in Chicago."

"Five months ago or so."

"Since you came back from New York, then?"

Tom nodded. "About then, yeah."

"Are you liking it?" Cross asked.

"Do you like acting as your father's underboss?"

"Two entirely different positions, man."

"My question remains the same."

Cross chuckled. "It's a lot of work. Busy days, I guess."

"Same here."

"I bet." Cross stepped into the office, and slammed the door closed
behind him. "I figured while I'm in the city, I should come over and say
hello. See what you were up to since you don't know how to use a fucking
phone."

"I call you."

"Once in a blue moon. I think you talk to my sister far more than you
talk to me. I don't know if I should be offended about that, or not. I mean,
considering you're supposed to be *my* friend and all."

"Offended or jealous? You do know they're not the same thing,
right?"

Cross barked out a laugh. "Fuck you, you prick."

Tom rounded the desk, and grabbed hold of Cross's reaching hand.
Despite what Cross said, Tom did call him every couple of weeks just to
chat. He still missed his friend, though. The two gave each other a quick
one-armed hug before letting go.

"It's good to see you," Tom said.

Cross shoved his hands deep into the pockets of his leather jacket. "We should do something, Tommaso. I'm going to be in the city for a couple of weeks before I'll head back to New York."

Tom cocked a brow. "A good week and a half of that will be spent with you on a gun run, right? I know the run for the cartel is coming up. A deal Theo made in exchange for two shipments of cocaine next month."

"So?"

Cross posed the question so flippantly that it made Tom want to laugh. His friend had no idea the constant silent fight he had been having with his father for months now about guns and running them.

For as hard as his father tried to keep him away from the gunrunning side of the Outfit's business, Tom still got word of what was going on every once in a while. Usually, one of his uncles would let the information slip when he asked the right questions.

"Not sure a gun run would be smart for me to get in on right now," Tom admitted.

Cross scoffed. "What, like sitting behind this desk all day is doing anything for you? You can't tell me that it is, Tom."

No, it really wasn't.

"Fact remains, Cross, I am way too busy right now to be up and going for something like that."

"You sure?"

No.

"Yeah," Tom forced himself to say.

Cross rocked on his heels, saying, "Suit yourself, but the offer is still open should you want to take me up on it. I've got a couple of days before I need to get on the road, you know."

"Don't you have a partner for these runs?"

Cross *always* used a partner, or he should be using one. It was one of the first things the two had learned when Theo taught them about the business of gunrunning. A partner could make all the difference in a good, clean run, or a failed one. A partner could save your ass in more ways than one, honestly.

"Haven't used a partner in a year or more," Cross said, shrugging.

"Kind of playing with fire, isn't it?"

"I don't have patience for people's shit, man."

"Or they don't have patience for yours."

"Same difference," Cross grumbled. "Is the fact you're busy the reason you haven't headed back to New York to see my sister, or what?"

Tom smirked. "That's real smooth of you, man."

"Wasn't going for smooth."

Yeah, Cross never did.

Blunt to a painful point.

Never failed.

"Cam's not asked me to come back," Tom admitted. "I mean, we talk and whatever, but that's not come up yet."

"You need her permission or something? It isn't obvious she likes you, or what?"

"It's obvious. I'm not blind or a fool."

"So, it is a permission thing."

"Something like that."

More like, he needed to know Camilla actually wanted him there. Tom didn't need to be wasting his time, or hers. When she let him know something worth knowing, then he would make an effort.

Cross's gaze darted to the clock on the wall. "You busy right now? We could grab some food."

Today was supposed to be payday for Tom … in a way. Whatever money the crew had made over the last week needed to be on his desk before night fell over the city. It was his rule, and he didn't allow his guys to bend it, no matter what. He had learned over the last few months that if he gave any of those fuckers an inch, they would not hesitate to take another mile.

Even so, Tom didn't want to refuse Cross's offer.

Cross stood still, waiting for an answer.

"Well?" his friend asked.

"Do you mind ordering it for here?"

Two birds, one stone.

Cross passed a look at the flat screen television. "There anything good to watch on that?"

"Any channel you want."

"Find me a game to watch. I'll order pizza."

Tom headed for the couch that faced the television. He dropped down on one end, and Cross took a seat on the other. Both used the coffee table as a footrest while Tom flipped through satellite channels. Cross's voice carried over the noise of the television as he ordered from his favorite pizza place in Melrose.

"That's going to be cold by the time it gets to here," Tom told him.

Cross wordlessly pointed at the microwave across the office. Soon, his friend had hung up the phone and shoved it back in his pocket.

"So, hey," Cross said.

Tom looked over at him. "What?"

"Are you sure you don't want to go on that run with me?"

"Don't tempt me, Cross."

"You should go."

"I should," Tom agreed.

"But will you?"

Tom chuckled. "That's the million dollar question."

It was a while later before Tom's crew started filtering into the warehouse one by one to pay their dues for the week. Half of his attention was on counting the money while he ate pizza. The other half was on the hockey game.

"Fuck, come *on*," Tom groaned. "You know that was a damned goal, you asshole."

"I saw the playback," Cross argued, never turning around. "It didn't go over the line all the way."

"It did."

"Nope."

"See you on Monday, Skip."

Tom waved a hand at Dale to excuse him from the office just as the machine on the desk beeped to say it had finished counting the bills. Dale had just reached for the door when Tom looked down to see the number on the cash counter.

He hesitated.

Took in the number again.

And *again*.

"Dale, you're short," Tom said.

Instantly, Cross reached for the remote on the couch, and turned down the television. Tom discarded the piece of pizza he had been working on, wiped his hands down on his jeans, and fished the cash out.

"I double counted, Skip," Dale said.

His tone sounded weak even if his words came off sure.

Tom didn't miss it, but he opted to ignore Dale as he started slipping through the bills in his hand. He counted them once, and then twice. Finally, Tom set the money down on the corner of the desk, feeling a numbness settle into his bones at the realization settling through his mind.

There was only one reason Dale would be short on cash.

"What were your pickups this week?" Tom asked.

"The three bookies, and a couple of pickups from the Heights."

Tom nodded. "You know I'm aware how much cash should have come in from those payments, right?"

Dale cleared his throat. "One of the bookies said he didn't get the total owed from one of his—"

"Bullshit."

"That's the story I was told, Skip."

Tom yanked a drawer open on the desk, and reached for the weapon inside. He placed the gun carefully on the top of the desk, and stared hard at the man across the room. Dale kept glancing at the door like he was going to bolt. Tom had no intention of letting the fucker get that far—

thieves had a habit of spreading, after all.

"Those bookies know to make up what they don't have because we allow them to keep the other part of the cut when it does come in. All the Capos have a good working relationship with their bookies because we have to. A little bit of trust goes a hell of a long way in this business. Try again, Dale."

Cross pushed up from the couch, and grabbed a couple of napkins from the desk. Still, he stayed a couple of feet back from the two men conversing, and didn't try to join in. Tom appreciated it.

Dale, however, couldn't seem to stand fucking still. His gaze darted in all directions like a wild cat caught in a corner. He shoved his shaking hands into his pockets, and edged closer to the doorway.

Tom palmed the butt of the gun. "Adriano thought someone might be skimming off the top of his money a while back. He thought some of the payments coming in were a little short, and that's why he started rotating pickups between different guys. Some of these payments are bottom line, and don't change a damn dime. Ones like these, Dale, when I already knew ahead of time from the bookies because they call in to let me know what to expect. I bet you didn't know that, huh?"

Dale swallowed hard. "I—"

"Is it because I'm young that you all treat me like a fucking idiot? Or is it because I was born with more zeroes in my bank account than you'll ever have?"

Cross snorted under his breath at that one.

Dale inched closer to the door again.

Fuck this shit.

Tom was done talking.

Talking did *nothing*.

Not in this case.

"A thief is a thief is a thief," Tom said. "And do you know what the only good thief is, Dale?"

The man didn't answer.

Cross did. "A dead one."

Exactly.

Fast as a blink, he lifted the gun, aimed, and pulled the trigger.

It was only after Dale's blown out skull hit the floor that Tom realized a couple of other guys on the crew were waiting outside the office.

Tom figured this was what his father would call a teachable lesson for all. It was good for these fools to see that he wasn't playing around anymore, and he wasn't going to take any of their shit after today.

"Come on in," Tom told them with a cold smile, "and don't mind the mess, guys."

Tom laughed as one of the guys helping to pack up the guns into the false bottom of the eighteen-wheeler fell flat on his ass. The icy ground had no mercy for the men trying to work.

"Want some skates?" Tom called out.

"Fuck you, Rossi."

"Want a hand up, then?"

"You would just let me drop back down."

"Likely," Tom agreed.

"Asshole."

Tom chuckled when the guy tried to get back up, but only fell once more. February was one bitch of a month. Nearing the end of winter, it fooled people into thinking spring was nearing, but it was never near enough.

He did end up helping the guy up. Another one of the guys working to help load up the smuggled guns starting tossing a salt and gravel mixture over the ground. It would help a little bit, but not a whole lot.

"Shit, can we get out of this cold for five minutes?"

"Yeah, let's do that," Tom agreed.

The group headed inside the warehouse, and Tom pulled down the bay door. It effectively closed the cold outdoors off, and left them inside the heated warehouse. Up above their heads, the heaters turned on full blast.

"Warm up for a bit," Tom told the guys, "and then we'll finish up, okay?"

"Sounds good."

"Sure, Tom."

He waved two fingers over his shoulder, and headed for the back of the warehouse. He knew exactly where he would find Cross, and he wasn't wrong.

At a metal table, Cross had a map spread out. The guy was meticulous on the details when it came to his gun runs. Every single thing was planned out to the finest of details. He planned for anything, and everything.

When something went wrong, Cross had three backups on hand to fix it. Tom respected that, and frankly, he had learned a lot from his friend's ways when it came to gunrunning. It was just too bad he would likely never get to put it to use.

Cross glanced up from his work as Tom approached. "Still not up for going with me on this run?"

"After that mess last week, you should know I really can't leave my crew for too long."

"It'd only be a week, maybe. I'm sure you've got someone to handle them for that long."

He did.

Lou. Adriano.

Plus, Tom could delegate tasks. The guys on the crew would be kept busy, and then they wouldn't have even a second to find themselves in shit. Still, he heard his father in the back of his mind warning him, and drawing clear lines in the sand.

Gunrunning was one of those lines.

"Not this time," Tom said.

Cross nodded at the guys near the front of the warehouse. "Thanks for helping them, anyway. An extra pair of hands is always needed."

"It was good—like old times. You know, back when we first learned how to do some of this shit with Theo."

"You think? It's definitely not my favorite part of the job."

"Hey, you're the bigwig gunrunner now, Cross. You don't have to worry about dismantling weapons or packing up guns. You get all the money and glory while they do the grunt work."

Cross cocked a brow. "And put my ass on the line every time I make a run, Tom."

"Yeah, I know. I'm fucking with you." Tom shoved his hands in his pockets, finally feeling warm enough to maybe open the bay doors and finish packing in the last few cases of guns. "Besides, I'm starting to realize I needed something like this."

Cross's attention was already back down on the map. "What's that?"

"Just … being around people I actually like, and don't want to kill."

A laugh echoed from his friend. "Yeah, that makes all the difference when you're working, doesn't it?"

"Makes it less of a chore."

And all his crew felt like was one big, useless fucking chore added to his daily life.

Tom didn't admit it out loud, though.

"Maybe you're in need of another break, man," Cross said, never looking up from his work.

"Hey, if I don't have the time to head out on a run with you, then I don't have time to take a break to do something else."

Cross shrugged. "Make time."

Easier said than done.

So was his life.

"Tommaso. I heard you were in this part of the city."

Tom spun around at the sound of his father's voice. Across the warehouse, Tommas headed in Tom's direction. At his father's sides, the man's right and left hands flanked him. Damian Rossi, the underboss for the Outfit, and Theo, the front boss and the man who controlled the gunrunning portion of the business.

He shot Theo a look, knowing that was likely how his father found out he was here. After all, Theo had been at the warehouse earlier when Tom first arrived, but left shortly after saying he had business to handle.

Right.

Business.

"Had to call him, huh?" Tom asked Theo.

"Be nice," his uncle, Damian, said.

Technically, Damian was a cousin, but Tom had grown up knowing the man as an uncle. Same with Theo, really. All of them—and even Adriano—were terribly close friends. It made it very difficult for Tom to do anything without one of them telling the other, and then the information almost always made it back to his father somehow.

"How's this run looking, Cross?" Tommas asked.

As usual, Cross was focused on his work. He answered, of course, but didn't look away from the maps. "It's looking fine, Tommas. Nothing to worry about."

"Good, good." Tommas's gaze turned on Tom. "I thought you had work to do on your side of the city today?"

"Someone needed an extra pair of hands."

Damian strolled past Tom, and clapped him on the shoulder. He didn't say anything, though.

"As long as the extra pair of hands is all he needed," Tommas said.

"I could use a partner on the run," Cross said.

"You didn't tell me that," Theo replied. "You rarely use partners now."

Cross looked up from his work, and his gaze darted between Tom and the other men. "It's good for Tom to keep up on his skills, that's all. Wouldn't want him getting rusty when he might need to be your backup someday, right?"

"Tommaso doesn't run our guns," his father said. "You do, Cross. Concern yourself with that at the moment."

"I am, but I'm just saying—"

"Either way," Tommas cut in, making sure his voice was heard, "Tommaso will not be the one going on the run. I'm the only one who gets to make the choice."

Tom shot his father a look. "I wasn't going on the run to begin with."

"Had to make sure."

"Of course you did," Tom muttered, "because apparently my word means fuck all."

Frustration and irritation ran rampant through Tom, but he shoved it back down. He knew why his father was doing this, but that didn't mean he particularly fucking liked it. He didn't need a reminder about who was in charge.

Tommas frowned. "I didn't say your word—"

"You don't have to."

Tom shook his head, knowing this was the one thing he and his father were never going to see eye to eye on. Every single thing else between them was as good as gold, and smooth fucking sailing, but not this. Tommas couldn't just take that his request to his son would be heeded. No, he had to do shit like this, too.

It drove him nuts, *and* made him defensive. Two things he hated the most.

"I'm heading out," Tom said, done with the whole show.

"Tommaso, wait a damn second."

Tom headed past his father with a wave. "Nah, I get it, Dad. You made your point. Later, Cross. Good luck on the run."

Cross didn't answer him.

Nobody followed behind.

Thank God for small miracles.

"It's not a bob anymore."

Camilla's dark eyes lit up, dancing with amusement on the screen. "No, it's grown out a bit."

To make a point, she flipped her hands through her shoulder-length brown—*now*—locks. Seemed she had changed the color again, too. Tom didn't know how to keep up with this girl.

He kind of liked it, though.

"Did you see my brother?" Camilla asked.

"A couple of times last week, yeah."

"Lucky him."

Tom raised a brow. "What's that supposed to mean, Cam?"

"Nothing. So hey, I like this Skyping thing."

He did, too. Much more than chatting on the phone or the occasional text. She was crystal clear on the screen, giving him a nice view of the sports bra and tiny shorts she was lounging in. She sat cross-legged on her couch with the laptop set up on the other end. Tom had settled into his bed before making the Skype call.

"It was a good idea," Tom said. "At least I actually get to look at you like this, and not sit here and wonder."

"Wonder what?"

Tom grinned. "The usual—what you're wearing, and all that shit."

Camilla laughed. "My eyes are up here, Tom."

His gaze drifted on the screen to look up at her face. He found her smirking, and she'd arched a brow high in response to his leering.

"What?" he asked. "You can't get on Skype half naked and expect me not to look, Cam. That's unfair."

"It's not like I'm indecent or anything."

"Nice try, girl. You could make a fucking paper bag look indecent, and you know it."

Her grin deepened, turning sexy and sinful in a blink. Just the sight alone was enough to make Tom's dick hard beneath the sweats he'd thrown on after his shower.

"Oh, I forgot to tell you," she said.

"What's that?"

"I got that piercing done. You know …" Her finger pointed downward, and she flashed her teeth. "Down there."

Tom's brow lifted high, and his throat tightened. "Did you now?"

"Wanna see?"

"You're wicked, Camilla."

She winked, and didn't deny it. "It hurt, but not as bad as I thought it would. The girl who did it made me sign this stupid waiver saying I understood that I might lose all feeling in my—"

"You didn't, right?"

"Sign the waiver, or lose feeling in my clitoral nerves?"

"*Camilla.*"

She gave him a little shrug, and then dipped her hand between her thighs. On the screen, he had the sexiest view of her fingers edging beneath cotton panties. The speakers caught the sound of her fingers stroking through her sex, and the wet sound it made. Her lips popped open in a perfect O shape as her breath caught in her throat.

"Oh, I still *feel.* Quite well, Tom. Better now."

"Oh?"

Oh?

He sounded like an idiot.

He didn't know what else to say at the moment.

Camilla nodded, and her teeth cut into her bottom lip while her fingers kept working between her thighs. "It's something new, you know? I'm always aware that it's there now, even walking down the street. I could probably wear something tight enough, and it would make me come just by walking."

His gaze was still firmly locked on her fingers moving under her panties. She'd made a damp little spot on the cotton from her juices. Her fingers moved from a thrusting motion, and then up higher, circling and tugging.

On that damn piercing.

He would really like to be the one playing with that fucking thing at the moment. Not watching her do it on a screen.

"Jesus Christ. You're killing me here."

"What do you want me to do, then?" she asked.

She was teasing him, and Tom was helpless to her game. He liked it a little too much to stop her from doing it.

"Well, moving those fucking panties aside so I can see what's mine would be a great start, Camilla. Get on that, babe. If you're going to tease me, at least make it worth my while."

"Tom—"

"Let me see your cunt, Cam."

She didn't hesitate after that to use her other hand, and pull the cotton aside. The wet, pink sliver of her sex peeked out at him. All bare, waxed, and pretty. The tips of her finger smacked gently against her clit as a shiver raced over her skin.

"Let me see the piercing, Cam."

"Sure you want to?"

Yeah, killing him.

Dead.

"Don't make me turn off this screen," he told her.

She gasped. "You wouldn't."

Probably not.

He wouldn't tell her that, though.

"Let me see it, babe."

She sucked on the fingers she had been using to fuck herself. Then, she made a V with her fingers around the hood of her clit. It allowed her to show off a tiny vertical bar that went straight through the hood of her clit. Two small balls were attached to each end of the bar. One rested on the top of the hood, and the other, right on her clit.

"You lie," Tom said, "because no matter how good it looks—and it really, really does—that had to have hurt a whole hell of a lot."

Cam shrugged. "Or maybe the pretty girl who did it was enough to keep my attention—"

The growl-like sound that came out of Tom surprised even him. The flood of jealousy that coursed through his system was a shock to his soul.

"I was kidding," Camilla whispered, grinning in that way of hers.

"Better be."

"I *was*. Care to show me yours now?"

"I don't have anything new to show, Cam. It's the same cock that had you coming a half of a dozen times."

"Yeah, but I bet it would get me off faster to watch you play, too. Don't you want to watch me get myself off while you come, too?"

How was Tom going to refuse her?

She was already back to toying between her clit, and the little barbell she had added to her body. Tremors rocked over her skin. Her shoulders shook. The lust darkening her gaze was enough to make him fucking wild.

"Yeah, I'll play, babe."

Camilla wet her lips. "When are you going to come back to New York, Tom?"

He hesitated to answer.

She had never asked him that question outright before.

"Do you want me to?" he asked.

"What do you think?"

"I'll be back."

"When?" she asked.

"Soon," he promised.

Somehow.

Tom flashed her a smile. "Now show me how wet your pussy is, Cam. And start telling me how those fingers of yours can't even compare to my cock."

She did.

He loved it.

CHAPTER TEN

"YOU'RE COMING to dinner tonight, right?" Camilla asked. "I told Ma you probably would."

She darted through the flood of students weaving around the halls inside the college. A blonde bumped into her, and didn't even bother to apologize. *Bitch.* The exit door was just a few feet away, thankfully.

"Did you hear me?" August asked.

"Sorry, just give me a second to get outside," Camilla said. "I don't know if the college suddenly got two hundred more students, or what."

In the cold March air outside, Camilla took a deep breath. The refreshing chill relaxed her far more than the stuffy halls of the college. Most times, she didn't mind. Today had been a different story altogether.

Maybe she just needed a damn break.

"All right," she told her friend. "What was that? Are you coming, or not?"

"Mom and I are for sure. Dad might end up working late."

"Good, so I'll see you then. Or did you want me to pick you up?"

"I'll drive with Mom," August replied. "I'm heading over there to drop off my dirty clothes anyway."

Camilla almost laughed, but managed to hold it back. August was grown up in a lot of ways, but she was still like every other eighteen year old fresh out on their own, too. Her mom washed her clothes once a week, and came over to clean her place when needed. August didn't like to have that pointed out, however.

"Okay."

"Love you."

"You, too," Camilla told her friend.

She hung up the call, and headed for the parking lot. She was able to remote start her car from inside her last class of the day because of the proximity to the lot. The taste of spring hung heavily in the air with the damp sprinkle of rain, and the disappearing snow. Still, winter kept clinging to the weather with the bite of cold and occasionally snowflakes.

Camilla was ready to put away the thick jackets, ugly boots, and wool hats. She needed to get back to cute dresses and strappy heels.

Anytime now.

She checked her watch as she slipped into the warm Mustang GT. By the look of the time, she had lots to spare before she needed to be at her parents' Newport home for a dinner her mother planned. It gave her time to get home, change out of the scrubs she had to wear for school, and maybe relax a bit.

She *loved* school. Loved to learn, and the challenges it posed. Her goal of becoming a NICU nurse was still very much alive and well in her heart.

Lately, though, school felt like a fucking chore. Something she had to do, and not something she really wanted to do. Getting up early and staring down six or more hours of classes a day was becoming more and more daunting.

School had never felt like that to her before.

She wasn't sure what exactly was causing her restlessness and lack of interest, but she needed to shake it, and *fast*. Before it became a problem she couldn't handle, and it began bleeding over more into her school work.

At least it was finally March break.

Camilla had one whole week to do *nothing*. That was exactly what she planned to do, too. A couple of her friends were heading to Cuba. Another was going to the Dominican with her family like they did every year.

She had been invited to join both, and she refused them.

What she really wanted to do was absolutely nothing.

Nothing for school.

No demands. No classes. No papers due. No group work.

Nothing for life, either.

No shopping, partying, or *adulting*.

She just wanted to chill.

Camilla's tires spun on the wet pavement when she pulled out of the parking lot. Familiar city streets passed her by as she made the thirty minute drive to her apartment. Inside her place, she turned on some music to bleed the lecture and group work she had participated in out of her damn head. She took a quick shower, pulled on dark-wash skinny jeans and a silk blouse, and fixed her makeup.

By the time she had pulled on the knee-high suede boots, she heard the faint hum of a ringtone filtering through the rock song blaring in her apartment. She darted out of the walk-in closet to find her phone had gotten buried beneath her bag and coat.

"Shit," Camilla said as she saw the name on the screen.

The missed call taunted her, and teased her. All at the same time. Her month had been crazy busy. She hadn't been able to talk to Tommaso a lot after their Skype call because of it. Once or twice, but it was always short and to the point. It kind of felt like he had been busy doing whatever he did in Chicago, too.

He never complained, though.

He never asked for more from Camilla.

She could see he had called twice while she was in the shower, and then the third time that she had heard, but missed.

Tommaso's number instantly lit up the phone again, and she picked it up before the first ring even finished. "Hello?"

"Hey, babe."

Her grin grew wide damn near instantly. "Hey, you."

"You busy right now?" he asked.

"Not right now. I've got a few minutes to chat."

"I'm not actually interested in talking at the moment, Cam."

"Why would you call, then?"

What the hell else did people do on the phone?

Tommaso's laughter echoed through the speakers. All dark, rich, and dangerous at the same time. A deep bass that rumbled through the phone, and vibrated into Camilla's bones without even trying.

She didn't know what it was about this man, but he had some kind of hold on her like nothing and nobody else. She wasn't sure how to get him out from under her skin, or if she even wanted to.

"Are you going to come get me, or what?" Tommaso asked.

Camilla stared dumbly at her reflection in the mirror of her vanity, unsure if she had heard him correctly. "What?"

"My flight landed at LaGuardia thirty minutes ago. I need a ride."

"You didn't think to let me know ahead of time that you were coming into the city? I would have already been there waiting for you when you landed."

Six long months had already passed since he had been in New York. Of course, she would have jumped at the chance to pick him up had he told her.

Camilla briefly wondered if her brother had known about any of this, but figured it didn't really matter.

Tommaso was back in New York.

That was all she wanted.

Now, he was just waiting for her ...

"I was thinking you might like a surprise, actually," Tommaso said, chuckling. "Are you going to come get me, Camilla, or what?"

It took her all of one second to answer him that time around.

"Don't move a damn muscle, Tom."

Camilla's heart thundered as Tommaso strolled her way at a leisurely pace. His lips curved into one hell of a smirk that probably ruined her panties. The glint in his gaze as his stare drifted down her body had her blood heating, and her skin tingling. He wasn't the least bit ashamed to be checking her out like he was. He wasn't even close enough to touch yet, and she was already on fire with her want for him.

Yep.

Poof.

Ovaries destroyed.

God, what was it about this man that made her kind of crazy?

Phone sex, racy texts, and Skype were not nearly enough to sedate the need she had for Tommaso Rossi. Camilla had figured that out quickly enough. Now that he was here, she couldn't wait to get him somewhere private, and satisfy the lust pooling in her gut.

Damn.

The spot didn't even have to be private.

She really didn't care at this point.

All of his confidence, danger, and sex appeal radiated with every step he took. He had a small duffle bag slung over his shoulder that he held by the strap with a single finger. Like an afterthought he was bringing along because for the moment, all of his attention was fully focused in on her.

He'd given her the arrival gate to meet him at, but nothing more. He'd been sitting on a bench, and already looking her way when she finally spied him.

Despite all the changes she went through over the past six months— from her hair, to her makeup, and even style—Tommaso was still the very same. Dark smile, dark suit, and dark intentions.

Especially when it came to her.

Seeing him coming her way was both overwhelming and terrifying. In good and bad ways. She had missed him terribly, and phone calls were not the same thing as actually seeing him. It also scared her to death because of how much she *had* missed him.

It was never more apparent to her just how much she wanted to see him again than in that moment. So yeah, that scared her a little. For the moment, she pushed the confusing feelings aside. This was not the time to deal with them.

Camilla's excitement spilled over, and she bolted forward when she couldn't contain it any longer. Tommaso laughed, and dropped his bag just in time to open his arms for her oncoming hug. She expected him to just embrace her, but instead, he lifted her right off the fucking ground without a bit of hesitation.

Her shriek of surprise was drowned out by Tommaso pressing a bruising kiss to her lips. A kiss that burned through her bloodstream like a forest fire intent on killing any reservations her heart might have been feeling in that moment.

Camilla tangled her hands into Tommaso's hair, and wrapped her legs around his torso as their kiss deepened. She didn't care about the catcall that echoed, or the laughter from nearby. It wasn't like they were the first people to make a public scene at the airport.

All too soon, Tommaso was setting Camilla back on her feet. She stared up at him with a wide grin as his hands cupped her face. With a husky chuckle, he kissed her smiling lips three times in quick succession.

"Missed you," he said.

"You did, huh?"

"Of course. Like you didn't already know that."

Camilla winked. "I thought *maybe* you missed me."

"Cam, you know good and damn well you were driving me crazy all the way in Chicago. Don't even try to pretend differently."

"I won't."

Tommaso let out a hard laugh. "I didn't think so."

"How long are you going to be here?"

A huge part of her wished she could take the question back as soon as she asked it. Another part of her wished he wouldn't answer. She didn't want to learn he was only going to be there for a couple of days.

Hell, a week wouldn't be long enough.

Yep.

Heartsick.

It had only really been sex—that's it. A couple of conversations thrown in, and nothing more. She wasn't even sure how a hookup had turned into something else entirely.

Camilla didn't know what to do with any of it, so she ignored it all instead.

"We'll see how long I'm here before somebody calls me back," Tommaso said, offering nothing else.

She had a mind to push him for more information, but convinced herself not to. They had lots of time to talk about all of that later, anyway. It didn't have to be right now.

"Do you have a hotel booked or something?"

Tommaso shrugged. "This was all kind of last minute. I just booked a ticket, and came. Here I am, babe."

Camilla wet her bottom lip, and asked, "Do you want to stay with me?

I mean, I'm on March break for a week, so I don't have anything else to do but stay in with you."

And *shit*, that sounded like gold to her.

Silky, hot, and priceless.

She would probably still be left wanting more.

"If you want me to," Tommaso replied.

Yeah, she did.

She really did.

"Stay with me, Tom."

His warm palms slid along her throat and jaw again, and he pulled her in for one more kiss that felt anything but innocent. He held her tighter, and all she could do was surrender to the taste of him, and the way his tongue teased hers.

Like a promise, she thought.

She couldn't wait to get that tongue of his working somewhere else. She had missed that little talent of his.

All over again, Camilla's heartbeat was racing out of control, and her chest grew damn tight. Still, she didn't stop kissing Tommaso until he was the one to pull away first. Like the first time, he placed softer, sweeter kisses to the seam of her lips as she watched him through lowered lashes.

An errant thought reminded her of something important. A promise she had made, and couldn't be late for.

"We have to go to dinner," she whispered against his lips. "But then you are all mine. Understood?"

Tommaso's thumb stroked her jaw line. "Where?"

She didn't miss how he didn't give her a response on the second part of her statement.

"My parents' place. I can't get out of it, or I would. Especially because I would really like to go anywhere with you where I could just get on my back or climb on top."

Tommaso bared his teeth at her brazenness. "That so?"

"Yep. You'll have to come with me to the dinner, but I don't think my parents will mind very much."

"Sure, babe. I'll do dinner with them."

Her gaze drifted over his features, taking in his grin and gray-blue eyes. The shadow of stubble on his cheeks and jaw tickled against her fingertips.

"They'll probably make a big deal out of you being there. Or maybe they won't, but who knows. Cross is supposed to be coming, too, so maybe you'll have somebody else on your side if they do try to be cute with you. Just ignore them if they say anything."

"Why would it be a big deal at all?" he asked.

Camilla refused to look at him, then. She didn't really know how much of her dating profile he knew, but it wasn't anything good to look at. She had made it clear to him once that this wasn't supposed to be very serious between the two of them.

Or rather, she didn't do serious.

Hadn't, her mind taunted. Truth was, she hadn't been with anybody since meeting Tommaso months ago. Nobody seemed to catch her interest.

But they weren't something—they didn't have titles.

So it didn't matter.

"I don't bring home dates. This would be a first for them."

Tommaso smirked. "I'm not really a date, Cam. I'm a friend."

He was not just a friend. He was far more than a friend.

Camilla liked it *and* hated it.

She just wasn't ready to admit it yet.

"Cam."

The surprise in Calisto's voice was only matched by the widening of his eyes as he opened the front door. His gaze darted to the man standing beside her, and then quickly back to his daughter. She pressed her lips together to keep from laughing out loud at the effort her father was putting forth to put his calm composure back together.

Her dad, the crime boss.

Her dad, always smooth and collected.

Her dad, currently looking like he had swallowed a fly.

Oh, she loved her father. She was absolutely what some people might consider a daddy's girl, and always had been. She probably always would be.

Camilla still got far too much enjoyment out of shocking her father. She was pretty sure it was only his kids who could actually do that to him. She had yet to see anyone else do it the same way they did.

It was just a little too hilarious.

"You brought a ... friend," her father said.

"I did," she replied.

Calisto's gaze drifted back to Tommaso.

It was only then that he finally decided to speak up. "Evening, boss."

"Just Cal tonight, Tommaso."

"Sure, Cal."

Calisto widened the door, and stepped back. "Come on in. I don't know why you bothered to knock, Cam. You never do."

Because she had greatly wanted to see the look on either her mother or father's face when they opened the door to see what awaited them on the other side. It had not been disappointing.

"Your mother is in the kitchen," her father said. "I'll be in there when you're ready."

He gave a little wave, and then headed back down the hallway.

Tommaso looked to her with a cocked eyebrow. "What was that about?"

"He's going to warn Ma that I brought someone."

"Come on, now."

"No, I'm pretty sure that's what he's doing."

"Should we give them a minute?" Tommaso asked.

Camilla shrugged. "It's been long enough. Let's go."

She slid her hand into Tommaso's, and wove their fingers tightly together. He brought her a little closer to his side as they headed for the kitchen.

The closer they got to the kitchen, the better Camilla could hear the whispering hisses between her parents.

Yep.

Her dad was absolutely giving her mother the heads up on Camilla's extra guest. Just like she said. All she could do was shake her head.

"Told you," she said to Tommaso.

He laughed lowly, and pressed a kiss to the top of her head.

Camilla walked into the kitchen with a wide smile, and Tommaso was right behind her. She didn't miss how her father's gaze dropped to the two's connected hands. He quickly looked back to Camilla's mother.

Emma, on the other hand, didn't look away as fast.

"Oh," Emma mumbled. "Well, hello."

Camilla held back her grin, and Tommaso tightened his fingers around hers like he had seen her amusement. Seemed even with a warning from Calisto, her mother was still shocked.

"You don't mind putting an extra plate on the table, right, Ma?" Camilla asked.

Emma recovered quickly with a nod. "Yes, of course."

She expected nothing different.

Her mother was a lot of things, but rude was not one of them.

"So, do you want to introduce us properly, or ...?" Emma let her sentence hang out in the open as she nodded in Tommaso's direction.

Tommaso only chuckled under his breath.

"I mean, if you want to," her mother added.

Camilla was well aware her mother knew who Tommaso was without needing proper introductions. The two had more than a handful of conversations about the Chicago-born man, and sometimes those chats were because her mother wouldn't leave her the hell alone. Not to mention all the information her mother had been fed from August and Calisto.

But fine, if that's what her mother wanted …

Camilla would play that game.

"Ma, Daddy," Camilla said, not even bothering to hide the roll of her eyes, "this is Tommaso. He made a special trip down from Chicago to see me. Since I was already having dinner here tonight, I figured he could join me."

Emma nodded. "Okay. Hello, Tommaso."

"A special trip?" Calisto asked, not giving Tommaso the chance to respond.

"I kind of missed New York," Tommaso said.

He shot Camilla a smile.

She returned it with a wink.

"Huh," her father said.

That broke Camilla's daze.

The awkward silence echoing in the kitchen certainly didn't help.

"All right," Camilla said, side-eyeing her father, "We are going to take a walk through the back property until dinner is ready. Shoot me a text, in case we're too far to hear you yell, Ma."

"Sure," Emma replied. "I can do that."

Camilla gave Tommaso's hand another squeeze, and then tugged him to follow behind her as she left the kitchen. The silence from before stretched on. She didn't hear either of her parents say a single word.

She had no doubt the very second the back door closed, the two would be whispering to one another again in the kitchen like earlier.

"That wasn't so bad," Tommaso said as they headed for the trails on the back property. "I think you made a big deal out of nothing."

"No, I really didn't. They just hid their surprise better than I thought they would."

"Maybe."

Tommaso tugged her in close again, and Camilla hugged him around his torso as they headed onto the trail. On the trails, they couldn't be seen from the windows because of all the trees. Camilla took the opportunity of privacy to stop Tommaso, and pull him down for another kiss.

"What was that for?" he asked when she pulled away.

Camilla shrugged. "For coming here."

"To the state, or dinner?"

"Maybe both."

"Mmm, I don't mind. Someone is worth the trip."

Camilla arched a brow. "Someone?"

"Definitely you, Cam."

Her smile grew sly in a blink.

"Keep in mind, dinner hasn't even begun yet, and most of the family is invited. You could still be grilled yet."

"Not concerned," Tommaso said.

"I bet."

Then, he smiled wider.

"I have something for you," he told her.

"You didn't have to bring something for me, Tom."

Tommaso shook his head, and dug in the pocket of his black tweed coat. "It wasn't anything big, so don't worry about that. Mostly, Chicago wanted to remind you … and thank you."

Camilla's brow furrowed. "What are you talking about?"

He grabbed her hand, and flipped it over so her palm was up and open. Then, he placed an item in her hand that he had kept hidden after pulling it from his pocket.

Camilla peeked at the item the second Tommaso had pulled his hand away. A small, rectangular keychain rested in her palm. It was simple in design—white background, black letters, and a little red heart. It hung from a silver chain that a person could attach to a keyring or whatever else they wanted.

I heart Chicago, it read.

Because of course he would remind her of that conversation.

Camilla bit her lip, and her shoulders shook with the force of the laughter bubbling its way out of her chest. Tommaso's laughter filled up the trail with hers. She reached for him, and fisted his jacket in order to pull him close enough that she could kiss his smirking lips. Then, she pushed him away just as fast, and smacked him lightly in the chest for being such an ass.

It was a stupid, silly gift. A cheap keepsake you could probably buy right off the street, and forget about it before it even made its way to the bottom of your luggage. She was pretty damn sure she had one that said something similar about New York, actually.

It would be nothing to somebody else.

It was a perfect memory of a day out with Tommaso for Camilla.

"You are terrible," she said, "and I kind of hate myself for it, but I love this."

"Someday you'll admit Chicago is better," he told her, "and you will be grateful that you already have this to show your love."

"Lies," she told him. "Nothing about Chicago is better than New York, and you know it."

He grinned—sexy and dark in a blink all over again.

"Something about Chicago is going to be making you *very* fucking happy tonight, Cam. Do you want to try that again?"

A shot of heat and need drove through her body. From her toes, to her fingertips. She was entirely hot, needy, and unashamed all at once. Damn him for making her that way, too.

"You're just about the only thing Chicago's got going for it," she said, meeting his gaze. "Just so you know."

Tommaso nodded. "You know what, I'll fucking take it."

CHAPTER ELEVEN

THE BEST wakeup call Tom had ever gotten was waking up to Camilla sucking him off. Already wet between her thighs, hot for him, and wanting to be fucked all goddamn morning. He was more than happy to go along with that plan.

Right after he got what he wanted, of course.

What he wanted was to shoot his load down her throat, and then get a taste of her pussy. Something he had missed over the last few months, and was pretty sure his memories didn't do the taste of her justice. He'd barely gotten her through the door of her apartment last night before he had her bent over the back of the couch to fuck her silly. He hadn't taken time for anything else—not when she had kept begging for him to just keep fucking her.

So yeah, he wanted that taste.

At the moment, though, he was a little preoccupied with Camilla's mouth on his cock. She took his length in all the way to the back of her throat, and then sucked hard enough to take his breath away when she came back up. She did this fucking thing with her tongue, swirling it around the head of his cock, and then flicking it against the throbbing vein on his shaft.

One of her hands stroked his balls while her other teased his abdominal muscles with her fingernails. Every grunt—each groan—that came out of his mouth was accompanied by one of her sweet little hums. A vibrating sound that rocketed through his dick, and straight into his balls.

She'd smile each time, too, or as best she could. It seemed she liked eliciting some kind of vocal response out of him, and he didn't seem to have much fucking control over his own body at the moment to stop the sounds. With each one, she peered up at him through dark, long lashes, and her lips curved just enough to tell him she liked it.

Tom wove his fingers into Camilla's brown, bed-mussed hair, and grunted hard. "*Fuck*, Cam. You're gonna make me come, babe."

"Mmm."

That was all he got back from her. Another one of those sexy little moans that only made him want to come more.

He thought she might only tease him by sucking his dick, and let him finish off by fucking her, but that didn't seem to be the case. She planned on getting something from him, so fuck it. He would damn well give it to her.

Keeping his gaze locked on Camilla's as she took his cock all the way into her mouth again, Tom tightened his grip on her hair. She stilled, and he felt her throat muscles constrict against his dick in the best way.

"You want me to come, Cam?"

She only blinked at him—lust swirling in deep chocolate orbs.

"Do you want to *make* me come, Camilla?"

The slightest curve of her lips answered him back.

Tom grinned, too. "Are you going to be my good girl and take it all for me—every last drop?"

She arched a brow, and her tongue teased at his shaft. That earned her another one of Tom's husky groans.

"Do you want me to fuck your pretty mouth, babe? Is that what you want, huh? Your eyes to water, and my cum down your throat?"

She stroked him slower with her tongue, and her hand squeezed his balls a little firmer. Not enough to hurt, but just enough to make his words catch in his throat with the unspoken promise.

"*Fucking hell.*"

Tom tugged on Camilla's hair, and brought her mouth all the way up to the tip of his dick. Her teeth grazed along the sensitive skin of his cock, and all he could do was suck in a sharp breath at the sensation it left behind. He couldn't remember a time when the sight of someone sucking his dick had ever made him as hot as Camilla was making him right now.

"Christ, woman," Tom grunted.

Camilla winked.

His little bit of control flew out the window.

At first, he used the grip he had on Camilla's hair to bob her head up and down. Her silky lips, and a rough tongue massaged his dick as he fucked her mouth. All the while, she never looked away from him. Those glinting eyes of hers danced with want, even as the head of his cock hit the back of her throat hard enough to make her tears gather.

It wasn't enough, though. Not to get him where he needed to be.

Tom brought Camilla down his cock harder, and flexed his hips upward at the same time. Her hand teased his balls, her tongue and teeth dragged against his shaft, and her pleased, muffled hum vibrated from her throat.

It didn't take long at all for the pressure to start building in his spine. The promise of release dug its claws into his gut, and it only made him fuck Camilla's mouth faster and harder.

The second he felt the pressure release, he held her down on his cock as his cum shot into her mouth. With each swallow she made, taking in his release, her muscles constricted in the best way around his dick. It only added to the sharp pleasure stabbing through his gut.

"*Fuck, fuck, fuck.*"

Tom let Camilla go, but she didn't immediately release his cock. Instead, she sucked him clean, and then licked his shaft from the base to the tip while she watched him through dazed, watery eyes.

Finally, she smiled at him.

Sweet, yet sexy, in a blink.

"Morning," she whispered.

Pink, swollen lips.

She smelled like the peppermint wash in her shower.

Messed hair and trembling shoulders.

"Morning," he replied with a grin.

"My turn, don't you think?"

"Fuck yeah, babe."

Tom grabbed Camilla around her waist and pulled her into him. His mouth crashed down on hers as he turned them over on the bed. Her tongue warred with his while she spread her legs wide, and grinded her wet, bare pussy against any part of him that she could. She pulled away from his kiss just to whisper in his ear.

Filthy, sinful words that drove him crazy.

Damn, he missed this girl.

"Eat me, fuck me, and use me, Tom. Won't you make me scream and shake for you? Fuck me until I can't move? *Use me.*"

Like he needed more of a reason to want to keep this woman forever.

Like he didn't already want to.

Tom's thumbs stroked Camilla's pierced, taut nipples as he kissed down her toned stomach. She arched against each and every one of his kisses. Her skin tasted like salt, sex, and peppermint against his tongue. The lower he got, the more his mouth watered for a taste of something else.

Once Tom was eye-level with her cunt—and the little silver balls peeking at him from her newest piercing—he glanced back up at her.

"I missed your pussy, Cam."

"I bet you did."

All glistening pink, and ready to be fucked, her sex felt like wet, hot satin under his fingertips when he stroked it. Camilla sucked in a hard breath, but didn't give him anything else. That was just fine—he'd get more noises out of her soon.

"Fuck me, you're damn wet. I think your pussy missed me, too."

She laughed a tinkling sound. "Someone's very sure of himself."

"Someone has a reason to be, Cam."

"Shut up and eat my pussy, Tom." She winked and added, *"Please."*

"Only because you said please."

"What do I get for the attitude, though?"

Tom smirked. "A red ass and my cock filling up your cunt."

Camilla sighed. "Sounds lovely."

This woman had no shame.

He kind of loved that, too.

Tom buried his face between Camilla's thighs, and lapped up all those tart juices of hers. God, he had missed the taste of her on his tongue. He used that new piercing of hers to tease between his teeth and flick with his tongue. He didn't think he had ever heard her shout his name as loud as she did, not to mention how hard her muscles tensed when she came that first time.

He went in for a second round just to hear her sound like that again.

The black and white checkered floor of the Brooklyn diner matched the pattern on the wallpaper, and the tabletops. He felt like he had jumped back a century in time just sitting there eating, but it was still comfortable. He gave props to the owners for being polite and welcoming. It certainly helped the atmosphere of the place.

"Do you come here often?" he asked Camilla.

She took the small bite of syrup covered pancake he offered. Once she swallowed the bite, she said, "Me and August, yeah. Usually a couple of times a week or so."

"You two seem ..."

"Hmm?" Camilla arched a brow, waiting.

"Close."

"I've known her since I was like fourteen or something. She was new to my private school, some big shot girls though they could pick on her because she didn't look like them or sound like them."

"Let me guess, you kicked their asses?"

Camilla barked out a laugh that made Tom smile even wider. "Nope. She did, actually. She didn't need me to do a thing for her—that girl saves herself."

"Nice."

"Right?" Camilla shrugged. "So yeah, I was like, I want to know that girl. The rest is history."

"Friends like that are hard to come by."

"Yeah, I know."

Tom offered another bite, and Camilla took it between her pretty lips with a wink. There was something about the way her lips wrapped around the fork that reminded him of their escapade earlier. It made his dick hard in an instant. He pushed the thought aside, determined to *talk*.

Who knew how long he would have with Camilla this time around? There was a lot he wanted to do with her while he could. Talking was definitely one of them.

"You could have invited her to come with us this morning," Tom said.

Camilla shrugged her dainty shoulders, but a sadness colored up her gaze. "August is busy with her internship. She used to spend like four nights out of the week at my place, but with this internship and the couple of classes she's got, it keeps her away."

"Sorry," Tom said lamely.

"It's okay."

"It's not really, though, is it?"

"Part of life, isn't it? You get busy, have shit to do, and make time when you can. Just something else to deal with, I guess."

Tom reached over to stroke Camilla's cheek. Her small smile made him do it a second time just because. "By the way ..."

"What?"

"Your family is pretty awesome."

Camilla's brow shot up. "Oh?"

"They're sneaky as hell, and I have to respect that."

"How so?"

"They were grilling me left and right last night whenever you left the room."

Camilla's laughter filled up the small, quiet diner. "I bet."

"They remind me of my family, actually."

She chewed on her lip, and glanced away.

"What?" he asked.

"I just ... thought to ask about your family, or whatever. Then I thought maybe you wouldn't want me to, or something."

"Camilla."

She still wouldn't look at him.

Tom pressed a finger under Camilla's chin and turned her head, so he could see her eyes again. "You can ask me *anything*."

In fact, he wished she would talk more than she did.

"Do you have any siblings?" she asked after a few quiet seconds.

"Two little sisters."

Camilla's gaze rolled upward. "Do they drive you as crazy as I did my brother?"

Tom chuckled. "They're quite a bit younger than me. Sara is almost ten years younger, and Rebeka is twelve years younger than me. So, I'm beyond the age where they drive me up the wall, I think. It probably helps that my mother and father basically require me to look after the girls, or take one day a week to do something with them."

"You know, I bet even though you're so much older than them, they still feel close to you because you make time for them, Tom."

"Is that why you're as close as you are to Cross?"

Camilla nodded. "Partly, yeah."

"Don't leave me hanging, now."

"I guess … he's always been like my hero or something. I mean, I remember when we were younger and would fight like cats and dogs. Then one day, that just stopped. He quit telling me to get out of his room every time I looked in the door. He let me play with his guitars even when I scratched the faces or chipped the wood. He would read me books I brought home from school until I fell asleep just because I asked him to. He never let guys treat me like shit, and he made sure I knew how much I was worth, and to demand people treated me like I had worth. It's a lot of things, Tom."

"Sounds like your best friend, really."

Camilla tipped her head to the side, saying, "Yeah, he is. He made time for me, no matter what he was going through, and he's been through some shit. I couldn't have asked for a better brother than Cross."

Tom flashed a grin. "Don't tell him that, though."

She scoffed. "Fuck, no. Do you know how big his goddamn ego is? He doesn't need me filling it with more hot air, believe that."

Their laughter rang out in the quiet diner again.

Then, Camilla asked, "And what about your mom and dad?"

"Tommas and Abriella are … like a king and queen in Chicago, you know what I mean? They live in this huge fucking mansion that used to belong to my mom's family, and hold court for everybody like royalty. Sometimes I think it's strange how they are, but my dad quickly tells me to mind my business. They earned the right to do whatever the fuck they wanted for the rest of their lives. They love each other like crazy, and sometimes fight like they're going to kill each other. My mom and dad are always keeping an eye out for the other one—they've got each other's backs like nobody I have ever met before. Kind of makes me think, sometimes."

"About what?"

"Just that it would be nice to have something—someone—like that to be with someday. One person to love and fight with, but know at the end of the day, they're the only person you can always trust to take care of you, and be there."

Camilla glanced away. "Yeah, I get that."

She picked at the two caramel drizzled strawberries on the plate, and then lifted one up for Tom to take a bite. The fruit tasted sweet with a hint of salt from the caramel, but it was nothing compared to the taste of her.

"So, Chicago must keep you busy, then," Camilla said.

"Busy enough."

"Work is all you do, huh?"

Tom wiped his thumb across his lip to remove the last bit of caramel, and grinned. "Are you trying to hint at something there, or what?"

"What would I be hinting at?"

"I don't know. Maybe trying to see if I was running around with somebody over these last six months."

Camilla cleared her throat. "Not my business to ask."

"But you *could*."

"Not my business."

"Cam." Tom grabbed her wrist in his palm, and tugged gently to make her look at him. She did, but he could see she didn't really want to hear his answer. "I didn't ask for a damn thing from you—I don't expect *anything*."

"I know. I extended you the same respect, Tommaso."

He shook his head. "That's not how I work, though."

Her brow furrowed. "What?"

"Just because I didn't expect shit from you while you were here, doesn't mean I held myself to that standard, Cam. I've got an interest in you, and intentions to see whatever the fuck this is through. I wasn't looking at anybody else."

She cleared her throat. "Huh."

"And you don't need to explain anything to me."

"But I haven't." Camilla shrugged. "Been with someone, I mean. Blame it on being busy, or not having any interest."

"Or you could blame it on me."

Camilla sucked air through her teeth, nodding. "Yeah, we could do that, too."

"How's school?"

"That really what you want to talk about?"

Tom smirked. "I want to talk about anything that has to do with you, Camilla."

"That so?"

"Yep."

"You still didn't tell me how long you're staying this time," she said. Because he still didn't know.

Tom got three uninterrupted, perfect days with Camilla before he finally got a phone call from Chicago. Well, his father, actually. His gaze drifted over Camilla's sleeping form as he picked up the call from Tommas.

"Hello?"

"Where are you?" his father demanded.

Tom let his fingertips drift over Camilla's naked shoulder. She didn't stir beneath the soft beige sheets keeping her covered.

"Why?" Tom asked. "Did you need something from me?"

"Yes, Tommaso, for you to *be in Chicago*."

"Figured out I was gone, huh?"

"Nice try on telling Adriano you needed a couple of days to clear your head," his father said, "but it didn't take a genius to figure out you left the city when I couldn't get ahold of you."

"I did need to clear my head."

"You didn't say you were leaving the city, son!"

Tom sighed, and scrubbed a hand down his unshaven jaw. "Everything on my end was handled. The crew is taken care of. There's no reason why I couldn't take a couple of days to relax or—"

"Because you didn't think to talk to *me*, Tommaso. That's why it's unacceptable. You have responsibilities here, and you know that. A crew to manage—*your* crew, not someone else's. You have duties to take care of, and not pass onto someone else. How can I reasonably believe you're anywhere near ready to move up in the business when you pull stunts like this?"

"It's not a stunt. I had other things I wanted to deal with."

Like Camilla.

And whatever they were.

Tom didn't tell his father that, though.

"You need to come back to Chicago."

"Dad—"

"That was not a request, Tommaso."

"To what, Dad? Run a crew I would rather not? Deal with men who behave like children and think I'm too young to be where I am? Handle a part of the business that you know I've never had any interest in? I needed a couple of fucking days to recharge, and then get back at the shit you wanted me to do."

His father let out a hard breath of air. The speakers crackled at the volume of the noise.

Really, Tom knew that he had probably gone a little too far, but he also knew that he could get away with it, too. Being the son of a boss—and a man who loved his children—meant that Tom knew exactly where his father's lines were drawn in the sand. He would never pull this kind of shit on his father otherwise, but he had left Camilla hanging for far too long.

Not to mention, he really did need a break from the fucking politics of the mafia in Chicago. Every man did, occasionally.

"What do you *want*, Tommaso?" his father asked. "What would make you happy, son? Can you figure that out and give me an honest answer?"

There were a lot of things he wanted.

Camilla, mostly.

Tom didn't think that's what his father meant. "For the Outfit?"

"Yes, for the Outfit. Tell me."

"Not what I'm doing."

"I figured."

"It's not meant for me—being a Capo, I mean."

"For some, it isn't. The crew has been better, haven't they?"

"Sure, but only because the fear of God, is me, currently."

His father chuckled dryly. "But you also know—"

"Fear doesn't breed respect, only contempt. I can't help what they won't accept. You know Lou would be far better to run that crew for Adriano, Dad. Make him—give him his button, and let him run the crew. He comes from the same streets those guys do. He's run with them and worked alongside them since he was a teenager. They respect him for it. That crew could *be* something worth having if they had the right Capo running them. Right now, it's just a pain in the ass, but it doesn't have to be."

Tommas sighed. "See, and there you go, son, showing your worth and how much you know in this business. Sometimes I think you don't listen to a thing or see what's going on around you."

"I see and hear everything."

"What do you want me to do for you, Tom?"

"Give me something worth doing, but it isn't this."

"You need to come home, son. Soon. It's not a request."

"Yeah, I know."

"You went to New York, didn't you?"

Tom laughed. "How did you know?"

"Call it a hunch. Say hello to the Donati girl for me."

CHAPTER TWELVE

CAMILLA LEANED against the frame of the hallway entry, and scrubbed her palms over her eyes in an effort to rid them of sleep. The watch on her wrist said it was close to noon, and she wasn't even surprised that she had slept damn near all of her morning away.

After the night before with Tommaso, she was lucky that she still wasn't sleeping. That man was a workout, but in the best of ways.

She had only woken up because of the constant murmurings that kept filtering through her dreams. It seemed like Tommaso was making or taking one phone call after another. It was the first time in the three days that he had been in New York where he actually spent any time at all on his phone. Mostly, he kept it tucked away in his pocket, and it rarely rang.

Tommaso's next words drew Camilla out of her thoughts, and back to his current phone call. With his back to her as he looked out the window of her apartment, and chatted on the phone, she knew he likely didn't have a clue she was there listening in.

Camilla knew better than to eavesdrop.

Spying never did any good.

She still didn't move.

"Shit, I would have to leave in …" Tommaso glanced down—likely at the watch on his wrist. "Well, a couple of hours to make that flight."

Camilla stiffened.

He was leaving?

Tommaso hadn't mentioned a thing to her the night before about him leaving again. In fact, she had asked him every single day since he came back when he had to leave, and he never seemed to be able to give her a proper answer.

Camilla wasn't sure why that bothered her as much as it did, but she didn't like it at all. Like maybe he had been purposely keeping something from her. But why, she didn't know.

She didn't have time to think on it for long. Tommaso's conversation with whoever was on the phone continued.

"I mean, he wants me back as soon as I can get there," Tommaso said, "so just book the flight for me. Email me the boarding pass once you have it, all right?"

A beat of silence passed. The other side of the conversation that Camilla wasn't privy to.

Then, "Thanks, man."

Tommaso hung up the call, and tossed the phone aside to a nearby stand. One Camilla used to rest her coffee on while she read or worked on a laptop. Still facing the windows, Tommaso scrubbed a hand down his jaw, and sighed heavily.

She could hear his stress in the exhale.

His disappointment.

Maybe he really hadn't known at all when he would need to go back, and that was why he hadn't given her a proper answer these past three days. She decided to at least give him the benefit of the doubt.

"You're leaving?" Camilla asked.

Tommaso's shoulders stiffened briefly before he turned around to face her. His posture relaxed, and one of his sexy smiles welcomed her. It didn't matter—she had seen and heard enough to know something was going on. No amount of charm and sex appeal was going to change her questions now.

"Are you?" she pressed.

He flicked a hand as if to wave it off. "Yeah, I got a call this morning. I'm needed back in Chicago."

Camilla nodded, but something still didn't sit right with her. "All right."

"What's wrong, Cam?"

"I don't know. Nothing?"

Tommaso lifted a single brow. "You sure?"

"Why wouldn't I be sure, Tom?"

"You just don't sound like you are, that's all."

Camilla hugged her lower half, and stayed leaning against the frame of the entry. "No, it's fine. You've got to go back, so go back. New York isn't your home, right?"

"I hear you saying nice words that seem like you understand why I'm leaving, but the way you're saying them is a little … defensive."

"No, it's not."

It totally was.

Tommaso simply stared at her. "Cam."

"What?"

Very defensive.

Jesus, what was wrong with her?

"Are you pissed at me or something?" Tommaso asked.

Camilla scoffed. "No, not at all."

"Okay, again, your words say no, but your tone says—"

"It's *fine*, Tom. You came to see me, and now you have to go back to where you actually live. Don't worry about it. I'm not. It's not a big deal."

"Is that it?"

"Is *what* it?"

"That I only came to visit, and now I have to go. That maybe it'll be another six months before we can get a couple of days together. That you'll be stuck waiting and missing somebody when that's really not your style. Is that what it is?"

Camilla blinked, silenced.

Tommaso only waited her out.

Something had already started making its way through her body like a weed. Its tendrils wrapping tightly around her soul and heart to squeeze tight and suffocate her from the inside out. She did *not* like how it made her feel. She did *not* like how it left pain behind.

It was the same thing she felt the first time Tommaso headed back to Chicago. It was the same thing she felt when her brother had left New York years ago. It was the same thing she felt whenever August wasn't around and Camilla needed her.

Like something was gone.

Something important was missing.

Something Camilla *cared* about.

That's what Tommaso Rossi had done to her without barely doing anything at all. That's what months of missing him, and messing around, and late night conversations with him had done to her already fucked up heart.

A part of her kind of hated him for it. Another part of her was scared to death to admit she felt anything at all. She didn't do this kind of thing, and she didn't know where to begin anyway—not serious, not commitment, and certainly not *love*.

As it was, she didn't even know how to do a relationship with a guy when he lived on the next block. And now because she caught some kind of feelings for Tommaso, her stupid ass heart wanted to try some kind of relationship with a guy in *Chicago*?

How the hell was she supposed to explain that to him when even she didn't understand the mess her heart and feelings were when it came to him?

She chose the coward's way out because she wasn't ready to deal.

"It's fine," Camilla said.

It was not fine.

She was not fine.

Somehow, she managed to keep the confused chaos her heart was hidden from her tone. She bet her eyes told a different story—she couldn't hide shit there. Tommaso didn't call her on it, and she wasn't sure how she felt about that, either.

Camilla was a damned mess.

A real, honest to God, *mess*.

"All right," he said quietly.

"Do you know when you'll be back?"

Every part of Camilla that was not ready to deal with her new emotional reality screamed at her not to ask that question. Yet, there it was. Out there for Tommaso to hear, dissect, and answer with something that could break her apart even more.

His answer did just that.

"I don't know," he said.

"Of course," she replied with a wave.

Not giving him a chance to respond, Camilla headed for the kitchen. She was already turning on the electric kettle and pulling a cup and coffee from the cupboards by the time Tommaso came in behind her.

"Of course," he echoed. "What's that supposed to mean, exactly?"

"It doesn't mean anything, Tom."

"I think it does, Cam."

She set the coffee mug to the counter a little harder than was necessary. She didn't miss the way Tommaso cocked an eyebrow at the action. It probably wasn't helping her whole *I'm fine* routine.

What did it matter now?

"I guess a little more time with you would have been nice," she settled on saying.

There. Let him make of that what he wants.

Tommaso came closer, and his hand skimmed over her back until he was holding tightly to her side. Just his touch alone relaxed some of her overactive, angry nerves. She wasn't sure what to make of that, either.

"You are on March break for another few days," he pointed out.

Camilla went about pouring teaspoons of coffee and sugar into the coffee mug. "What about it?"

"You could come with me to Chicago."

She stilled in place, freezing up instantly at his suggestion.

Tommaso let out a dry chuckle.

"Wow, that went downhill fast, huh?" he asked.

"I can't go to Chicago with you, Tom."

"Why not? You've got time."

"Because I still have a couple of things for school that I need to work on even if it's March break. My mother and father are here, and I don't just up and leave without giving them some kind of notice."

Not to mention her father was still having some health problems. She didn't offer that information to Tommaso, however, as it was still something their family was dealing with privately.

"Plus, August and I have some stuff planned this weekend," Camilla added. "I'm not going to blow her off just to head to Chicago with you."

"*Just* for me," he deadpanned.

His flat tone hit her like a nail straight through the heart.

"I didn't mean it like—"

"Nah, it's fine, Camilla. I get it."

Tommaso let her go, and took a couple of steps back. Instantly, she wanted to reach out and pull him right back into her. Stupid pride kept her from doing it, if only because she thought this might be easier.

Like ripping off a fucking Band-Aid.

That Band-Aid being him.

She could indulge the idea that they might possibly be something someday, or she could just face the hard facts head on.

Camilla didn't live in delusions.

It was very unlikely that they would go anywhere together. Not being apart like they were, not with Camilla living her life like she did, and not when she was terrified to even admit she cared about this man.

It wasn't his fault.

Not really.

This was all her.

"I can't go to Chicago," she told him one last time.

The hard set of Tommaso's jaw told her that his defenses had come out to play now, too.

"Can't or won't?" he asked.

"Tom—"

"I mean, at least be honest with me, Camilla. Be fucking *real* with me. Tell me what it actually is so that I know, and I can make a choice where you and I are concerned. You could give me that decency. I would respect that, babe."

She tried as hard as she could to let his words bounce off her. They were just words, after all. Not weapons, or something that should feel like they were physically assaulting her heart and soul. Still, they hurt.

It all hurt.

When she didn't respond to him as fast as he wanted, Tommaso spoke again. His next words hurt just as much as the last because once again, he was making her take a hard look at things she wasn't ready to see just yet.

"Why won't you try?" he asked. "With us, I mean. Take a risk, Camilla, and figure out what this is, or if it's going anywhere. If it's not, then fine. We had some fun, and fuck the rest. We can go our separate ways, and let it be done. But we can't even do that because you won't—at the very least—*try.*"

"It's not about trying, Tom."

"I think it is."

No, it really wasn't.

It was about her restless heart and not being ready. It was the fear of the unknown, and a future that seemed uncertain because she didn't believe stability was a real, tangible thing. It was about him pulling her in, and her pushing him out. It was the monster of her habits that liked to bite at her back, and the comfort of the familiar which never let her down.

It was a lot of things, but it was not about her inability to try for him. After all, she had been trying for six whole months.

Look where that got her.

Here.

Fighting with him.

In her fucking kitchen.

Like lovers; like they were *something*.

Instead of saying any of that to Tommaso, or explaining the swirling chaos inside her head, Camilla chose another coward's way out.

It was just easier.

She turned away from the counter and her coffee, and reached for him. Fisting his shirt, she pulled him into her, and kissed him hard. It took a second, and then two, before he started to respond. Shocked, likely.

Camilla didn't care what it was.

They were predictable—whether they were something or nothing—in the way that anything physical between them would always override the rest. Call it a connection, or some kind of manipulation right then, but it was just *easier.*

Easier than feelings, talking, and fighting.

Easier than fear, shoving him away more, or letting him bring her closer.

Camilla didn't do hard. She didn't do anything with anyone except for this right here. It was the only thing she could promise, and keep.

Sex was the only thing she knew well.

"Fuck," Tommaso murmured against her lips.

In a blink, Camilla found herself lifted from the floor, and set down on the counter. The boyshorts she had slipped on after getting out of bed were tugged down her legs, and discarded somewhere on the kitchen floor.

Never once did Tommaso's lips leave hers—a now familiar dance whispering along her mouth while a war waged in her mind. His hands skimmed over her thighs, and his fingertips pressed into her flesh just hard enough to make her sigh.

"Open up," he demanded. "Take me."

Two husky words that took her to a different place entirely. One where things like love didn't get much of a say when pleasure and lust was on the table instead.

Camilla's legs widened. It spread her wide, and flashed her pussy. Already wet, and already wanting. Not that it was anything new, really.

She bit his jaw while her hands made quick work of undoing his pants, and pulling his cock free from dark gray boxer-briefs. Already thick and hard in her hand, her fingertips couldn't even touch when wrapped around his cock.

She loved the size of him. The weight of him heavy in her palm. How he filled her full, and stretched her open.

Tommaso dug in the pocket of his shoved down slacks, and pulled out an item that hadn't even crossed Camilla's mind in those moments—a condom. It wasn't like her to be reckless, or stupid.

And yet here she was ...

Being all of those things.

Camilla shoved those thoughts aside, and let her needs and wants take over instead. Selfish, sure, but easy.

Familiar.

Once that condom was rolled down Tommaso's length, Camilla reached for him again. She pulled him in for another burning, bruising kiss. She opened her legs to him, and dug her heels into his lower back as he slid his cock through the lips of her pussy.

He smeared her juices all over her pussy. He teased the head of his cock at her entrance, only allowing her to feel just a little bit of him there, and not nearly enough to satisfy the hunger beating against her ribs. His tongue struck hard against hers as his hips flexed forward.

One thrust.

One groan.

One cry.

She was home again—flying again.

High again.

A fast, unforgiving pace began between them. Her fingernails dug into his neck and jaw, while his hand cupped her throat and forced her head back to the cupboard door. That way, she was forced to look at him while he fucked her. This way, she could see it in his eyes that he knew exactly what she had done by trying to distract him.

No kisses.

No filthy words.

No teasing or fun or promises.

Just a hard fuck that left her aching in the best way, but hurting more in her heart.

But this was Camilla.

And she didn't know anything different.

Camilla was still sitting on the counter and nursing her coffee when Tommaso came back into the kitchen. She hadn't gotten down to grab her panties, or even bothered to fix her hair. She could still feel him hard between her thighs, and the stinging bite mark he had left on her lip.

At least he had the decency to fix his clothes, she guessed.

That made one of them.

Dangling from his hand was the duffle bag he'd come with. In his other hand, his phone. His gaze narrowed at the screen of his phone momentarily before he looked to Camilla.

"I've got to head out."

Yeah, she figured.

Camilla waved a hand. "Give me a call, or something."

Tommaso smirked, and shook his head. "So that's it, then?"

"What else is there?"

Ripping that Band-Aid right off.

Tommaso nodded to himself. "All right, Cam. Just so we're clear on this one thing before I leave this time around, I'll get it out there for the both of us."

She didn't reply, simply waited him out.

Nursing her cold coffee all the while.

"I'm not disposable, Camilla."

She hesitated on her next drink. "Excuse me?"

"I'm not some toy for you," he said quietly. "I'm not something you get to play with and then dispose of when you're bored, or had enough. I won't be some new and shiny thing to keep your attention for a while before something else comes along to take my place. I'm not *disposable*. Just so that's clear—you're not to treat me that way, either."

"I—"

"This little game you play was fun at first. I don't mind a good cat and mouse chase when I know there's something worth waiting for at the end of it all. Problem is, you haven't shown me that there's going to be anything at the end. Oh, you're absolutely worth the fucking chase, sure, but you have to *be there*, too. I don't think you're going to be."

Tommaso shrugged, adding, "So that's where I stand, Cam. I think I could love you—fuck, maybe I already do, but you won't give me the chance or time to figure it out—but love's not a one-sided thing. Not for me. It can't be."

He kept staring at her, waiting.

She didn't know what for.

Camilla looked away.

The coward's way out presented itself once more. Only this time, she would really hurt him by using it. She knew it even before the words came out of her mouth.

"Have a good flight, Tom."

"Have a good life, Camilla."

She didn't look away from the wall until she heard the door of her apartment click when it closed. She held it all together—kept all the hell inside—until she heard that one sound. She blinked, and the tears fell.

She cried, and drank cold coffee all the while. She let the pain out while she was alone, and no one was there to see it or help. The hollow space in her chest filled with the air from her sobs, and the ache it caused spread outward like an infection threatening to poison the rest of her.

She shouldn't feel guilty.

She shouldn't have regret.

Camilla looked for a fun time, not a long time because that was supposed to be easier. Wasn't this supposed to be easier?

The Band-Aid was gone.

The pain should be over.

Or maybe it was just her.

Maybe she was broken.

CHAPTER THIRTEEN

TOM DRAGGED—more like forced—his way through another round of phone calls. To some made men, sitting behind a desk or being the Capo out on the street making the rounds and calling the shots was like being at the top of the world.

Not to Tom.

If anything, work was another fucking chore to add to his days now. Something else he had to do, and not something he particularly wanted to do. He had been somewhat getting better with the crew and Capo position, and then New York happened three weeks ago.

Or rather, Camilla happened.

Tom's gaze darted to the cell phone on the desk. His personal one, not the burner he was currently talking on for business.

Not once had his phone rang.

Not once had Camilla called.

Not in three long weeks.

Not one fucking word.

Tom's irritation spilled over into the phone call to a fellow Capo. "You know what, fuck it, go to Theo, then."

"That's what you want, Tommaso? Me to take this to the front boss?"

"If that's what you think is going to get this settled, then do that."

"Or is it because you know you're so shoved up Theo's ass, he'll just bend to whatever the fuck you want?"

"Theo's not going to bend to whatever I want, Marty," Tom replied, barely keeping his cool. "If anything, he'll come back on me harder because he thinks I should know better. But go ahead and make my fucking day. It'll be one more thing for me to have to deal with right now. At this point, I don't give a fuck. I am done talking about it."

Tom hung up the phone, and tossed it to the desk without care. He was pretty sure it cracked the screen when it landed on the face, but who gave a shit? Not him.

The damn thing was eighty bucks.

It could and would be replaced.

Tom was coming to learn not everything could be fixed or replaced so easily in his life. Actually, he had known that for a while. It was Camilla that had yet to get up to speed with shit like love and whatever else.

Fuck.

Tom scrubbed a hand down over his face and jaw, determined not to get in another one of those moods again. The last one had lingered for a couple of days, and spilled over onto anyone who came too close to him.

He was trying to keep this shit controlled.

He *tried* to keep people out of his business.

"You look like you're ready to kick somebody's ass."

Tom turned fast at the new voice, and found Lou leaning in the warehouse's office. "Marty is still being a fucking cocksucker, that's all."

"About the whole truck thing last week?" Lou asked.

"Yeah, that nonsense. He was under the impression that his guys would get the goods to sell, and we would get a cut of the profits. I figured since my guys nabbed the truck, even if it was on his territory, he would get the cut, and we would get the right of sale for the goods."

"I mean, that's how shit usually goes with other Capos and crews," Lou said.

"Little late, anyway. The goods are all gone."

It wasn't like they could keep a whole truck's worth of stolen luxury goods on hand. Anything with a designer label had to have the serial number filed off—if they could—and it needed to be turned around on the street, and fast. Otherwise, they were risking the cops getting a lead on the stolen goods, and finding them in one of their warehouses. That spelled bad news all the way around the damn board.

"The guys got the last of it sold today, right?" Lou asked.

Tom nodded. "First time in forever they actually decided to get off their asses and do something correctly."

"Come on, Tommaso. They're a good crew."

"Yeah, when they want to be, and we both know they don't want to be good for me very fucking often."

Lou sighed, and leaned against the doorjamb. "They *have* gotten better."

"They don't respect me, Lou. They fear me, and that's why they behave now. Because I killed a couple of them, and beat the shit out of a couple of others."

"It did settle them down, though."

"Sure," Tom agreed, "but for how long? Fear and respect are not the same things, and it won't get me anywhere with them in the end. If even one of them thought they had a chance to get rid of me, or whatever, I don't doubt for a second that they would pull the trigger on it. As long as they could get away with it."

"Give them a bit of trust. Turning on you likely means somebody's coming after them. Or hey, turning you over to the cops likely means some of their friends on this crew might get caught up in that mess, too. I don't think that's something you have to worry a whole lot about right now, man."

Tom chuckled. "Like I said, as long as they thought they could get away with it. Right now, they can't. I'm safe at the moment."

Again, *for how long*?

Sadly, Tom wasn't even exaggerating. It was just a sad fact of the business. Capos either had really good relationships with their crews, or they had a shitty one. Tom was the latter, and he knew exactly why that was.

"I'm from a whole different world than them," he said. "I grew up in a mansion, and they were brought up in crowded, rundown apartments. I attended a private school, and some of them didn't even graduate public high school. I drive around on their streets in my Benz, and they're … yeah. Trust me, I get it, Lou. I don't ask why. I know why."

Lou cleared his throat. "I'm from their world, too, man. I still respect you."

Tom smirked, and came close enough to his friend to clap him on the shoulder. "Yeah, well, you saw something through the pretty rich boy exterior, I guess."

"Nope."

"No?"

Lou shrugged. "A lot of these guys on the crew forget, Tom, that regardless of where you came from or how much money you have, you're still made. You still earned your spot just like every other made man in the business. That's how it works, and that deserves some kind of respect."

Tom laughed, and smacked Lou on the shoulder again. "You know that's the kind of shit that gets you the button, right? That's the kind of attitude that gets you *made*, Lou."

Lou let out a bitter laugh. "Doubtful, Tom. How many made men do you know come from the streets; guys who come from nothing?"

Tom knew a lot. They weren't from his generation, but from his father's. He didn't tell that to his friend.

What mattered most, was that Lou would eventually be rewarded and recognized. It would happen someday. Tom would make goddamn sure of it.

"You know what, fuck this whole place," Tom said.

Lou cocked a brow. "That's not very … Capo-like."

Nope.

"And fuck Marty, too."

Lou chuckled. "Someone's thinking about causing trouble, Tom.

Pretty sure you're the one always telling us to stay the hell out of trouble."

"Maybe, or maybe I just need to blow off some steam."

Get out of this mood.

Get Camilla out of my head.

Move on.

"You got something in mind?" Lou asked. "Or do you trust me to take you somewhere good?"

Tom shoved his friend out of the office. "Fuck you for even asking."

"Hope you like whiskey, man."

Tom did like whiskey.

Quite a lot, actually.

He also tended to favor the cozy, homey feel of the small bar that Lou had brought him to. Sure, the tables were a little wobbly, and the leather stools had a couple of rips, but that gave the place its history. The dark wood paneled walls and neon lights that spelled out different drinks reminded Tom of a time when he hadn't even been alive.

The bearded, massive man behind the bar liked to scoff when someone asked him for anything other than a spirit or a beer.

Understandable, really.

Nobody was coming here for specialty drinks.

Unfortunately, as much as Tom liked the place, and the top shelf whiskey burning his throat with every sip, it just wasn't doing it for him. *It,* being thinking about something other than the fact Camilla hadn't once tried to call him in three weeks.

That girl was under his skin something bad.

He just didn't realize how much before.

Or maybe he hadn't wanted to really think about it because of what it would mean in the end. That he had allowed himself to become attached to a woman who was in no way available. That he had somehow fallen in love with Camilla, and she couldn't offer that back to him.

Fuck his heart for hurting.

Fuck his chest for aching.

Fuck his life for all of it.

Tom tipped up his glass and swallowed back the remainder of the amber-colored whiskey in his glass. It burned all the way down his throat, and he sucked air through his teeth in an effort to soothe the sensation as he set the glass back down on the bar.

"Another?" the bartender ask.

Tom nodded, and waved two fingers over his glass. "Double it, though."

"You got it, man."

The white bearded man topped Tom up, and then headed down the way to a girl in a too-tight dress standing on wobbly legs.

"Are you going to hug the bar all night, or what?"

The feminine voice came off sweet and yet concerned at the same time. Tom turned around on his stool to face a woman he had never seen before in his life.

The first thing he thought?

She's not Camilla Donati.

She was tall, black-haired, and blue-eyed.

Thin as could be.

Pretty, sure.

"I beg your pardon?" Tom asked.

The woman smiled.

"Your friend ..." She pointed at Lou across the bar currently playing a round of pool with a guy and another girl.

He'd asked Tom to join, too, but he hadn't been in the mood. Instead, he stared at his phone for a good hour and a half while he got drunk on whiskey. Seemed like the right thing to do at the time.

"He said you were a little lonely, and I thought maybe I could cheer you up," the woman said.

Tom cleared his throat, and wet his lips.

He usually appreciated a bold woman.

Hell, bold was what drew him to Camilla.

Camilla.

Fuck. His. Life.

Pushing off the stool, Tom gave the woman a smile.

Every bit of it was forced.

"Tell Lou thanks for the concern, but I don't need cheering up," Tom said.

"You sure?"

Baby blues and painted red lips.

He didn't doubt she would be a fun time.

She just wasn't Camilla.

"Yeah, I'm sure."

With that, Tom headed out of the bar without a goodbye to his friend. His phone was still dead to the world in his hand.

No calls.

No texts.

Tom had to hide the phone in his pocket, and busy his hands by running them through his hair in order to keep from calling her.

Fuck Camilla, too.

Fuck her for making him feel like this.

Fuck her for ruining him like this.

"Apparently you get to be the lucky fuck who drives my ass around today," Adriano said as he peered into the car's passenger window. "I could have used an enforcer, but you make for better conversation."

Tom gave his uncle a look. "Yes, lucky me. I get to drive around the spoiled Capo because he doesn't want to use a rental while his car is in the shop."

"I hate rentals."

"We're going to completely ignore that I called you spoiled, then?"

"Shut up. It's not like you have anything else better to do, Tommaso."

"Get in the car, Adriano."

"Tommas wants you at tribute next week," Adriano said as he slid into the young man's car. "Usually I show up for both of us, but he's asked for you to show face, too."

"He didn't mention that to me when I went over there yesterday."

"Sunday."

Tom nodded. "No business on Sundays."

"Well, not in your father's house, anyway."

"Fine." Tom steered the car onto the road, and headed in the direction that would lead them back into the heart of the city. "Any reason he wants me to show up?"

Adriano glanced at the black bag on the floor of the Benz. "Money, Tommaso."

"Well, yeah. That's why there's tribute. I mean, you usually pay my tribute."

"Except you're the main Capo now for the crew, so you need to be doing that."

Ah.

Tom sighed.

More politics.

"Why does your face look like you smelled something bad?" Adriano asked.

"What?"

"Your face, Tommaso. It's like saying tribute was as bad as dumping shit on your car."

"No, I'm just … not in the mood to play mafia politics with other made men. Not lately, anyway. Plus, I've got that issue with Marty, and I know he'll bring it up at tribute just to make a fucking show of it."

"Huh."

Tom glanced over at his uncle. "What?"

"You used to love going to tribute when you were younger. Never thought I would see the day when you dreaded it."

"I don't *dread* it."

"Sounds like it."

Tom sighed. "I'm just …"

In a fucking mood.

Or rather, he was still in a damn mood.

"Ignore Marty," Adriano said, shrugging. "I know all about the truck scheme, and what happened between the crews. Listen, you were in the right on that, Tommaso. Did he threaten to call Theo on you? Like the fucking front boss of the organization would step in and slap you on the wrist or something?"

"Basically."

"Of course, he did, the asshole. You think he's going to bring that up, seriously?"

"Why wouldn't he? Seems like anytime someone has a chance to knock me down a peg in this business, that's exactly what they try to do."

"He's not going to bring it up just to look like a foolish prick, Tommaso."

"You say that, but—"

"I say it because I know it." Adriano shook his head, and stared out the window as they headed onto the highway. "You did the standard thing all crews do when it came to that, and you even offered him a higher cut of the profits to make him relax when he did try to throw a fit. He's just pushing you because you're young, and he thinks he can. Trust me. I know—I have dealt with dozens of fuckers just like him."

Tom's shoulders loosened a little from the stress that had been weighing them down lately. He kept his gaze on the road as he asked, "How did you do it?"

"Hmm?"

"All those years being the youngest Capo controlling a crew. I mean, I know a lot of your friends had moved up in the organization by then—my dad, Damian, and Theo. So that left you managing a crew, right?"

Adriano smirked when he glanced over at Tom from the passenger seat. "You know, there was a time when all my father wanted was to be the boss of the Outfit."

"Wasn't he for a time?"

"A very short time."

"So what's that got to do with you being a Capo?"

"The position was only supposed to be a stepping stone for me, Tommaso. At least, from my father's perspective. Eventually, he saw me being like him. A boss—at the very top, doing what *he* thought I would do best."

"Him, not you."

"Exactly." Adriano turned back to the window, saying, "Some men are meant to be bosses, and some are far better on the streets with a crew, and the soldiers of the organization. It just depends on the man, Tommaso."

"You still didn't answer my question."

"How did I manage being the youngest Capo?"

"Yeah," Tom said.

Adriano laughed under his breath. "White knuckles, Tommaso."

"Huh?"

"I white-knuckled my way through a lot of it. I got older, gained more experience, and a fuck lot more patience along the way. All traits that helped in different situations."

"And you have no interest in taking over for Damian, or even Theo when they're done?"

Adriano scoffed. "Hell no."

"Why not?"

"They've gotten used to the politics of this business, Tommaso. They know how to handle other organizations, and make deals. They talk, talk, and talk more every single day just to keep peace and get shit done. Me? I'll do politics, but I want to do them on the streets. It's where I work best."

Tom drummed his fingers to the steering wheel, considering his uncle's words. "Maybe it's just the politics I've been dealing with, then."

"Pardon?"

The two men glanced at each other before Tom's attention went back to the road. He wondered how to phrase his next statement, as he didn't want to come off as ungrateful for the position he had or the work he had been given in the Outfit.

"The politics of a crew, the streets, and the Capos," Tom said. "I think it's the wrong kind of politics for me, Adriano."

"Probably."

"You don't sound surprised for some reason."

"You're a hell of a lot like your father, Tommaso."

He scowled. "What's that supposed to mean?"

Adriano rested back in the seat, unbothered, and seeming pleased to be driven around by someone else to do his business. "It means, there was once a time when your father was one of the best Capos in Chicago."

"And then?"

"Then, he became a boss. He did that for one reason—something he wanted more than anything."

Tom's brow dipped in his confusion. "My mom?"

Adriano nodded once. "Yeah. See, he went into the boss thing because he had no other choice, but that man would be a damn liar if he ever said he thought he could go back to what he used to be."

"Funny."

"What?"

"I don't think I could see my father as anything other than a boss."

Adriano chuckled. "See? Like I said when we started this conversation, Tommaso, some men are simply made to be a boss. They're not meant to be fucking around with all the other nonsense that makes this organization what it is. They work better at the top."

"Yeah, maybe."

His uncle reached over and hit his shoulder.

Tom looked over at Adriano. "What?"

"You might just be one of those men, Tommaso."

Who knew?

Not him.

Tommas's hands landed heavily on Tom's shoulders. His father leaned over him to see what was on his plate. "Nice spread."

Tom stabbed the fork into an egg, but his interest in food was very little. "I have to keep my energy up somehow, don't I?"

"I suppose. Adriano says you've been throwing yourself into work, and keeping your head down. Any reason for that?"

"Nope."

His father moved around the table, and took a seat in front of him. Tom continued shoving his face full of food in an effort not to have this conversation with his dad. Especially not now, and not there, at tribute. There were too many other men around to hear their conversation, and he wasn't up for that.

"You haven't been over to the mansion more than twice since you got back from New York," his father noted.

"Work," Tom reminded him.

"Mmm. How was it, anyway?"

"Work is fine."

"Nice try. New York, I meant."

Tom cleared his throat. "Fine."

"I don't think so—something's different with you since you got back. I'm not the first person to notice it. A mood, Adriano tells me."

Tom shot his uncle a look. Beside him, Adriano pretended like he hadn't seen or heard a thing. *Asshole.*

"Adriano should learn to keep his mouth shut," Tom said, shrugging.

"I take it you're not going to fill me in on whatever is bothering you, then?"

"It won't make a difference if I do."

Tommas nodded, and stood from the table. "All right, son. Enjoy your breakfast."

His father left the table, and headed to his own where his underboss and front boss were waiting with their food. It was another twenty minutes, after tribute had been paid and the men were well into eating, before Tommas spoke again.

"Marty, I heard you're having some kind of problem with another Capo. Care to fill me in?"

Tommas's voice carried over the chattering Capos in the restaurant. Instantly, the men quieted, and looked to Tom's father. A few glanced between the Capo Tommas had called out, and the boss himself. One or two glanced at Tom before looking away.

It made him think Marty had probably been running his mouth a bit. Not that it would be a surprise.

"No, boss," Marty said from two tables away from where Tom sat with Adriano and another Capo. "There's no need, really."

"Can I assume the issue has been corrected, then?" Tommas asked.

No.

Not even close.

Tom kept quiet just to see what Marty would say.

"I can't say the issue has been fixed," the balding, bulging Capo replied, "but I can't say a conversation here would fix it, either."

Tom's father tipped his head to the side like he was considering the man's words. "And why is that, Marty?"

"Well, I suppose to start—"

"Do you think I'm not objective when it comes to my men and their issues?" Tommas asked, not even giving the older Capo a chance to speak.

"I didn't say that, boss. I was going to say—"

"How you already went to Theo, and were told to take the offer the other Capo offered because it was a better deal—*far more*—than any other Capo would have given you, considering?"

Marty cleared his throat, and his gaze shifted to where Tom sat. "I don't mean to be rude, boss, but—"

"You should know by now, and at your age no less, that adding a *but* into a sentence you start with "I don't mean to be rude" actually means you very much intend to be rude, Marty."

"I … my apologies."

Tommas cocked a brow, but never once did his gaze leave the older Capo. He didn't single Tom out, or even make it seem like his son was involved at all. While Tom was almost certain there were a few Capos in the room who knew that the other Capo his father meant was him, he appreciated the way his father was handling the issue.

At the same time, he really didn't need his father to handle it.

Tom could do it.

He certainly didn't need anyone thinking he needed his father to come to his rescue, either. He didn't think that would do any good for him at the end of the day.

"My offer still stands, Marty," Tom said, joining the conversation. "Twenty percent for the truck being on your territory, as it always is, and another five percent on top of that for the misunderstanding you think we had."

"I don't *think* anything, Tommaso. You know damn well what we agreed to."

Tom sucked air through his teeth, refusing to show his irritation or frustrations in the presence of so many made men. "Yes, that my men would steal the truck, and sell the goods. They had the scheme worked out, and I brought it to your attention because of territorial lines. Not one thing was mentioned about *who* would handle the goods—you were only interested in money. My boys did the work, and so, they get the payoff from it."

"As I told you, Marty," Theo, the Outfit's front boss, said.

"Any other Capo in here would—"

"Agree that if they wanted to handle the goods, it would have been brought up in the first conversation," Adriano put in. "I mean, I've done these boosts between our territories before, and you didn't try to pull this shit on me."

Marty's face reddened. "I didn't pull anything on Tommaso. I can't help that the *boy* doesn't know how business works when a man who has been in it for longer than he has asks for something, Adriano."

Tom stiffened, but still refused to let his anger bleed into his tone when he said, "That's it, right?"

"I beg your pardon, Tommaso?"

"Because I'm almost twenty-two now, and you've got forty years on me. So it's easier for you to think you can screw over a young gun like me because I won't speak up, right? I'm a Rossi—my dad's the boss—and you had it in your head I probably wouldn't run to the boss because it would make me look like a boy who needs his daddy to fix shit for him.

"Nobody is fixing anything for me," Tom continued, unaffected. "My offer stands, Marty. Twenty for the territory, and five for the misunderstanding. And since you tried to pull this nasty shit on me this time, you can trust that I'll never work with you or your crew again on anything else."

Finally, Tom's father decided to speak up again. It was not like Tommas to stay quiet when his men argued. He usually culled that nonsense as soon as it started.

"Take the extra five, Marty," Tommas said, "because if it were me, I would have dropped you back down to fifteen just for thinking you were smart and could pull one over on me."

Nods passed around the room.

Confirmative agreements echoed from several men.

Tom had not been in the wrong. He could handle his business. He fucking hated being a Capo, but he knew how to be one.

Sometimes, the politics weren't such a bad thing. At least, not when they kept him distracted from something else. Like the phone in his pocket that still hadn't rang in a month with a call or message from Camilla.

Fuck his life.

CHAPTER FOURTEEN

THE WORDS on Camilla's laptop seemed to be bleeding together the longer she stared at them. She blinked, and when that didn't work, she rubbed the heels of her palms into her eyes just for good measure.

It also did nothing.

The words were there, sure. Black strokes in Times New Roman font against a white backdrop. Her essay due on the correlation of lack of available healthcare to women living below the poverty line, and inadequate maternal care leading to premature births. She had been given the assignment a month ago, and should have had it done already.

This was one of the areas she excelled in. This was a topic she could discuss for days and days. She knew the ups and downs, and exactly how she wanted to handle the posturing of the essay. It should have been done already, yet here she was, still looking at the damn thing and wondering what else she could write into the opening paragraph.

It was due in …

Camilla checked the date at the right hand, lower corner of the laptop's screen.

One week.

It was due in a fucking *week*.

She tipped her head to one side, trying to stare at the words from a different angle. Then, she tipped her head to the other side.

She probably looked like an idiot.

August confirmed it. "What are you, a bird?"

Camilla straightened on the couch. "No."

"Why are you looking at your screen like that?"

Knowing she wasn't going to get anything done going on like she was, Camilla sighed and closed the laptop screen. She set the computer on the coffee table, leaned back on the couch, and rubbed at her temples.

"You okay?" August asked.

The scents of bergamot and chamomile wafted through the apartment. Compliments of a chamomile tea August had brewed from loose leaves, and a bergamot oil she had put in a diffuser. Apparently, Camilla's stress wasn't only visible to herself, but also to her best friend.

August's way of helping was tea and oil, and quiet.

Lots of quiet.

Except now, her friend seemed ready to talk.

Camilla didn't know if she was ready, too.

"I don't know what I am anymore," Camilla whispered.

She didn't even know if August had heard her, but she felt slightly better the moment she let the words slip past her lips. It was the first time she had admitted them out loud. It was the first time since Tommaso walked out of her place a month ago that she told someone else in her life that she was *hurting*.

August had heard her.

Loud and clear.

Camilla wasn't all too surprised.

This is what best friends were for.

August came to sit on the edge of the coffee table. She moved Camilla's laptop further away, and picked up the chamomile tea that had long gone cold. Peering into the almost-full mug, her friend let out a heavy exhale.

"Do you want to talk about it?"

"Not sure what to say," Camilla replied.

"Well, anything you haven't told me would be a great start."

Camilla laughed, but it came out strained and bitter. It even left behind a bad taste in her mouth. Fuck everything because she couldn't even laugh lately without it being something awful, too. So was the way of her life, it seemed.

"You were trying to talk to me earlier, weren't you?" Camilla asked.

Maybe she wasn't ready to talk about Tommaso, or what happened. Maybe she wasn't ready to admit out loud that she had purposely hurt him, and then forced herself not to call him for a whole month despite every single part of her wanting to hear his voice.

Maybe Camilla just wasn't ready to say she had been wrong.

Old habits died hard.

Hers died even harder.

"It wasn't anything important," August murmured. "I was just telling you about a spread I got to help with for Bared Brand's magazine."

Camilla stared at her friend.

Heaviness weighed down her heart.

Regret filled her stomach.

Sadness clenched around her lungs.

"Aug," Camilla said quietly, "that's fucking amazing, and you know it is."

August shrugged. "It's nothing big."

"No, it *is*. It really is. And you were trying to tell me about it, but I was just over here off in my own world."

"So you've got a lot going on."

"No, I'm just being a shitty friend lately."

August gave her a look. "Cam, you're not being a shitty friend. I think you've just got some stuff to figure out in your head, that's all. We all go through that stuff sometimes."

"Not me."

"Well, maybe you don't usually go through it with a *guy*."

And there her friend went …

Calling her out.

Without actually saying Tommaso's name, of course.

August cleared her throat, and stood up from the coffee table. "Do you know when I figured out something was up with you after last month?"

"When?"

"You had an appointment to get your hair done up in those mermaid colors you wanted, and you totally flaked. You've been talking about that style for months now."

Camilla blinked. "Shit, is Chilla—"

"She's fine with you missing one appointment, Cam. I might have mentioned you were a little out of it lately."

"So my missed hair appointment clued you in, huh?"

August laughed. "You *don't* miss those. I saw you go to one once when you had the Norovirus."

Camilla made a face. "I did do that once, didn't I?"

"Puke everywhere, Cam."

Yeah, Chilla was not pleased about that. Not that Camilla blamed the woman.

"Hey, my hair looked good, though," Camilla pointed out.

"That was about the only thing you had going for you."

Camilla smiled, and for the first time in a month, it didn't feel forced. Still, as quickly as it had come, it faded. Just like that, her moment of happiness was gone. It was far too easy for her to lose happiness lately than it was to keep it.

August didn't miss Camilla's sudden change in mood again. Her friend bent down, patted a hand against her cheek, and made Camilla look at her. Familiar russet eyes told her shit was rough, but it could get better.

One of the many reasons she loved her friend.

"What happened when he came down to visit last month?"

Camilla shrugged. "Things felt too serious, I guess."

"And you bolted?"

"Like a baby deer."

August cocked an eyebrow. "You do know there's nothing wrong with

... falling in love, right? Being with one person. Whatever."

"I know that."

"Do you? Because I don't know that you do, Cam."

"I know I freaked out a little." Camilla made a noise under her breath, and stood from the couch. It made August take a couple of steps back to give Camilla room to move. "But he knew I was like this anyway—I didn't want serious, Aug, I wanted *fun*."

"I think you're trying to convince yourself of something that no longer applies, Cam."

"I—"

"And maybe you should give him the benefit of the doubt, too."

Camilla glanced at her friend, confused. "What?"

"Tommaso—give him the benefit of the doubt. You said it, Cam. He knew you were kind of a little crazy when it came to commitment and relationships. Like you're fucking allergic or something. Some part of him probably expected this to happen, or something like it. He might be a guy, but he still protects himself from getting hurt. Walls, you know?"

"We all have them," Camilla filled in what her friend didn't say.

August shrugged. "Yep."

Well, all things considered, Camila figured it was too little, too late now.

"It's been a month," she told her friend. "I haven't called, or texted. He hasn't made any effort to contact me. I think we can safely say I fucked up, and it's done."

"Mmm, I don't think it is. At least not for you."

"I'm not him."

August nodded. "Nope, but he waited six long months for your crazy ass the first time. What's one more month, Camilla?"

"Who even says I want to see him or whatever? Maybe I want to go back to doing what I did before I met him."

"I say it," August deadpanned.

"Yeah, but—"

"Staying in a comfortable place isn't courageous, it's easy."

"Sure, but—"

"Take a risk, Cam. One that doesn't involve some stranger you seduced in a club."

"Hey."

August waved a hand. "Just saying."

"Again—"

"Don't make me tell you that you can't be helped," August interjected with a severe look. "Don't open your mouth and make me say that, Cam."

She laughed again.

It didn't taste so bitter that time.

"Cam," Emma said, her smile growing wider at the sight of her daughter in the kitchen entryway. "I didn't know you were coming over today."

Camilla fiddled with her nails, acutely aware that they needed a good manicure. It was easier than looking at her mom. If she stared too long at Emma, her mother would know something was wrong. She didn't want her mom to worry.

"I was in the neighborhood, Ma."

"Didn't you have classes today? It's Tuesday."

"I took a day off."

"That's not like you."

Shit.

Camilla chose the wrong words. She could hear the concern in her mother's tone already. It wasn't that she didn't think her mother could help her, or make her feel better, but this was something she wanted to do alone.

Besides, just coming to her parents' home and being close to them was a huge help to Camilla's mess of emotions. Her childhood home, and all the good memories it had, soothed her without barely trying at all.

That's why she had come today.

Just to *be here*.

Looking up from her nails, Camilla tried to shrug it all off for her mother's benefit. "We all need a day or two to recharge sometimes, right?"

"Sure," Emma said. "Is that what it is, though?"

"Yeah, Ma. That's what it is."

"Are you going to stay for lunch?"

"I could eat."

"Just like your brother—neither of you refuse food," Emma teased.

"Well, we don't refuse yours."

Emma smiled, proud as could be. "That's very true. By the way, your brother is here. He's in talking to your father."

"Where?"

"The office."

Camilla nodded.

This was a good change. It allowed her to get out of her mother's sights without Emma prying for too long, and figuring out what was wrong.

"I'll go say hi," Camilla said.

"Do that," Emma called from behind her, "and make sure to talk to your father about whatever's up with you, too. Don't think I can't see it, Camilla Emma Donati."

And there her mother went using her full name.

Camilla winced, but kept walking.

She should have known better.

Her parents always knew.

Camila had been fooling herself thinking she could come here just to be comforted by a familiar place, and nothing more. But maybe that was exactly why she felt drawn to her parents from the second she woke up that morning.

"Well, look who came all the way to Newport today," her father said when she walked into his office.

Sure enough, both her father and brother were there. Calisto, sitting behind his large desk as he usually did. Cross, on the other hand, was sitting on the corner of the desk, and looking over something inside a folder.

Camilla opted to throw herself down on the leather couch against the far wall. "Thought I should come over and say hello before you forgot what my face looked like."

Calisto scoffed. "I can't forget what your face looks like—not when I stare at your mother every single day."

Cross chuckled. "She does look like Ma."

"Darker hair."

"Donati eyes."

"Acts like her, too."

"Jesus, have you seen how clean her place is? What nineteen-year-old girl keeps *that* clean of an apartment? Just like Ma."

"Okay, we all know I look and act just like my mother, thank you," Camilla grumbled. "Let's not make it into a speech or something."

Two pairs of eyes darted her way.

Her father's brow shot up at her attitude.

Cross's gaze narrowed.

Camilla looked away.

Fuck.

So maybe she was in a mood today, too.

It wasn't unusual for her family to tease her about the likeness she shared with Emma. In fact, it was a regular thing that got brought up almost every dinner, or occasion. Camilla didn't typically mind it.

It was no surprise that her brother and father picked up on her attitude, and thought it strange, considering.

"Just … don't ask," Camilla said.

She rested back on the couch, and used her arm as a shield to cover her eyes. That way, she didn't have to see her father and brother staring at her.

No, she only had to *feel* their eyes burning into her.

"Someone's in a mood," Calisto muttered.

"Sounds like it," Cross agreed.

"Any idea why?"

Camilla pointed a finger wildly in her brother and father's direction. "Don't even start. I don't want to talk about it."

"Sure you don't," Cross deadpanned, "because we all know to come here to this house when we don't want to talk about our *feelings.*"

"You say that like it's a bad thing," Calisto grumbled.

"Sometimes, people just don't want to talk, Papa."

"Yeah, well, then don't come here. You know how your mother is. She's a fixer. She likes to *talk.*"

About everything, Camilla added silently.

"I guess we're going to pretend like you didn't make us sit opposite to one another and talk about why we were mad, or offended, or got our feelings hurt, and how it made us feel when we were growing up, huh?"

"Don't be a smartass, son."

"You did do that," Camilla pointed out.

"Yes, and now look at the two of you. I actually have children that don't want to kill each other every time they're in the same room. Don't act like how I raised you two was a bad thing."

"Didn't say it was," Cross said.

"Nope," Camilla agreed.

"Wait."

Camilla stiffened on the couch. "What?"

"Is this about Tommaso?" her brother asked.

Her teeth gritted so hard that her jaw hurt. "I don't know what you're talking about."

"Mmhmm, I bet you don't."

"What did I miss?" her father asked.

"I'm assuming," Cross said, "but last month, Tom came down from Chicago. He didn't go anywhere except Camilla's place. He didn't even call me when he was down, but he left a few days after he got here."

"Three." Camilla sighed, and rubbed at her eyes. "He left after three days."

"I know he was here last month," Calisto said. "He came here for dinner."

"Bet you didn't see him after that, though, did you?"

"Well, no."

"Yeah, and come to think of it, he hasn't answered any of my texts this month. I was hoping to get some information from him about something for work, and … silence."

Camilla cleared her throat. "Just leave it alone, Cross."

"Camilla."

It was her father speaking that time—soft, caring, and yet still firm and sure. He used to use that tone on her when she was being particularly stubborn or difficult as a young child. Just like how it did back then, it made her move her arm and look at him.

Both her brother and father were still staring at her. Neither had moved an inch.

"What?" she asked.

"Did something happen that I need to know about?" Calisto asked.

She could see the unspoken question burning in her father's eyes—*did he hurt you?*

Camilla shook her head. "It was me, Daddy, not him."

Cross nodded like he now had some great understanding that Camilla didn't know about. Her brother always had been a little too arrogant for his own good. She was pretty sure her father said more than once it would be Cross's arrogance that killed him someday.

Who knew?

"Tom's a good guy, Camilla," her brother said.

She shot him a glare. "I know he is!"

"No, I mean … Tom's a good guy. He's not the kind of useless fuck that treats women like garbage, or uses them. He's not really physical in his anger a lot of the time, and he's level-headed. He's clean about business, and about life. So when I say that he's a good guy, I mean, he's like a fucking unicorn in this business. It's hard to find good men who do the kind of shit that we do."

"That's true," her father said quietly.

"What about you—or Daddy, even?" Camilla asked. "Aren't you both *good* men?"

Calisto chuckled. "Well, Cam, as long as we're good to the women in our lives who matter, then that's all we need to do."

Cross was still looking at her, though. "Don't mess with Tom in a way that plays with his head, Cam. He doesn't deserve that, you know? He genuinely liked you. I mean, I only know one other person who has waited a long time to get a second chance with somebody they love, and it tells me that waiting means something."

"Who?" Camilla asked.

Her brother shrugged, and glanced away. "Somebody. Point is, give it a chance. See what comes of it."

"I did give it a chance."

No, you didn't.

Camilla ignored her inner voice.

"I agree with Cross," her father said, joining the conversation again. "Tommaso is a good man, Camilla. I think any man that is willing to kill for a woman he barely knows at all says a lot about his character."

She froze on the couch. "What did you just say?"

"Not a good time to bring that up, Papa," Cross said out of the corner of his mouth. "Not when you're goal is making her trust the guy."

Camilla sat up straight on the couch, and stared hard at her father. "Tell me what you meant."

"Cross can explain it better than me."

"I told you that shit so you would *know*, not so that you could tell her," Cross snapped. "You weren't feeling well when it first happened, so I had Tom keep his mouth shut until you were better, and I could tell you myself. It wasn't like you needed the extra stress at the time, considering you had another episode coming on. We agreed not to *tell her*."

"Do you want to discuss how that makes you feel, son?"

Her brother gritted his teeth, and then turned to her. "The morning after you met Tom that first time, one of the guys that hung around with Zeke made a comment about you."

"Which guy?"

"Doesn't matter."

"What did he say?"

"Listen, he only did it because you probably rejected him before."

"Not what I asked, Cross."

Her brother sighed, clearly annoyed. "A slut, Cam. He said other shit, too—you're not wife material, or whatever. Good for a fuck. You know, what people say sometimes."

Those words didn't sting Camilla like they used to. Now, she didn't care. She was quite aware that society liked to stamp labels on her because they didn't approve of her choices. A strong, independent woman was far easier to insult than to admire and praise.

It was what it was.

Men were even worse.

Except for men like Tommaso ...

Men like her father.

Men like her brother.

"And what did Tom do?" Camilla demanded.

Cross arched a brow, and asked, "What do you think?"

A cold chill slipped down her spine.

Her father said it.

Killed a man.

Her gaze darted between her brother and father.

Learning that should have scared her; it should have bothered her deeply. It did, in some ways. It also didn't bother her at all in other ways. It didn't bother her because sitting across from her were two of the best men she had ever known. Her father and brother. Men who were criminals, and who often did bad things, yet loved with all they had.

Good men.

"But why?" Camilla asked. "He didn't know me. He didn't have to protect my honor or some shit. He didn't have any reason to do that at all."

If anything because she had spent the night with him after simply meeting him, Tommaso might have actually had reason to agree with the guy he killed.

Cross shook his head. "You don't get it, Cam."

"I think she does," her father said, still staring at his daughter. "Answer your own question, Camilla. Why would Tommaso do something like that?"

Camilla's throat tightened.

Her heart hurt again.

She still answered.

"Because he's a good man."

And she was a scared little girl.

Calisto and Cross had not been lying.

Camilla's greatest pet peeve was dirt, dust, or clutter. Despite the mess she could be when it came to life and love, her apartment was not one. Cleanliness and tidiness in her personal spaces helped her to feel put together.

Even if it was just an illusion.

Plus, cleaning helped to keep her hands distracted. That way, she didn't have the worst urge to grab her phone, and make a call to Tommaso.

She wasn't quite ready to that.

She wanted to, sure.

Being ready was another story altogether.

Camilla heaved the clothes out of the dryer, and into the waiting basket. She had already swept and mopped every single floor in her apartment. She dusted every shelf, and corner. She rearranged the books on the shelves, and then reorganized a junk drawer that no longer had a lot of junk in it.

All she had left to do was one single basket of laundry to fold and put away. Then maybe she could get to work on the essay she had pushed aside a couple of days earlier. When—or *if*—she got that done for school, then she would consider calling Tommaso.

She was hoping to feel a bit calmer, then.

Less anxious.

Like maybe she would actually know what to say should he pick up the fucking phone.

But who was to say he would pick it up?

After what she did, she wouldn't blame him for ignoring her altogether.

Camilla climbed two flights of stairs to get back to her apartment from where the laundry room was situated in the building. By the time she got back into her place and put the basket on the bed, her fingers were itching again.

Frustrated, she shoved her hands down into the clothes to grab something to fold. Another distraction for her.

What she brought out made her heart stop.

A simple black band T-shirt. The faded logo on the front teased her.

Tommaso had been wearing that on the second day he was in New York a month ago. She had been sort of struck by how relaxed he looked in jeans and a tee instead of his usual dress shirts and slacks, or even a suit.

He'd still looked good, though.

Damn good.

Camilla held the shirt up, and stared at it.

Fuck it.

She grabbed her phone, but didn't make a call.

She checked flights instead.

Apparently, she could be in Chicago before supper time. A cancellation for a first class seat was now hers.

Booked.

Now, Camilla just had to figure out what she was going to do when she got to Chicago.

She did make a phone call that time.

"What, Cam?" her brother asked the second he picked up the call.

"I need some help."

"For?"

"Chicago."

Cross made an appreciative noise on the other end. "All right. Like what?"

"Anything. Everything. I mean, Tom I can handle. It's where to go, and who to know … get what I mean?"

"Yeah, I do. Give me thirty minutes."

CHAPTER FIFTEEN

LOU WAS a good middle man, Tom had come to find out. At least where the crew was concerned. It made things far easier on Tom to simply delegate certain tasks to his friend, as the men were more agreeable to Lou, and less difficult.

Things like collecting money for the week.

Or keeping an eye on certain schemes.

Tom wished he had thought of this trick sooner. It would have taken away a shit load of stress, and make things far easier on himself.

Lesson learned.

He got to relax behind his desk, and he barely said a word as man after man from the crew came into the office to hand over their money for the week. Lou took care of the conversation, and paying the guys their dues for whatever work they had done.

It worked for Tom.

Lou liked it.

The crew was agreeable.

He considered that a win all the way across the board.

Sometimes, he had come to learn, a Capo had to take what they could get. Simple things made the greatest difference when it came right down to it.

"Good week," Tom said to Lou when another guy headed out of the office.

Lou nodded as he flipped through the stacks of cash. "One of the better ones over the last few months, that's for sure."

"As long as they're making money, then I don't give a damn how we do it."

His friend laughed. "Yeah, I know."

"You would be good at this, you know?"

Lou glanced over at Tom. "Good at what?"

Tom waved at the room. "*This*, Lou. Doing this."

"Being a Capo, you mean?"

"That's exactly what I mean."

His friend scoffed. "Yeah, right. We both know I'm not going anywhere but right where I am, Tommaso."

"That's a shitty outlook."

"Not really. I like where I am, so I don't see it as a bad thing. I mean, being a made man used to be something I wanted. Then the deeper I got into this business, the more I figured out it wasn't likely to happen."

"You shouldn't assume things. Everybody gets their say on nominations when the time comes. Capos get a voice on who they would like to give their in to the family, so to speak. Would you still want to be a made man, if the opportunity came up?"

Lou shrugged, and took a seat on the edge of the desk. "Back when I was a teenager, I used to glamorize the mafia in my head. All the Capos drove black cars, wore suits, and controlled the city."

Tom chuckled. "That's a pretty accurate description. You just didn't think to consider the rest of the people who make up the organization, too."

"Sure, but my idea was based on some crazy notion where I could be one of those guys, Tommaso. A wise guy, you know what I mean? I started running the streets because we were dirt fucking poor, and our water got shut off in February. A month later, they turned the power off, too. I had two little sisters, and a baby brother. My father had fucked off somewhere with his latest piece of ass, and my mother barely held shit together. So I went out, and I hustled. I did deliveries, or ran errands. I did some drug drops when I thought it was safe enough that I wouldn't get caught."

"You never told me about that stuff," Tom said.

Sure, he had known that Lou's life had been stricken with poverty and rough times, but he hadn't quite realized just how much. He hadn't known how much his friend had sacrificed and suffered to be where he was—still quite low on a totem pole that they called the Outfit.

So was the fucking way of this business.

Tom was lucky—privileged as fuck. He knew it; he never denied it. Sure, he'd worked hard all his life to be a made man, but he didn't doubt for a second that Lou worked twice as hard just to survive and be sitting where he was.

Lou shrugged, and cleared his throat. "Before I went on the streets to work, I wanted to be a lawyer, or a doctor. Maybe a cop."

"That's a bad job to have in this city."

His friend barked out a laugh. "Right? One of the most dangerous cities for the blue line."

"A new cop is always coming up dirty on the news every other week, too."

"Yeah, I know, but that was one of my dreams. I ended up here instead, and I just substituted one dream for another. One dream that I likely wouldn't even achieve. How could I?" Lou asked, a bitterness coloring his words. "I was just some poor kid from the Heights with no dad, and a mother entertaining Johns on the weekend at the pay-by-the-hour motel down the block to make extra money that her two jobs didn't provide.

"That's what made me easy pickings to the guys on the crew that needed a young kid to deliver their drugs, or pick something up. Twenty bucks thrown at me went a long fucking way. It didn't take much at all for them to convince me into this business, despite the fact I could see some of them were three times my age and still going nowhere. Maybe that's why when I started doing this shit, I glamorized the idea of the mafia and made men in my head, and the dream changed to make it worth my while. Funny how that worked."

Tom swallowed hard, and glanced down at his clenched hands. "Sorry, man."

Lou waved a hand. "Nah, don't do that. Don't be sorry, or have pity. I fucking hate that shit, Tom."

"Nobody's victim, huh?"

"Nope. I made my choices."

"And you're still here doing this," Tom noted.

Lou shrugged a single shoulder, and pushed off the desk. "I guess you could say the dream is still very much well and alive for me in some ways. Like maybe if I keep working at it, somebody will see me as something other than that poor kid from the Heights that needed money to have water and heat."

Tom gave his friend a smile, but said nothing. Someone already did see Lou as more than that because Lou had seen someone else as more than a rich pretty boy.

Him, that was.

Tom was going to get his friend the button.

No matter what.

He'd do that for Lou.

Somehow.

The phone on the desk rang, interrupting their conversation from going any further. Another guy from the crew stepped into the office at the same time Tom picked up the call. He waved for Lou to handle the guy—as he was already going to do—while Tom turned his back to the two men exchanging cash in the office.

"Rossi here," Tom said.

"Son, are you busy?"

Tom relaxed a bit at his father's voice. "Not really. What do you need, Dad?"

"You should make your way over to the mansion as soon as you can.

Someone's waiting here to see you, Tommaso."

He stiffened.

"Who?"

"Someone I think you want to see."

Tom's throat constricted, and his heart raced. He didn't have any fucking reason to believe it was Camilla waiting for him. She still hadn't called. It had been over a month since he last talked to her. He gave her space hoping that she would figure her shit out and contact him.

Yet, here he was.

Still very much alone.

"Who?" Tom asked again.

"You were right about her," his father said. "What you told me about her the first time, I mean. She's very … different. In a good way, mind you."

Camilla.

"Don't let that woman out of your sight."

His father chuckled. "Right now, your mother is plying her with apple pie, and a promise to show her the library. Your sisters just got home from school, and are giving her the first degree. She's not going anywhere."

He heard his father's unspoken words loud and clear.

Take your time if you need to.

Tommas had known—even though Tom refused to talk to his father about it—that something was bothering his son. That something was wrong, and had been since he got back from New York the second time. Over and over again, his father pushed to know what it was. He asked him about Camilla. He questioned why Tom threw himself into work when he had barely got through the day before without wanting to blow someone's head off. He even suspected his father made a phone call to Calisto Donati just in case he could get information there.

Still, Tom had kept his issues private.

"I don't need time right now," he told his father.

He'd spent a whole month waiting.

That was enough time.

"She's not going anywhere, son," Tommas repeated.

Her hair was a deep shade of brown mixed with gold and red highlights. A little past her shoulders, her hair sat in beachy waves.

Longer than the last time he had seen her, but not by much. For anyone else, Tom probably wouldn't have noticed the half an inch difference in hair length, but this was Camilla.

He'd learned with her that even the slightest change was to be expected, and he needed to look for it.

The flowy, peach-colored dress was a good choice for the month of May. It fell just above her knees, and showed off the ankle boots with a four inch heel she wore.

Tom wasn't really sure why he thought to take in the way she looked, and the things she wore. Maybe because doing so gave him a few more seconds to simply look at her while she entertained his sisters, and not bring attention to himself just yet.

What was he supposed to say?

How did he open this up now?

Tom didn't know.

His brain decided to misfire like a fucker, and his mouth opened before he could stop it. "Cam."

Camilla looked up from the photo album she was flipping through, and smiled at Tom. A shy smile, he thought, and not one of her usual bright, brilliant grins he was accustomed to. No, this was hesitant, like she wasn't sure what his reaction would be when he looked at her, or something.

It still made her brown eyes light up, though.

"Hey," she said.

"Tommaso!" his two little sisters shouted in sync.

And just like that, his momentary daze was broken while his sisters leaped from the couch to get closer to him. He took a few minutes to calm Sara and Rebeka down—or the best he could—and all the while, tried not to look at Camilla for too long.

"Camilla came to visit," Rebeka said.

"She lives in *New York*," Sara said, stressing the state like it was a big deal.

Tom grinned. "I know. Hey, why don't you two go find Ma, and let her know that we want something special for supper."

"Ma's having a dinner," Sara said seriously.

"A dinner?"

Camilla spoke up, then. "She wanted to invite some people over."

Tom cocked a brow, and then sighed. "Not surprised."

"Do you want us to go, so you can be alone with Camilla?" Sara asked.

He looked to the oldest of his two sisters. She was a bright girl—looked like their mother, but acted like their father. Little got past Sara at the end of the day.

"A little bit, yeah," Tom said, smiling.

Sara nodded as though she already knew his answer. "Okay,

Tommaso."

She grabbed Rebeka's hand just as the younger of the two girls tried to dart back to the couch where Camilla was still sitting. She pulled her little sister along, and headed for the hallway.

"Come on, Rebeka," Sara said, "let's go get pie."

"Yes! Pie!"

Tom waited until he could no longer hear the voices of his sisters before he turned to Camilla again. She was still sitting on the couch, but now her gaze was turned down to the photo album in her lap.

"Which album is that?" Tom asked. "My mother seems to make it her mission to document every single little thing about our lives."

"Birthdays from last year," Camilla said.

"Huh."

Camilla peered up at him, and said, "I guess today's your twenty-second birthday, Tom. May seventh, right?"

He blinked, unsure for a moment.

"Is today the seventh?"

Camilla's smile turned sly. "You forgot your own birthday?"

"It's just another day."

"No, it's *your* day, Tom, and I almost missed it."

He didn't miss the sadness in her tone, or the way her eyes dropped back down to the album.

"You have a huge family," Camilla said after a moment.

"Yeah, it's big."

He didn't know what else to say.

He didn't know what to ask her.

Tom just … stared at her.

Finally, Camilla looked up from the album, and smiled at him. Brighter than before, and less hesitant. "Your dad is kind of imposing."

Tom nodded. "For people who don't know him, sure."

"Your mom is really sweet, though."

Tom laughed at that. "Yeah, until she's pissed at you. I mean, then you might as well just get the hell out of the city. At least until the storm passes."

Camilla laughed, too. "I can't see it."

"Well, no, you're the woman her son loves, and this is the first time she's ever met you. It's not a huge surprise that she's being especially nice to you."

Her eyes widened.

Tom realized what he'd said instantly.

The silence stretched on between them long enough for him to clear his throat, and look away. "Love shouldn't be a scary thing. Loving someone shouldn't be hard to do, even if it's hard to find. Love should be effortless."

Easy.

Right.

"I know, Tom," she whispered.

It was the humans who made love hard, he knew.

"It's women like you who make the thought of being in love with you something to fear because no offense, Cam, but you're kind of a fucking flight risk."

Her laughter came out soft and light.

"Am I?" she asked.

"Just a little bit, babe."

"Yeah, I guess I am."

"I don't mind taking that risk, though, Cam. I want to take it, but only if you do. I don't mind the effort actually being something needs, but it's a give and take. I cannot be the only person giving while you just take from me."

She let out a quiet exhale, and closed the album in her hands. Tom waited her out, and didn't move an inch when she got up from the couch and came closer to him. He stayed still even when she was close enough to touch, and she reached up to cup his jaw with her warm palm.

"I'm here, Tom."

He nodded. "I can see that, Cam. A call might have been nice."

"It's been a rough month."

"Oh?"

"Really rough," she admitted. "But I *am* here … with a little help from Cross, but don't tell him that because then he'll want to be thanked. I like to keep him honest."

Tom chuckled. "So, what does being here actually mean for you?"

"I guess it means what you did for me, I'm trying to do for you. I'm here. Who are you, Tommaso Rossi? Care to show me your world?"

"Anything you want."

Anything to keep her.

At least for now …

Camilla's hand slid from his jaw to behind his neck, and she pulled him closer. She had to stand all the way on the tips of her toes to reach up and press her lips to his. It was only once her mouth touched his that he wrapped an arm around her waist, and crushed her to him.

Her body.

Her mouth.

All of her.

Her fingers tangled into the hair at the nape of his neck, and tugged hard enough to sting. He answered that back by biting her bottom lip, and then kissing the same spot. Her breathless laugh whispered along the seam of his lips before he hushed her with another kiss—harder and deeper than hers had been. She didn't seem to mind. Her lips parted to let his tongue snake into her mouth.

There, he found a familiar taste. A sweet heat. Their kiss was now a familiar dance that could make him ache and burn all at the same time. It was a damn shame that now his cock was hard, but he was going to have to wait to do something about it.

The whole dinner thing, and all.

Yes, Tom had most certainly missed Camilla. He wondered if that feeling was mutual. Her hands that wouldn't let him go, and her lips still on his, said it probably was.

"So, Camilla, what brings you all the way to Chicago?"

Tom shot Adriano a look. His uncle, and his aunt Alessa sitting right beside the man at the table, only grinned right back at him.

"Thought I would like the city, actually," Camilla said.

"Not *someone*, then?" Eve, Theo's wife, asked.

"Someone, too, sure." Camilla gave Tom a smile. "I mean, Tom's *okay*."

"Ouch," Tom muttered.

Camilla flashed her teeth in a wicked grin, and that sent laughter echoing down the table.

So was the way of his life.

When he wasn't getting shit from people on the streets, his family picked up the slack. Of course, Tom didn't mind this so much. He could handle his family.

"What are you studying in school?" Damian asked. "Last I heard from your father, you had gone into nursing."

Camilla nodded. "Still am. I have a few more years to get where I want to be, I think. Or, with all the programs I want to take, it'll make it easier to get on a NICU ward without all the seniority that usually clogs up time."

"NICU," Tom's mother said. "Why a NICU nurse?"

"I was premature, and so was my brother."

"Oh." Abriella frowned, and her gaze darted to Tom as though she were trying to see if she had crossed some invisible line. "I'm sorry."

Camilla waved a hand. "It's okay. I went back to tour the hospital where I had been born. I was about fifteen or so, and the nurses actually remembered me because a lot of them were still there working."

"Is that common?"

"I think it depends on the nurse, and how working NICU affects him or her over time," Camilla replied, smiling softly. "I guess a lot of preemies that were born as early as me don't get to go back—fifty-fifty chance of survival. My dad told me once that for every baby that got to leave the NICU during my stay, another one never did. It was a big deal for the nurses to see me again, and that's what did it for me."

Under the table, Tom squeezed Camilla's thigh gently. She hadn't needed to share that kind of personal information with his family—people she barely knew—but he was grateful that she had. He'd only known some of the reason why she had chosen a nursing career, and her explanation certainly filled in any blanks he might have had left.

"You've still got a while to go yet with school, then," Abriella said.

"A little while, yeah," Camilla agreed with a laugh. "I don't mind. I work hard because I want to. I have a goal, and I intend to reach it."

"A good mindset to have," Tom's father said. "And just how long are you staying in Chicago, Camilla? Seems you have something to get back to."

That, Tom wanted an answer to as well.

Camilla stuck her fork into the pasta dish she had half finished, and said, "We'll see, I guess. I don't like leaving things unfinished."

Again, Tom squeezed Camilla's thigh.

He appreciated her willingness to indulge his family and their questions because she didn't have to do any of that at all. He was sure her intentions when coming to see him had very little to do with his family, and yet, here she was.

A screech from Sara took attention away from Camilla and Tom for a moment.

"Rebeka!"

"Oh, it was just a mistake," Abriella said, pushing her chair away from the table to stand up.

"Yeah, a mistake, Sara," Rebeka said, huffing at her sister.

A large red splash of sauce covered the front of Sara's pink dress. If there was anything his sister hated, it was someone ruining her clothes.

"Go to the kitchen," Abriella told Sara, "and I'll be in to clean it off."

Sara gave Rebeka her meanest glare before heading for the kitchen like she had been told to. Tommas shook his head as he too stood from the table.

"I'll go grab something else for her to wear," he told his wife.

"Thanks," Abriella replied. Then, she turned to Rebeka. "You sit right there, and don't you move."

Rebeka was already shoving her mouth full of food again. "Okay, Ma."

"Don't talk with your mouth full."

Tom's youngest sister showed off more chewed pasta when she

repeated, "Okay, Ma."

More laughter filled up the table.

Camilla laughed beside him, too. "Sometimes I wish I had younger siblings."

"To gang up on your brother, or what?"

She winked at him, sexy in a blink. "One reason, sure."

"Probably the only reason."

Camilla shrugged. "Probably."

A firm tug on Tom's pant leg took his attention away from the conversation he was trying to have with his father, and Tommas's men. At his side, little Rebeka looked up at him with her big blue eyes, and a worry line creasing her tiny brow.

"I think Camilla is lost, Tommaso."

He almost laughed at how serious she sounded.

"What makes you think that?" he asked.

"We can't find her. It's been ten whole minutes, and Ma says after ten minutes the person hiding wins. We called to her, but she didn't answer us."

Oh, Christ.

He left Camilla alone with his sisters and the other women for a few minutes to chat about something important, and look what happened.

"We were playing hide and seek," Rebeka said.

"Yeah, I figured that out. She doesn't know how to get around the mansion. Nobody thought to say that was a bad idea, Rebeka?"

The place was a two-wing, three-level *monster*. He could fucking get lost in it.

Rebeka shrugged her little shoulders. "She said yes."

Behind him, Tom's father chuckled as he'd clearly been listening in. "Go find her, Tommaso. We can finish this conversation later."

He turned to his dad, but shook his head. "No, just consider what I said about Lou, and the crew. It needs to be done, and it's your best bet to make that crew successful. It's only running smoothly right now because of him."

"I'll consider it, Tommaso. I'll talk it over more with Theo and Damian, too, and see what they think of it. Maybe a seat could be made for another man seeing as how we don't have one that needs filled at the moment."

"All right."

It was the best he could ask of his father. Tommas was the boss, after all, not him. Only his father could make those choices at the end of the day, as they usually ended up impacting the entire organization as a whole and not just one piece of it.

Things like that couldn't be done lightly.

Tom understood.

"Did anybody see which direction Camilla went?" he asked.

Rebeka nodded. "The front."

Great.

That left him with about fifteen halls to search, and at least ten rooms. Not to mention bathrooms, coat rooms, and closets.

Fuck.

"Go play with Sara, and I will find Camilla," Tom told Rebeka.

"Okay!"

Rebeka darted off, and Tom headed for the front wing of the mansion. If he was lucky, he would find Camilla and be able to finally sneak her away for a night he had waited a whole damn month for.

If he wasn't so lucky …

Well, he'd just have to find her.

Tom spent a good thirty minutes looking around the front wing of the mansion. It took him up to the second and third floor, but eventually he made his way back down. He called Camilla's name out several times, but got no answer back.

He was starting to think someone was playing a trick on him. Or someone had gotten mixed up in which direction Camilla went. Either way, Tom couldn't find her.

And now he was starting to worry …

Tom rounded the foyer stairs, and headed down a hallway that was rarely used for guests, but was a shortcut back to the middle of the mansion. It cut the time in half to get back to the dining room and kitchen.

His best plan now was just to get everybody to start looking for Camilla. What the hell else could he do?

A muffled knock stopped him.

And then another.

"Camilla?" Tom called out.

"Tom?"

Just from the direction her quiet voice came, he knew exactly where she was. Tom went back the way he came, and opened up the last door on the right. From the outside, that door could be opened easily.

But from the inside?

The doorknob jammed.

Every single time.

The only way to open it from the inside was with a little knife his father kept hidden up above the doorjamb. They only used that small room as extra storage for coats or whatever else when they had parties at the mansion.

Sure enough, Tom found Camilla on the other side.

Instantly, she smiled sheepishly at him.

He barely held back his laughter.

"Got lost, did you?" he asked.

The door closed behind him, but he wasn't worried about it. He knew how to get out.

Camilla made a face. "Nope. I did not get lost. I just knew that eventually the girls would go find someone—likely you—and you would come get me. Now, look, Tom. I've got us all alone. See what I did there?"

Her cheeky little response was all bravado, and he knew it.

"You got lost, and then stuck."

"No, this was entirely intentional."

"Mmhmm."

He came closer to her, one small step at a time.

Camilla's grin kept growing all the while.

"It was," she said firmly. "That's the story I'm going to tell."

"Because you don't want to admit you got lost, and then stuck."

"Stop saying that." She gave him a fake glare. "Let me keep my pride, Tom. It's all I've got right now."

"Oh, is that what it is?"

"Yep," Camilla said.

They were only a foot apart, now. He could reach out, grab her, and do all the sinfully good things that had been running through his mind since he saw her.

"Maybe you need a lesson on learning how to swallow your pride, then."

She licked her lips.

His dick hardened.

"Maybe I do."

Her whisper coaxed him.

Encouraged him.

Challenged him.

Tom never did know how to back down from a good challenge, and he wasn't about to start now. He jolted forward, grabbed Camilla's face, and pulled her in for a bruising kiss. Her grin curved wickedly against his lips, and then her tongue peeked out to tease him, too.

"Probably shouldn't be doing this here," she said against his mouth.

"Probably shouldn't have gotten yourself lost in one of the most private rooms in the mansion, then."

"Asshole."

Tom reached around and smacked her ass. "Say it again if you want another one."

Camilla stood up on tiptoes, and her mouth grazed his ear. "Ass—" *Smack.*

Her laughter pulsed against his ear. *"Hole."*

He slapped her backside again.

Camilla made a sexy noise in the back of her throat a second before her hands pushed against his chest. She shoved Tom back against the door that had previously kept her locked in. The second time her lips met his, he already had his hands up her skirt, and two fingers stuffed up her wet pussy. He muffled her cries by sticking two of his fingers in her mouth. Her tongue swirled around the digits while he fucked her with his other hand.

And *damn*, was she wet.

Hot and silky against his palm.

The suckling noise her pussy made every time his fingers thrust in told him that her panties were probably already ruined. Camilla grinded her cunt against his hand as he added a third finger, and rubbed his palm into her clit at the same time.

She tipped her head back, and made his fingers slip from her mouth. They wet a trail of her saliva from her chin to the column of her throat where he grabbed tight. Her happy little sigh, and the way her pussy clenched around his fingers said she was damn close.

"Make me come, please make me come," she chanted. "Make me come, Tom, and then eat my pussy until I come again."

"Only if you lick my cock clean after you come all over it first."

Glinting brown eyes met his. She grinned again, and came hard at the same time. "You got yourself a deal, Tommaso."

Good God.

This woman would kill him.

He didn't mind a bit.

Tom pulled his wet fingers out from between her thighs. Camilla took that chance to bring his hand to her mouth, and suck his fingers clean.

He loved the taste of her pussy.

But he liked the taste of it more on her lips.

"Fucking missed you like crazy, Cam."

Through lowered lashes, and a sinful smile, Camilla said, "I bet you did."

Then, she lifted up to her tiptoes, and kissed him again.

"And I missed you, too," she whispered. "Now bend me over something, and fuck me before someone comes looking for us."

Tom had her bent over an empty, small circular table before her next breath. He was balls-deep in her pussy the second she yanked her skirt up, and spanked her wet center just to tease him. Camilla knew exactly what her teasing did to him, and how insane it made him feel.

She was still perfect.

So crazy fucking perfect.

CHAPTER SIXTEEN

"YOU HAVE *no* respect for sleeping in," Camilla mumbled.

God, she tried so damn hard to sound irritated, but really, her voice just came off high and airless. Not whiney, but close. Still just a little bit too needy for her liking.

It probably didn't help that Tommaso's lips were kissing a tantalizing path down her stomach. He'd started at her cheek, then her throat, and focused on her breasts for a while. He teased and flicked the small hoops in her nipples until they were taut, and her back arched off the bed.

Then, he moved lower.

And *lower*.

"How can I respect sleeping in when I have you in my bed?" Tommaso asked. "Besides, I don't know how to sleep in. I wake up before dawn. Get used to it."

Get used to it.

Words like those might have scared Camilla before. They kind of implied something long-term was on the horizon. Something beyond a one-time deal. The first thing she would have done after getting her fill was bolt, and stay gone.

Not this time.

Those words teased.

They made her anticipate.

They *promised*.

His lips touched down just below her navel, and his tongue flicked out to lap at her skin. He went lower still, kissing her pubic bone, and hooking one of her legs around his shoulder. Camilla knew what was coming, and couldn't find a single part of her that wanted to stop him.

No matter how much she pretended to like sleep.

This would always be better.

Again, his tongue flicked out to lap at her skin when he kissed just above the hood of her clit. Camilla let out a slow exhale, and steeled herself. She wasn't going to show a damn thing to Tommaso.

It didn't matter how good his blue gaze looked as he stared up from between her thighs with a sexy little grin, his eyebrow cocked in challenge, and ...

"Why do you have to be like this?" she asked him.

Tommaso's grin deepened. "Like what?"

"I don't know ... sweet, patient, sexy as hell, gorgeous, and there's more but my brain is really just focused on how close your mouth is to my pussy right now. So, it's basically fucking useless at the moment."

His chuckle rocked them both on the bed.

"I mean, do you want to pretend like it's a bad thing where my mouth is right now?" he asked.

Camilla glanced up at the ceiling, and sent a silent prayer to the God she had been taught to revere and trust. A deity she gave all her faith to because everyone needed something to believe in—something good and beautiful.

Tommaso was kind of like that for her, too.

Finally, she peered back at Tommaso, and waved a hand at him. "Who do I have to blame for all of this, huh? Your mother, or father? Some person who took you under their wing and taught you how to be this amazing, perfect man, or what?"

"Uh."

That was all she got.

Uh.

Camilla stared at Tommaso, and waited for a response. "Well?"

"I'm confused, Cam. You act as though it's a bad thing I'm a decent guy."

He dropped his upper body down, rested between her legs, and set his chin to her stomach. Like that, the two looked at one another until she felt like she was capable of making full sentences that made sense.

"It's not a bad thing—it's just not something I'm used to. Yeah, that works."

She mentally patted herself on the back.

Tommaso shook his head. "Yeah, well, that's a shame."

"Maybe you're not perfect at all."

"Ouch."

Camilla laughed, and reached down to stroke his unshaven cheek with her palm. "No, I mean ... maybe you're just perfect for me. Every little thing about you seems to break down my walls, right? Things about you that would usually send me running for the hills actually draws me back in. I don't know. I'm rambling."

Wordlessly, Tommaso pushed up from the bed, and rested on his hands. He hovered over Camilla with a smile that was still sexy, but also soft and *knowing*.

Like he knew exactly what she was scared to say.

Tommaso bent down, and grazed his nose along Camilla's cheek. She tipped her head back, and answered his soft touch with a kiss. A sweet, slow kiss that burned through her body. From her toes, to her fingertips, she was on fire.

It wasn't so devastating, though.

It wasn't frightening.

It soothed and reassured and protected. It wrapped around her like invisible tendrils holding tight, and refusing to let go.

It was *just* a kiss, but it was everything else, too.

And that's when she knew for sure …

That's when all the things she had been wondering and waiting for slipped into place. All the answers she thought needed words and explanations actually only needed a kiss.

Because *that* was when she knew.

Camilla loved this man.

She almost wished she could stay like that—forever lost to the moment when she fell in love with Tommaso. She knew she would love him until the end of time, but this would be the one and only time when she first really *knew it*.

Tommaso smiled against her lips when Camilla stroked his cheek.

He knew.

She could see it in his eyes.

Camilla still told him.

"I love you, Tom."

"I know—I love you."

"It's not so hard to say, I guess. Not so scary."

"See," he told her, "love is effortless, Cam."

It was.

That, and perfect.

Like him.

The ruckus of laughter by men inside the warehouse quieted damn near the second Camilla stepped foot inside the building. A dozen pairs of eyes turned on her, and she let out a little laugh.

"What, have they never seen a girl before?"

Tommaso chuckled at her side. "Not in here, babe. Ignore them."

Camilla followed behind Tommaso as he headed for the far end of the warehouse. There, an office door was open, and inside were two more men.

One, Camilla recognized as Adriano—apparently, Tommaso's uncle. He had been at the dinner the evening before.

"Camilla."

She smiled at Adriano's greeting.

The other guy pushed off the desk, and shot Tommaso a questioning look. "Camilla?"

Tommaso shrugged. "Yeah, Camilla."

"This is … a little weird. Mostly because I don't understand what's happening."

Adriano waved the other two men's conversation off as he stood from the chair behind the desk. "Don't mind them. I hope my nephew is showing you around Chicago properly."

Camilla cocked an eyebrow at Tommaso. "Not yet."

"Working on it, actually."

"You better," Adriano said, grinning. "It's hard to sell a New Yorker on Chicago."

"Let's not get into that old conversation," Tommaso said, shaking his head. "It's not worth the effort."

"Because New York is—"

"Not the best," Tommaso interjected fast.

Camilla rolled her eyes, saying under her breath, "Says you."

"And me," the unknown guy added.

"Me, too," Adriano said, shrugging. "It's a little dirty, Camilla. That's all."

"Yeah, well, fuck all of you, too."

Laughter rumbled through the room. Their teasing didn't really bother her. If anything, it made her feel more welcome. She certainly didn't want Tommaso's family and friends tiptoeing around her.

"Are you going to introduce us, or what?" the unknown guy asked.

Tommaso waved between Camilla and the man. "Cam, this is Lou. We've been friends for years. Lou, this is Cam. She's none of your business."

Camilla smacked Tommaso on his arm, and then held a hand out to Lou. "Nice to meet you, and ignore him."

Lou flipped Tommaso the middle finger after he shook Camilla's hand. "You could have mentioned …" The guy trailed off, and nodded in Camilla's direction. "You know."

"None of your business."

"Tommaso," Camilla said.

Tommaso only shrugged, but said nothing.

Adriano sighed heavily, and came around the desk. "Someone—not saying who, but it's Tommaso—doesn't like to share things. We blame it on the age difference between him and his sisters. He was spoiled rotten for too long by his mother and father, and it shows every day of his life."

"It is not pick on Tom day," Tommaso muttered. "Give me the paperwork you wanted me to drop off to Tommas."

"Every day is pick on you day when you bring a girl to work," Lou said, smirking.

Camilla hid her smile by looking away. Apparently, she didn't need to worry about a damn thing, or feeling out of place. It was … good.

Easy.

"Seriously, get me the paperwork before I leave without it," Tommaso said. "I'm not staying here for longer than I have to, if I have to listen to this shit."

Adriano pointed a single finger at Tommaso, but started digging in the desk. "Watch it, *nipote*."

Tommaso wasn't even paying attention to his uncle. He had already moved onto his friend again.

"Pick on me, huh?" Tommaso asked.

Lou nodded. "Yeah, sorry, man."

"I'll remember not to give you a call when we all head to Joe and Cory's club opening up tonight, then."

"The new one downtown?" Lou asked.

Tommaso shrugged. "Not for you."

Camilla knew Tommaso was just bothering his friend, but she decided to step in. After all, she might need the guy on her side someday. She pulled out her phone, and turned the screen on.

Handing it over to Lou, she said, "Plug your contact in. I'll call you when we're leaving."

"Cam," Tommaso said, looking like she'd just punched him in the gut. "What the hell, *donna*?"

"Hey, I'm making friends," she replied.

Lou grinned, and punched his number into the phone. "I like her, Tom. You should bring her around more often."

"Yes," Adriano agreed as he handed over a red file to Tommaso. "I agree."

"He's been up there a while," Camilla said, glancing upward at the high ceiling.

"Business," Tommaso's mother replied.

Camilla nodded, and went back to the bread she had rolled. Using a knife, she cut a cross-cross pattern along the top part of the loaf.

"I don't usually cut it like that," Abriella said.

"Sorry."

"No, it's fine."

"I can roll it up again, if you want."

Abriella laughed, and patted Camilla's cheek with a floury hand. "I just meant to say, that's a new way to cut the loaf."

"Oh." Camila set the knife aside, and brushed her hands off on her jeans. It left flour handprints behind, but she didn't mind. Abriella had asked her to help with the bread she had been baking, and Camilla didn't want to refuse. "Well, my mom does it like that because it makes it look like a cushion after it's done."

"Huh." Abriella picked up a bit of flour, and sprinkled it over her rolled dough, and the countertop. She went about rolling the dough again. "I like it. How are you liking Chicago?"

"It's all right. I mean, it's not New York or anything."

Abriella smiled. "I feel the same way when I leave this city. It takes some getting used to."

"But I like it here. Tom took me around today, and showed me different places."

"Met some people, too, didn't you?"

Camilla nodded. "A lot of them were at dinner, but yeah. It was nice to meet everyone again—one on one."

"We are a large family."

"Not like mine," she admitted. "It's just my mom and dad, brother, and a couple of aunts that moved away years ago."

"No grandparents?"

Camilla shrugged. "My mom's parents, but I've never even met them."

She could see the question lingering in Abriella's gaze, but the woman didn't ask for more. She was grateful because honestly, she didn't even know what to say about her mother's parents. All she knew was that they were not nice people.

"We've made our family big over the years," Abriella said quietly, still working away at the bread. "Tommas's mother and father are dead, and so are mine. What we had left were relations made by marriage and friendships."

"Makes for peaceful business, I bet."

At least, Camilla assumed it would. She knew the closer a family was, the less likely they were to fight on the mafia side of things. Or, that's what her father liked to say.

Abriella glanced up from the dough with a sly smile. "And just how much do you know about business, Camilla?"

She laughed. "Enough to know my place."

"That's a start. What about my son?"

Camilla cleared her throat. "I ... never really asked Tommaso, to be honest."

"Why?"

"Because it didn't matter to me if he was connected, or not. It didn't make a difference to how he treated me, or the things he did for me. I knew he was a good man, and the rest were just details."

Abriella's hands slowed in her work. "What made you come to that conclusion?"

"I was raised by a good man who lives in shades of gray. To people who only see his name come up on the news, he's a criminal. He sells drugs, evades taxes, and puts guns on the streets. But to me, he is just my dad. It was the way he treated me that mattered. Not the rest."

As she spoke, Camilla kept her gaze focused on the next dough she was rolling into a perfect loaf just the way her mother had taught her. It was easier to be honest that way, as then she could simply speak and not worry about how her words might sound to Abriella.

"You didn't consider at all that Tommaso is the son of a boss—the only son? That someday, he might sit where his father does because those expectations have followed him around for his entire life?"

"Not really," Camilla said.

She *knew*, of course. She wasn't a stupid girl.

Camilla just didn't think it mattered.

"Do you think that's because you're a bit naive, or perhaps you grew up in this world of ... business?"

"Definitely not naive," Camilla replied.

"And the other one?"

Well ...

Camilla didn't think it was entirely because she grew up inside the suffocating world of Mafiosi, either.

It was something else entirely.

"As long as he loves me, then I don't care about the rest," Camilla said, finally looking up to meet Abriella's gaze. "I never went looking for a man who lives his life on the right side of the law. I never went looking for a man at all. A *good* man found me and something about me was good enough for him. That's all I want to know. It's all I needed to know about Tommaso."

Camilla sighed. "That doesn't mean I went into this blind, or that I'm moving forward with blinders on, either. It just means I know what I signed up for here."

"Do you? Do you know how hard it is to love a man who can be taken away with one misstep—in a single second? Do you know how difficult it is to build a life around a man whose very nature could leave you entirely without because he is not an easy man?"

"I do now," Camilla said.

It was scary.

It was also their life.

"And?" Abriella asked.

"And I still love him."

Once more, Abriella reached across the counter, and patted a floury hand against Camilla's cheek. "I like you, Camilla Donati."

"Do you?"

"It's hard not to."

Tommaso's mother smiled in a way that said she knew something Camilla didn't.

"I can see why he found you," Abriella murmured. Then, louder, she added, "You can stop hiding around the corner, Tommaso. I know you're out there, son."

Sure enough, Tommaso stepped into the entryway of the kitchen. His striking blue gaze fell on Camilla, but his face was blank. No emotion—nothing to give away he had been listening in to their conversation.

She didn't need to see it in his face.

She found it in his eyes.

Questions he had answers to now. Things he hadn't asked her.

Abriella gave Camilla a wink, and a smile. She understood what the woman had known that she didn't. Even men like Tommaso needed reassurance—they simply didn't ask for it. His mother had known he needed something he wasn't going to say he wanted, and so she gave it to him.

Camilla took that as a lesson to learn, and one to keep close. A lesson from a woman who probably understood what she was talking about better than anyone knew.

Joe Rossi was built like a brick shithouse, and his younger brother Cory was just as big. That was the first thing to come to Camilla's mind when she was introduced to Tommaso's cousins.

She was fucking *dwarfed* by them.

Sure, she had to stare up at Tommaso because he was tall, but it would take three of her easily to make one of them.

"You sure she's legal to be in this joint?" Joe asked.

Tommaso gave the older of the two a look. "Is Cory?"

Cory grinned at Camilla, dangerous in a blink. "I'm not legal to be here, either, but I own half the place. No worries."

Joe shook his head. "Don't let her drink, Tommaso. I don't need an underage drinking charge or some shit. I would never get my alcohol license back."

"Can't drink tonight anyway," Camilla said.

She didn't give a reason why, though.

"Lou!" Cory shouted.

The man in question broke through a small crowd of people near the entrance with a wide grin on his face. Camilla looked up at Tommaso, and shrugged.

"Seems he didn't need me to get him in here, huh?"

Tommaso chuckled. "He knew I was fucking with him. Cory is a good friend of his, too."

Camilla figured that one out about five seconds ago.

Lou and Cory greeted each other with a handshake, and a smack on the shoulder. Cory pointed at something across the floor—a secondary bar of some sort, and then gave the rest of them a nod.

"Nice to meet you, Cam," he said. "And Joe, don't be an ass to everyone tonight. The whole point of this business is to keep people *in* the club."

Joe made a noise under his breath, but didn't fully respond. Cory was gone with Lou a couple of seconds later.

"Dad's always telling me to look out for him. Like Cory has got somebody else to worry about coming after him when he's not looking or something," Joe muttered. "Who he's really got to worry about is me kicking his arrogant ass."

"You should meet my brother if you think Cory is arrogant," Camilla said.

Joe passed her a look. "Cross Donati, right?"

Camilla laughed. "Let me guess—"

"The *most* arrogant fucker I have ever met."

"Knew it." Camilla shrugged one shoulder under her tight, black club dress. "Bet you still like him, though, don't you?"

"Cross is ... hard not to like. Or respect."

"It's usually one or the other with him," Tommaso agreed. "Find us later, Joe?"

"Sure, if I have time. Seems someone is going to spend his night showing off, and that leaves me to be the boss of the place."

"Knock it down to him being the younger one, man."

Joe nodded. "*Right*, that's what it is."

Tommaso's hand at Camilla's lower back guided her through the people, and closer to the bar. His gray-blue gaze drifted over her dress, and down to the black heels on her feet. "I did tell you how nice you look tonight, didn't I?"

Camilla scoffed. "Nice?"

"For the moment, I'm keeping this PG, Camilla. Don't push me."

Heat danced through her insides.

"You did tell me, Tom."

With that, she hooked a finger around the tie he wore, and pulled him in for a kiss. The black suit he had put on earlier did *everything good* for his body. It showed off his leanness, gave him that tall, dark, and handsome bit to accentuate.

She loved it.

"Did you have fun with my mother today?" he asked.

"I did."

"That's good." He pressed a kiss to her nose. "I knew she would like you."

Camilla smiled softly. "You could have asked me, you know, about business and how I felt. You didn't have to spy to find out."

Tommaso shook his head. "There is some stuff in this life you just don't ask. You find out one way or the other. This was one of those for me."

"Did you think I knew?"

"Entirely," he replied. "I figured you would have stayed the hell away had you found a problem with it."

"I see," she teased.

Tommaso winked, and tugged on one of her loose waves of hair. Then, he gestured at the wall-length, built-in bar for the club. Behind it, bottles on shelves seemed to dance under the lights and strobes. The bass from the music pumped through the floors, and vibrated Camilla's feet.

"You can drink, if you want," he told her. "Joe was just being a shit."

"You shouldn't encourage underage—"

His hand smacked her ass hard, quieting her. Still, a hot little squeak escaped.

"So much for PG," she told him.

Tommaso shrugged. "I went as long as I could. I make no apologies for anything that happens next."

Camilla's laughter melted into the sound of the music. "No drinking for me tonight, like I said. I have an essay I have to finish when I get back to your place, and then email it in to my professor. That way, I don't have to rush home. I can stay … a few more days."

He glanced down at her. "Really?"

She nodded. "Yeah, Tom."

"What's the essay?"

"Just a correlation between preemie births and lack of prenatal care for poverty stricken women."

"Heavy topic," he said.

"You can help me with big words, or listen to me key it out."

Tommaso leaned down to press a kiss to her head. "You don't need help, but how about I feed you snacks, and make sure you're watered every few minutes."

"Watered?"

"Coffee?"

"Will you switch it to wine when I'm almost done?"

Tommaso patted her ass again. "Whatever you want, babe."

"*Anything* I want?"

His gaze darted down to her as he gestured for the bartender at the same time. "What's your filthy mind getting up to now? I recognize that tone, Camilla. That tone means sex."

He was so right.

"I mean, it's kind of good you know the owners. You probably have a way into the office."

"Jesus Christ."

Camilla wet her lower lip and she looked up to the row of windows on the second level that seemed to be one-way, considering she couldn't see inside. "We could ... watch the show, too. Just not give a show."

Tommaso cleared his throat. "Let me have a drink first."

"Whiskey does taste better on your tongue."

"Bet it tastes divine on your pussy, too."

Camilla smirked. "Probably. Save some to bring with you and we can test that theory out."

CHAPTER SEVENTEEN

THE CLUB'S office door slammed shut, and Tom backed Camilla into it. He kissed a path down the delicate column of her throat, and sucked hard on her pulse point. It left a pretty red mark behind when he finally let go.

Already, his hands were skimming beneath the skirt of her black dress. Smoothing over silky thighs to find the waistband of the thong she wore underneath. He tugged, and she gave a little shimmy of her hips.

That was it.

The thong fell down.

"Should lock the door," she told him.

Tom kissed her stained red lips once more. "No way. Nobody's coming up here."

"They *could.*"

"They won't."

Tom considered lifting Camilla against the door to fuck her, but that hadn't been what she wanted earlier. The desk had a nice view of the one-way windows overlooking the club's floor, but it was too fucking high.

Damn, Joe.

Why did the fucker need such a big desk?

"Too bad you weren't a couple of inches taller," Tom said as Camilla's teeth teased his jawline. "Could have bent you over the desk."

Camilla fake gasped. "Don't point out my shortness, Tom. That's not nice."

His laughter rumbled. "I was just saying."

She waved a hand high. "There's a whole world up there that I don't even know about, okay. Don't rub it in."

He laughed even more.

Camilla gave him a look.

Tom couldn't stop. "Sorry, sorry."

"Do you know August got me a fucking stepstool as a gift when I moved into my apartment?" Camilla glowered at him. "So then I could *reach the cupboards.*"

"That's perfect."

"Stop laughing. This is serious, Tommaso!"

He tried—he really, really did.

The only thing that finally stopped his laughter was a hard kiss from Camilla, and the way her tongue slammed against his with sinful intent. Her hands pushed against his chest, and knocking him back from the door.

He didn't stumble, but he hadn't been expecting the move, either. Still, he managed to grab her as he took the couple of steps backward. He pulled Camilla along with him, dragging her over to the window ledge.

Flipping her around, he shoved her against the ledge. There was one for the window, and a smaller one on the floor. Camilla stepped up on the ledge at the floor, and it gave her just a few extra inches of height. His hand at her neck forced her upper body downward and forward. The side of her cheek rested against the glass, and her skirt rode up to show just a peek of her ass.

Camilla grasped the ledge with the first smack of Tom's palm against her ass. On the second one—a little lower where her ass melted into her thigh—she moaned. For the third, she pushed back against his palm when he slid it between her thighs.

"Christ, you're wet. Like a damn lake down here."

Her laughter came out airless and sweet. "I like it when you spank me."

"Say it again and I'll think about giving you another."

"*Tom.*"

"Say it again, Cam."

Her brown gaze darted over her shoulder to lock onto his. "I like it when you spank me, Tommaso. Give me another, please."

Pleasure and lust jolted through him.

He gave her another three slaps on the other side.

"There, now you match on both cheeks, Cam."

"All pink?"

"Little more red, actually."

She sighed happily. "Warm?"

"Just like your cunt," he said as his fingers slipped back between her thighs. Two of his digits thrust into her pussy, and her inner muscles hugged him tightly. One stroke, and then two. Three, and on the fourth he curled his fingers at her G-spot. The trembling in her legs every time he hit that spot had his grin growing. "You going to come, Cam?"

"You gonna make me?"

"You know it, babe."

It didn't take long at all to give her what she wanted. He was pretty sure thirty seconds was a record for him when it came to making her come, but who knew? At the moment, he was more focused on the sounds she made as she rode his fingers through the first orgasm.

"Holy shit," Camilla mumbled against the glass.

Tom was already using his other hand to undo his pants while the fingers still stuffed up her pussy massaged her G-spot through the orgasm. Her sweet juices slicked up his hand, and the scent of sex clung in the air.

He removed his hand from between Camilla's thighs because he would need two for his next task. Camilla read his mind before he could even reach for the item in his pocket.

"Don't," she said, letting go of the ledge long enough to grasp his wrist. "I'm on the shot—we don't need condoms."

"You sure?" Tom leaned over her a bit to kiss her cheek, and he felt her smile grow. "Because it's fine, Cam."

"I might like the feeling of you coming inside me, Tom. Actually *there*, you know? Wouldn't it make you hot to think about your cum in my pussy when we go back downstairs to dance?"

His thick groan echoed back to his own ears.

Heady.

Loud.

Raw.

"Fuck me, Tom," he heard her say.

Christ.

He couldn't get his slacks down fast enough, or his cock out into his hand quick enough for his needs. He kissed over her shoulder, and the back of her neck, and he fitted himself in behind her. Already hard as hell—painfully so—sliding into her warm, tight channel was heaven to him.

The sweetest relief slipped through his bloodstream with that first thrust.

Like he found home and happiness there.

Sin and love.

A hunger thudded in his ribcage right along with his heartbeat. A deep bass that matched the sounds pumping down on the club's floor. People moved below them while Tom grabbed both of Camilla's hips, and yanked her back into him. Over and over again.

Flashing lights on the ceiling helped to light up the fireworks already starting to burst in his eyes. Camilla's loud cries melted into the music, and drowned in his ears.

The harder he fucked her, the louder she moaned. The deeper his thrusts came, the more she begged.

This woman was *everything* to Tom.

Everything perfect.

Everything beautiful.

"Whose slut are you, Camilla?" he asked in her ear.

That sinful, sly smile curved her lips.

"Yours, Tom."

"And don't fucking forget it, babe."

It wasn't long before she was coming a second time. Tom let go of her right hip to fist a hand in her hair. He tugged Camilla's head back as she shouted his name through her orgasm.

"Beg for my cum, Cam. Tell me how badly you want it. Beg me for it."

She did.

Loud.

Repeatedly.

Hot.

She had been right. The thought of knowing he would be inside her all night long drove him fucking insane. It made him want to get her back to his place, clean her, and then fill her up again.

Tom never came harder in his life than he did at that moment. He'd never had an orgasm so strong—one that damn near brought him to his knees.

So perfect.

Tom cupped Camilla's face in his hands, tipped her head back, and kissed her once. Then a second and third time in quick succession. Her sweet smile grew, and she peered at him through her thick, dark lashes.

"Love you," she said.

"Feel good to know that now?"

Camilla laughed softly. "Yeah, it does."

Cool May air blew around them. People rushed from all directions, probably late and needing to get to their gates.

Tom didn't care. He wasn't quite ready to let go of this woman just yet.

"I might make you late," he warned her.

Camilla flashed her teeth in a grin. "Not too concerned about it."

"Pretty sure you have something coming up for school. A test, or something."

She shrugged. "I could afford to miss it."

"No, you can't."

"Yeah, probably not."

"And your parents might like to see you," he added.

"Yeah, they've called a couple of times."

Tom kissed her once more. "Thank you."

"For what?"

"Coming here. Spending time with me and my family. Keeping an open mind about Chicago."

"That last one was a joke, right?"

"Kind of," he said, "but not really."

Camilla's cheeks pinked in her amusement. "You're terrible."

"Yeah, well … what can you do?"

"I should thank you, too," she said quietly.

"For what?"

"Loving me."

Tom let out a hard laugh. "That was hard not to do, Cam."

"Okay, then … waiting me out, Tom. Giving me time. Letting me figure all this craziness out, and still being here at the end of it all."

"Of course, I'm here, Cam."

She patted his cheek with her warm palm. "So, fair warning. The next time you see me, I'll have mermaid hair."

Tom cocked a brow. "Mermaid hair?"

"Pink at the roots. Purple in the middle. Blue on the tips."

"Huh."

"It'll be nice."

"Mmhmm," he said.

What else could he say?

This woman constantly surprised him.

Camilla poked a finger right in the middle of his chest. "The only acceptable response you can give me when you see it is a compliment, or asking what I plan to do next. Understood?"

Tom gave a single nod. "Got it, babe."

"Do you think you'll be able to come visit soon?"

"I will," he promised. "Not sure when, but I will figure it out."

"And I can come up on some weekends."

"You better."

Camilla winked, and then her amusement faded fast. "We'll figure this out, won't we?"

"Hmm, what?"

"The distance. The space. New York and Chicago. Just … us."

Tom pulled her in for one last kiss—they really were cutting it close, and it was going to take forever for her to get through O'Hare's security. "We will figure it all out one thing at a time, Camilla. It's worth that, isn't it?"

"We're definitely worth it," she whispered.

"Thought so. Go catch your flight."

She hesitated for a second, and he knew that feeling well. Like he didn't want her to leave, but he knew life was set up elsewhere for her. It was things they would have to work on and figure out.

Worth it, though.

"Call me when you get settled," he told her.

Camilla nodded, and her hand tightened around his wrist momentarily. One last kiss between them, and she headed into the departure entrance of the large airport. Tom was left watching her go.

Fuck.

He already wanted her back.

Tom cursed under his breath as a text message rang through the Bluetooth in his ear. A message from his father, it seemed.

Head to my restaurant downtown. I need you for something today.

The guys on the crew were expecting him in less than a half an hour to go over their business for the week. He thought to text his father back and say he was on his way to the warehouse, but didn't bother. A boss was a boss—when a boss called, a man went. It was as simple as that.

Tom pulled an illegal U-turn in the middle of the road when traffic slowed, and hit the gas. He had been closer to the warehouse than the restaurant, but ended up making it in half the time. By speeding, of course. He didn't exactly need a speeding ticket, but it was what it was.

Parking in the employee spot, Tom shut down the Mercedes, and headed for the back of the joint. Tommas never worked at a table, but in a back office where he could have private meetings and whatever else was needed.

Sure enough, Tom found his father sitting behind a large desk. A steaming cup of coffee sat on one side, and a cell phone sat on the other. No paperwork or files like he would usually have. No employee from the restaurant was sitting in the chair.

Just Tommas, Theo, and Damian.

Tom stepped into the office. "You called?"

Tommas smiled. "Did you send Camilla off?"

"An hour ago, or so."

"Already figuring out a way to get to New York, hmm?"

Tom chuckled. "That obvious?"

Smirks passed between the older men, and left Tom out of the loop of what was so amusing. Well, he did know. Him. He was amusing to them because this was the first time they had ever seen him in this sort of ... mindset.

In love.

Tom checked his watch. "I was supposed to be at the warehouse in five minutes to meet the guys and get them set up for the week. If we get this over with, I can still make it in time so that most of them won't have already bailed on me."

"You won't be needing to go to the warehouse."

He looked up, and met his father's gaze. "What?"

"The warehouse—handling the crew, I mean. Not necessary after today."

Tom cleared his throat. "Kind of my job, boss."

He almost said *dad*, but thought better of it at the last second. It was clear this was a business meeting, and not something else.

Respect was needed.

Always.

"Actually, I need an extra pair of hands handling the gunrunning side of the business," Theo said with a shrug. "Mind, you won't be running the guns, but handling the business side of the operation. Handling deals, managing the shipments, and the guys who work in the warehouses."

"Like a new crew," Tommas added.

Tom's gaze drifted between his father, and Theo. "You don't want me running guns, though."

"You're not running them, Tommaso. You're doing something else, but in the same arena. Something better suited to you, son," his father said, leaning back in chair to seem more relaxed. At least, for the moment. "See, you're not like me, or like I was. You're not even like Theo or Damian back when they were young Capos. You're *you*. And I did not take into consideration that we have all treated you far differently than how we were treated. You've learned at a different pace, and your focus shows it. The way you know what is best for the organization, the crew, and you personally shows it, Tommaso."

"Cross has already brought up the fact that he can't handle every aspect of the gunrunning without some additional help. We all know you're suited to it." Theo pushed off the edge of the desk, and waved at hand at Damian. "Besides that, it's about time you start shadowing the underboss, don't you think?"

"It's good business to put men where they work best," Damian added.

"And where they deserve to be," his father said.

Tom liked all of this.

He just had one question …

"What about the crew in the Heights?" Tom asked. "Is Adriano going to step back in, or what?"

Tommas shook his head. "Adriano has been working on building another crew, actually. He's quite good at that—he knows where he does his best work."

"That crew needs a Capo, boss."

"It will have one."

"Who?"

Tommas picked up the cell phone, and held it out to Tom. "Call Lou, son. Have him meet *you*—do not offer more information—at the club Damian likes to work out of. The rest of the Capos have already been notified, and will be arriving at the club anytime now."

Tom glanced down at the phone in his hand, unsure but *happy*. "Got it."

"Lou has one hour to show up. He's not to be one fucking second late, and you are not to tell him what he's been called in for."

Yeah, Tom knew how initiations went.

His had been the same, only he had been made to run errand after errand for his father and uncles for days leading up to it. His had come in the dead of winter, and left him freezing as Capo after Capo threw question after question at him while he stood mostly naked in a cold warehouse.

Lou was going to get his button far easier, it seemed.

Tom was actually grateful for that.

"His time started two minutes ago," Tommas said. "Are you going to be the reason he loses his chance because you're just standing there like a fucking idiot?"

Tom laughed. "Nope."

"Call the man, Tommaso. Now."

"Tom!"

"Tommaso!"

Tom braced for the impact of the tornadoes coming his way. Sara and Rebeka barreled into him full speed, full of laughter and shouts. It didn't matter if he was gone for a day, or a month. His sisters still acted like he was their favorite person in the whole world whenever they saw him again.

"Where's Camilla?" Sara asked.

"Yeah, she coming?" Rebeka added.

Tom bent down on one knee to at least be closer to eye level with the girls. "Cam had to go back to New York, but we'll see her again soon."

Rebeka frowned.

Sara made a face.

"Well, okay," Sara eventually said.

"Hey!" Rebeka shouted.

Tom's eyes widened at the loud volume.

Jesus, his sisters were loud.

"I'm right here," he told her, "you don't need to shout."

And bust my eardrums.

"Ma says the new princess movie is showing." Rebeka preened, pretty as could be. "Will you take us, Tom?"

Both girls smiled.

They knew he couldn't say no when they did that.

"Yeah, I'll take you."

"*Yas!*"

Again, loud.

Tom stood, and put a hand on both girls' bobbing heads. "Let me go talk to Ma for a few minutes, and then we'll go. Okay?"

"Okay," both echoed.

Then Sara said, "Come on, Rebeka. Let's go get ready."

Rebeka happily followed along with her older sister. Despite Tom not growing up with siblings close to his age so that he had a friend, he was happy his sisters had each other. The two looked out for the other, and he hoped that continued on.

Quickly, Tom found his mother.

In her library.

She looked up from the book in her hands at his presence in the doorway.

"Tommaso."

"Hey, Ma."

"Where's your father?"

Tom shrugged. "He's got business to celebrate tonight."

A new made man.

The boss always had to celebrate a new recruit.

Abriella didn't ask questions, simply patted the seat next to her on the leather couch. "Come, sit with me."

"I told the girls I would take them to a movie."

"The princess one?"

"How did you know?" he asked, chuckling.

"They haven't stopped talking about it since I showed them the trailer." Abriella glanced over at him as he sat down. "But that's not why you came over tonight, is it?"

"How did you know?"

His repeated question made his mother smile. She touched his cheek with her fingertips, and then looked back at her book before she set it away.

"I just thought maybe you would come see me today sometime."

"Why?"

"Camilla went home today, didn't she?"

"This morning, yeah."

Abriella nodded. "Something on your mind, Tommaso?"

"Something is always on my mind, Ma."

"Something about *her*, I meant."

"Maybe."

Abriella smiled widely. "Thought so. Over in the desk, you'll find what you're looking for in the top drawer."

Tom gave his mother a look, but stood from the couch and headed for the desk. In the top drawer of the old desk, he found a black velvet ring box. Inside rested his mother's princess cut diamond engagement ring sitting on top of a crown of diamonds. The white gold band gleamed, telling him someone had recently gotten it cleaned.

For a long while, Tom stared at the ring, but said nothing. His mother was the first to speak.

"It's okay not to know *when*, Tommaso."

"Is it?"

"You know her, and that's what matters." Abriella tilted her head to the side as she stared at him, saying, "You're happier, now. Maybe that's what you needed, Tommaso. Maybe that's what you were looking for. Every man needs a good woman in this life. Seems you found yours a little earlier than most."

Tom kept looking at the ring. "I still can't believe you knew I was coming to ask you about this."

Abriella laughed. "Of course, I did, Tommaso. I was the first woman to have ever loved you—you're my boy, and I know you. I know your heart. She gets to be the last woman to love you, though. I'm glad it's her."

Tom crossed the room again, and dropped a kiss to his mother's head. "Love you, Ma."

She reached up and patted his neck tenderly. "Go, and take your sisters to the movie. Say hello to Camilla for me when she calls."

"I will, Ma."

CHAPTER EIGHTEEN

CAMILLA RIPPED open the top of the brown envelope, and took a deep breath. She had no reason to be nervous. There was no reason to think she had failed, or would be staring at bad grades for the final semester. Still, she took her sweet ass time pulling the records out.

She didn't bother peering over the individual class scores, and things that had been included by the professor. No, she went straight to the average—the GPA score.

Three-point-eight.

Camilla grinned.

Yes.

"Well?" August demanded.

Camilla gave her friend a look. "What do you think?"

"You failed."

"August!"

Her friend laughed, and snatched the papers right out of Camilla's hand. She looked them over, and nodded like she hadn't expected to see anything different than what she was looking at.

"I knew it," August said. "Five more years, Cam."

"Maybe four. Who knows?"

"You know. You've always known what you wanted."

Camilla nodded. "True. So hey, you want to hit the diner or something to celebrate? It's the end of May, school is all over, and I have nowhere to be."

August wrapped an arm around Camilla's shoulder with a laugh. "Sounds like heaven, right?"

"Yep."

"Well, I *would* go to the diner, but we should probably hold off just a couple of more minutes."

Camilla's brow furrowed. "What, why?"

"Because someone is coming over."

"Who?"

"Someone."

What was August playing at?

Camilla didn't invite people to her place a lot of the time. It was her space—she liked to keep everybody else's energies out of it.

August *knew* that.

"So hey, now that it's summer, and I finally finished that one-year internship for Bared Brands, what are we doing?" August asked.

Camilla dropped down on the couch, and her friend came with her. The two stared at each other for a long while. "It has been a big year, huh?"

"Busy," August said.

"That, too."

"I just feel like …"

"What, Aug?"

"We should *do* something together this summer. You and me. Maybe go to Europe like we wanted, and then make a trip to the Keys."

"That sounds fucking perfect."

Understatement.

It sounded like a whole bunch of relaxation time that Camilla could really use. Her whole year had been one damn thing after another. August had the best ideas.

"I just want to spend some time with you—one on one," August murmured.

Camilla glanced over at her friend, and her brow furrowed. "I know we've been busy a lot."

"It's not that, Cam."

"Then what is it? I don't understand."

"Chicago," August said quietly. "Tommaso. You're not going to be here forever, and whether you want to admit it or not, you'll leave soon. Except … you won't be coming back. At least not in a couple of weeks, you know?"

A tightening in Camilla's chest ached like nothing else.

She didn't know what to say.

August shrugged, and looked down. "Don't get me wrong, Cam. It's great. *He's* great, and I know he is. I can still be happy and sad at the same time about it."

"Yeah," Camilla said. "I know."

Then, August reached over and squeezed Camilla's hand to make the two look at each other. August was smiling. Camilla was sad.

"I can come visit, right?"

Camilla barked out a laugh. "I'm not even moving down there right now. It's not even a thought in my head for at least a year. I have school and—"

"It'll happen. I can come visit whenever, right?"

"Yeah, Aug. Anytime."

August's smile bloomed wide. "That's all I care about. Free food and board, and I get to consider it a mostly paid vacation."

Camilla rested back on the couch, and laughed loudly. "You almost made me cry, you asshole."

"Psht," August replied. "Says the girl with the heart of ice."

"Not anymore."

At that second, a knock echoed on Camilla's apartment door. Her gaze narrowed as she looked between her grinning friend, and the door.

"Who is it?" she asked.

August shrugged dramatically. "Who knows?"

"Bitch."

"Hey!"

Camilla laughed, and dodged the half-ass slap from her friend as she jumped up from the couch, and passed August by. She gave August a peek of her tongue over her shoulder when she stuck it out. At the same time, she yanked open the door without staring at it, or even checking the peephole.

It might have helped to prepare her heart had she done those things. It might have helped hearing the sound of his voice just a couple of inches away.

It might have helped …

It probably wouldn't have helped at all.

"Someone told me you're on summer break, Camilla."

Tommaso.

She spun around so fast, everything was a blur in her vision. And then her gaze landed on him standing outside her apartment door, and absolutely everything in her life was right again. The world's axis tilted back, and the globe began to spin in the right direction.

It had been too long.

Three weeks since she had seen him last.

Not *really* long.

Still, too long for her.

"Tom," Camilla whispered.

His grin deepened, and turned sexy in a blink. "Hey, babe."

"Surprise?"

Tom nodded. "Surprise. I'm here for the week."

She looked over her shoulder at a slyly smiling August. "Let me guess, this was who you meant?"

"Yep."

"What did you do?"

August looked over her fingernails. "Got his number from your brother, and thought I should finally introduce him properly to the best person to have ever graced your life. I mean, what else?"

194

Tommaso chuckled behind Camilla, and then he came closer. Close enough to press a soft kiss to the spot behind her ear, and make her fucking melt.

"Surprise," he murmured once more.

"Last night when we Skyped, did I tell you how much I loved you?"

"A little."

Camilla turned, and found Tommaso still watching her and grinning in that way of his. She wrapped her arms around his neck, and pulled him in for a hard, fast kiss. Too soon, she was pulling away because of their audience of one. They didn't need to be giving August a show.

"Love you," Camilla said.

Tommaso stroked the pad of his thumb across her whispering lips. "Say it again, Cam."

She did.

Only for him.

Two months later ...

"Happy birthday, happy birthday, happy birthday to you."

Camilla stayed hidden in the shadows of the hallway as her mother and father danced together in the living room. A sweet slow dance that had her mother wrapped in her father's arms as the two swayed to the song. A song her father had been singing to her mother.

The sight was cute enough for her not to intrude. It certainly wasn't the first time she had seen something like this between her parents. Calisto was not the kind of man who hid his affections, but especially not inside his home.

The love her parents shared was the one and only reason Camilla actually believed such a thing existed before she had experienced it herself.

That a man could love a woman so wholly, so entirely, and with everything he was that nothing could ever compare. That he could love her so much, she would become his entire world, and no one else would ever be able to ruin it.

She believed in love because of them.

Now, she knew love was real because of Tommaso.

"Want me to sing it again?" Calisto asked.

Emma's laughter rang out light and sweet. "To what, remind me that I'm getting older by the day, Cal?"

"Never. My beautiful Emma."

Her mother smiled softly. "Mmhmm."

Calisto pressed a kiss to Emma's nose. "Yes, mmhmm. Even when I didn't know, you were still mine, *amore*."

"You are something else."

"You love it, though."

In that moment, so much of Camilla's own characteristics stared back at her. The playful banter. Affection, sweetness, and love.

All of it, really.

Camilla figured—as much as she didn't want to interrupt their moment—she better make her presence known before the two went any further. While this moment was cute and sweet between her parents, she wasn't interested in anything their tones suggested.

She loved her parents, though.

Camilla cleared her throat, and neither of her parents seemed very surprised to see her standing in the entryway. Emma shot her a smile, while Calisto continued hugging his wife.

"Happy birthday, Ma."

Emma preened. "Thank you, baby."

"Tommaso said sorry he couldn't make the party tomorrow."

Calisto finally stepped away from Emma, although not before giving her one more quick kiss. "Did you take him to the airport this morning?"

"Yeah, he got called back to Chicago early."

Camilla tried to keep the sadness out of her tone, and failed miserably. It was what it was.

Emma gave Calisto a knowing look, and then turned back to her daughter. "You weren't supposed to be coming over today. Is something on your mind that you want to chat about?"

"Actually, yeah."

Calisto took his usual place behind her mother when Emma sat down in the chair.

"Go on," her father said.

"I'm considering moving."

Emma raised a single brow. "To Chicago."

It wasn't even a question.

A simple, understanding statement.

But not a question.

"Yeah, to Chicago," Camilla confirmed.

"And when would you consider making this move?" Calisto asked.

Again, there was no surprise to her father's tone. Just like her mother's. As though they had been expecting this from Camilla for a while. Like maybe they had prepared themselves for this conversation.

"Maybe ... a year?" Camilla shrugged, adding, "I could finish out this next year here, and get everything in order. Things like a new school and whatnot."

"Okay," her mother said.

Camilla looked to her dad even though her mother had been the one to talk. "Okay?"

Calisto smiled. "Yeah, okay, Cam."

That was that.

Two months later ...

"What are you looking at over there?" Tommaso asked from the kitchen entryway.

Camilla quickly shut down the laptop, and pushed the brochures aside. "Nothing."

"Mmhmm."

She heard his footsteps echo behind her, and then his fingers weaved into her hair. She tipped her head back to catch his kiss. A familiar rhythm that soothed and burned her from the inside out. At the same time. She never did figure out how he managed to do that to her.

As long as he kept doing it, she didn't care.

"Ma's asking when we're heading to the mansion," Tommaso said.

Camilla peered up at him. "My flight landed two hours ago."

He laughed. "That makes no difference to my mother."

"I thought we were just having dinner over there."

"The girls figured out you were already in town."

Camilla smiled. "They did, huh?"

"Someone let them in on the secret."

"It was you."

Tommaso winked. "It was me, yeah."

She loved Tommaso's little sisters. Sara and Rebeka were two little spitfires. The younger siblings Camilla had never been given in her own life. Every single time she got to spend a few days with the Rossi sisters was like making up for lost time, or something.

Being that she still lived in New York, and him in Chicago, they really only got to be together every so often. Sometimes, he went to her for a weekend, or a week, if he could spare it. Sometimes, she went to him for a few days.

It all had to fall into place to work. Between her schooling, family, and life, and his family, business, and everything else ... it was not a simple thing to simply get together.

It *was* work, sometimes.

Nothing was easy.

Camilla missed Tommaso all the time. The distance often ate away at her with every missed phone call, or *good morning* text message she didn't have time to reply to. Despite how hard it could be, she also knew it was still very much worth the effort.

The love was effortless.

Loving him was so easy.

Anything else was just details.

"We can head over," she told him.

"You don't mind?"

Camilla shook her head. "Nope."

He dropped another kiss to her lips, and then murmured, "You do know that now your five days here are going to be technically half with me, and half with them."

"Pleasure of doing business with you, Tommaso."

His laughter rumbled through the living room.

"Business, huh?"

Camilla shrugged. "Yep."

"Are you coming down with Cross next month when he makes the trip for work?"

"Maybe. Depends on what's happening with school."

Tommaso cleared his throat, and straightened. "Yeah, I guess."

"Probably be last minute, if I do."

"Don't tease me with surprises, now."

Camilla flashed a sexy grin. "I could show up with a trench coat, and nothing else on underneath. Pretty sure the TSA agents wouldn't think it appropriate, but maybe a little flash will—"

His hand still in her hair tugged gently. It was enough to elicit a laugh out of her, and then a squeak when he bent down to kiss her even harder and deeper than before. A kiss that burned her far hotter, and made her wish for something else.

"You better stop that," she whispered against his lips, "or we won't be going anywhere."

"Starting to think that might not be a bad thing."

Camilla patted his cheek, and then pushed him away. She stood from the couch, and gathered the brochures she had been looking over. One fell out of the pile, and Tommaso quickly picked it up. He glanced at it, and then did a double-take.

"Wait, is this—"

Camilla snatched it out of his hand. "It's nothing."

Tommaso stared at her for a long while, silent. "That's a brochure for a nursing school in Chicago, Cam."

"So?"

"You didn't tell me you were looking at schools here."

She fiddled with the edge of the brochures, unsure of how to explain the thoughts running through her head at the moment.

"I just … wanted to look," she said.

"Look, is that all?"

Camilla peered at him through her lashes. "It's inevitable, isn't it? Me moving here, I mean. You're not going to come to New York to live. It's getting harder and harder for us to find time to spend a couple of days together. I don't mind—it's what we have to do, right?"

"Yeah, I know, Cam."

He rounded the couch, and reached for her. In a blink, she found herself wrapped in his comforting embrace. He rested his chin on the top of her head, and she sunk into his hold. Here, nothing was ever wrong. With him, everything was perfect and still.

"You don't have to do anything," Tommaso told her. "Not move here, or start a new school. None of it, Cam. You don't have to do anything for me that you're not ready to do. Okay?"

She nodded.

And loved him even more because of it.

"Maybe I'm not completely ready to let go of New York, but I am ready to start looking."

"Set stuff up, you mean."

"Yep," she said, sighing. "I talked to my parents about it a couple of months back, too. They didn't even seem surprised. Everybody always sees shit coming before I ever do."

Tommaso's chuckles rocked them both. "That's … a little bit true."

"I guess I should finally admit, though, that Chicago is *slightly* better than—"

"*Yes.*"

Tommaso's shout echoed in the house. Camilla's laughter followed right after.

She leaned back in his embrace to look up at him. Cocking one brow, she tried her damnedest not to laugh or smile.

"You're terrible," she said.

"Maybe so, but I won."

"I think you won when you got me."

Tommaso made a noise in the back of his throat. "That, too, but the Chicago versus New York thing was big to me."

She smacked his chest lightly. "Ass."

"Right now, yeah. So, what finally did it for you, Camilla? What made you switch sides?"

Camilla grinned. "What do you think—*who* do you think?"

"Ah."

"Yep, you." She tapped a finger to his lips. "But it's our secret, and if you ever tell anyone, you will die a slow and painful death."

Tommaso returned her grin. "Deal, babe."

"I will hold you to it."

"You better. We could make some time to go around and look at the campuses while you're up here," Tommaso suggested.

Camilla smiled against his chest. "Yeah?"

"Anything, babe."

"Even if that means we'll spend all of our time together visiting family or driving around?"

"Worth the effort," Tommaso told her. "We're worth the effort, Cam."

With him, it definitely was.

It always would be.

EPILOGUE

TOM TUGGED on the sleeves of his suit jacket, and shifted on the chair for the fifth time. This whole meeting shouldn't be a big deal—he had been waiting for what seemed like forever and a day for this moment.

He was beyond *ready*.

Yet, he fidgeted.

"Stop bouncing around like that," his father said to him, adding a severe look to make his point. It only worked for a second, and then he was back to fidgeting all over again. "Why are you so nervous, Tommaso?"

"Don't really know," he admitted.

"Give him a break," Damian said from the other side of the table while he looked at the screen of his phone. "I think it's normal, all things considered. Joe damn near paced a hole in the floor when he had to talk to Lucian. Didn't seem to matter how many times I told him Lucian actually *liked* his dumb ass. There he was, pacing back and forth for a good hour or more."

"Yeah, cut him some slack," Theo agreed. "It's not like any of us understands how this feels for him. We never had to ask for this kind of thing way back when. I imagine it's enough to make him want to puke."

"All right," Tom said, "if we're going to start talking about our feelings and walking down memory fucking lane, I am out."

The other men at the table ignored him completely. Not that he was surprised when they continued on with their conversation like he hadn't even said anything at all.

"We only didn't have to ask because they were all dead," his father said.

"Lucky you, Tommas," Damian replied. "Mine was arranged, so my choice was do it, or die."

"You say that like you don't love my sister to death," Theo said, smirking.

"No, I love Lily. We were the lucky ones in that way."

"No, Alessa and I were the lucky ones back then." Adriano flashed a smile from the far end of the table. Tom was convinced his uncle's only reason for coming to the meeting was to watch him squirm. "And you know what, now that I think of it, Theo kind of asked. Not my dad, I mean. He was dead. Me, though. He asked me."

"Did I?" Theo asked.

"More told than asked, but I respected it just the same."

Tommas looked to Tom, and shrugged. "My apologies, son. Apparently, you can be nervous. What the fuck do I know?"

Tom stared up at the ceiling and wished it would swallow him whole. He didn't think that was asking for very much, considering. Right?

"It'll be over before you know it," his uncle said.

"And easier than you're making it out to be," his father added.

"Please, shut up," Tom muttered.

Chuckles echoed back from the men surrounding him at the table. Really, Tom didn't mind their jokes even if he did pretend otherwise. There were the men whose feet he had grown up under. These were the men who had guided him through every milestone in his life, and put him on the proper paths when he had lost his way.

He supposed, in a way, it made sense for them to be here for this milestone, too.

People passed by the front windows of the restaurant, distracting Tom for the moment. The men at the table went back to chatting with his father, but he wasn't paying them much attention. He was too lost inside his own head to care.

It took his father touching his shoulder to finally break Tom from the daze. Tommas gave him a knowing smile.

"He won't refuse you," his father said. "You know that, right?"

"Do I?"

"What reason would he have to refuse you, Tommaso?"

"The same reason any father with a daughter might refuse, Dad."

Tommas shook his head. "He knows you're a good man. You're worrying for nothing, son. He likes you."

Tom laughed dryly. "So?"

"He has probably known this was coming for a while now."

"Aren't all fathers the same?"

"How so?" Tommas asked.

"They find their daughters hard to let go."

"You're overthinking this, son."

"She was always his, Dad."

"Not when she became yours, Tommaso."

"New restaurant?" Calisto asked.

Tommas nodded. "It is, actually."

The Donati boss shook hands with Tom's father. Tommas waved at the open chairs waiting at the table for Calisto and the men he had brought along with him to sit. Behind the man, his underboss and consigliere waited for the greetings to finish.

Cross, still relatively new to being his father's underboss, nodded to Tom. Wolf Puzza—Calisto's consigliere—kept his attention on the meeting bosses.

"Sit, Cal," Tommas said with another wave.

Once everyone was seated at the table again, Calisto's gaze turned on Tom. "There's a very young Capo at the table today. Any particular reason for that?"

Tom's father laughed under his breath before replying, "The title is a matter of semantics for Tommaso, now. I've learned that my son doesn't quite fit the position. He does his best work for me elsewhere."

Calisto's gaze drifted toward Cross with a knowing nod. "Yes, they do have a way of surprising us like that. Don't they?"

"Seems so." Tommas waved a hand, and added, "Besides, Tommaso has agreed to begin shadowing Damian. One of the reasons he's sitting in on this meeting between our syndicates today."

"Already mentoring with your underboss," Calisto said, his tone offering nothing as to how he felt about that.

"Do you think he's too young for it?"

Calisto gestured to his own son. "I think some men are simply a better fit for the position, regardless of their age."

"Me, too," Tommas agreed. "Business, then?"

A single nod passed between the bosses; business was the first tall order of the day. At least one hurdle for the meeting was over. Tom could once again thank God for small miracles. Had Calisto been uncomfortable with Tom's presence at the meeting, he would have had every right to ask Tommas to make his son leave.

It was a test of sorts from Tommas. As far as Tom knew, his father was testing the waters with other syndicates regarding a far younger underboss readying to have a say in the Chicago Outfit. Mafia politics were what they were. Sure, Tom hated them most of the time, but they were still needed at the end of the day.

Tom stayed quiet—like he had been directed to by his father—as the business connections between the Donati Cosa Nostra and Chicago Outfit were discussed. All standard, usual things that continued to keep the peace between their respective organizations. Some upcoming deals that involved money for both families. More politics, but Tom found like this, he didn't mind them so much.

He didn't need to prove his worth.

He already had.

Before long, the meeting was coming to an end, and the Donati men stood to leave. After all, it was never a good thing for two organizations to gather together in the same place for too long. Feds took notice, and nobody wanted their picture on yet another corkboard in some suit's office.

All over again, with a single look from his father, Tom's nerves kicked into overdrive.

Now or never.

"I don't think there's anything else, is there?" Calisto asked.

"Tommaso has something to ask, I believe," Tommas said, looking to Tom.

All eyes turned on him.

Tom's mouth went dry.

Fuck.

"Well, what is it?" Calisto asked.

Tom spoke even though it felt like his heart was thumping hard enough in his throat to make him puke. "Camilla."

"What about my daughter?"

He was acutely aware of all the other men staring at him in that moment. None of them were strangers to him except for the Donati underboss, yet it still felt like it. He was beginning to think he should have done this in a more private setting.

"Tommaso," Calisto pressed, "what about Cam?"

Just spit it the fuck out, man.

Tom did just that. "I want to ask Camilla to marry me, and I would really like your blessing to do it."

There, he said it. Now, it was out in the open. No taking it back. His nerves started to ebb a bit. Not a whole lot, though. He still hadn't gotten a reply from Calisto, after all.

The silence stretched on while Calisto and Tom continued their staring contest. Someone cleared their throat, and Calisto finally glanced down at the table, breaking the tension.

"You don't need to ask me for that, Tommaso," he said.

"But I wanted to," Tom replied.

"What I said remains the same."

"Cal," Tom's father said, "all he's asking for is—"

"I know what he's asking for," Calisto interjected as his sharp gaze cut to Tommas. "He doesn't need to ask for it at all."

"Because you won't give him your blessing, or ...?"

Calisto looked back to Tom once more. "Tom thinks I don't know about a lot of things. He thinks I don't know about what he did to a man inside the office of a club when said man insulted my daughter. He didn't even think about defending her—if it was wrong, or not his place—he just did it. At that time, Tom barely knew Camilla at all. He still did it, though. And, while some might be angry with him for killing a man, and not coming to me with the information, he did what he was told by my son. Something else I appreciate for too many reasons than I care to name at the moment."

Tom looked to Cross, questioning silently. He had been unaware that his friend chose to share that information with Calisto. Cross only shrugged.

"He thinks I don't know," Calisto said, glancing back to Tom's father, "how Camilla can be, and how difficult and wonderful she is. He thinks I don't how he waited her out because despite her restless heart, she was worth it."

Calisto shrugged, adding, "I wish she still danced as much as she did when she was little, and that she still needed me as much as she used to. I wish she would travel more, see the world, and let life figure out the rest for her as she goes. Maybe I would have chosen a million different paths for my daughter, but these are the ones she has chosen for herself. *He* is the one she has chosen.

"So yes," Calisto murmured with a smile. "He thinks I don't know about a lot of things, but I do. I *know*. Tommaso does not need to ask for something from me that he already has."

Tom cleared his throat, but stayed quiet.

"What was it that I told you when you first approached me about Camilla, Tom?" Calisto asked.

He didn't even have to think about it. Not really.

"You don't make those kinds of choices for Cam because you love her."

Calisto ticked a finger in Tom's direction. "Exactly that. Don't ask me for something you already have. Although even if I did want you to ask me, you should already know, I think you have very much earned my blessing."

"Where are we going?" Camilla asked.

"For a drive," Tom replied.

"I didn't come to Chicago for the weekend to spend a whole day driving around, Tom."

He shot her a look. "Be nice, Cam."

She grinned right back. "I think you like me better when I'm kind of nasty, though."

"Depends on the kind of nasty, babe."

He squeezed her thigh high under her skirt. She laughed, but didn't bat his hand away.

"Are you planning on doing something between my thighs, or …?"

Tom winked. "Later, yeah."

"Boo, you suck."

"You're distracting, and I need to keep both of us alive at the moment."

"Mmhmm."

She moved Tom's hand even higher under her skirt, eliciting a thick groan from him when damp cotton met his fingertips.

"Killing me here," he told her.

Camilla pushed his hand away with one of her teasing little laughs. "You better make it up to me later."

"You know it."

"So I seriously can't do *anything* to convince you to tell me where we're going?"

The suggestive tone in her words couldn't be missed. Sweet Jesus, this woman was something else.

"You're pure filth, Camilla."

She smiled wickedly. "I know."

"Stop trying to bribe me with sex. It won't work."

She sighed. "You could at least indulge me to make the time pass by faster."

"Do I look fucking stupid to you? I know exactly where indulging you leads us."

Camilla didn't even deny it.

"Plus," he added quickly, "we're almost there."

"Oh?"

"Yep. So shut your pretty mouth, and behave for ten more minutes."

Her pout damn near had him yanking the car over to the side of the road. He could have given her something to really pout about then. He bet his girl would still like it, and beg for a hell of a lot more.

Tom chose not to tell any of that to Camilla because he knew exactly where that would lead them to, as well. She would take it as a challenge, and before he knew it … sex it would be. Maybe the two of them were just predictable in that way, but he still loved it.

Still, he had shit planned for them today. He intended to get it all done regardless of how good a roadside fuck—or even road-head—sounded.

"You just … sit there."

Camilla rolled her eyes. "And *behave.*"

"And that."

"I'll remember you told me that later."

"You are due for a hard fuck and a nice red ass."

Camilla preened. "Promise to put your silk ties to good use, too, and I'm in."

Yep.

Pure filth.

Tom hadn't lied. They arrived at their destination in a little under ten minutes. The brand new gated Melrose Park community was just beginning to be filled with newly built homes. Expensive, beautiful two- and three-level homes on sprawling acreages. Tucked away in Melrose Park, the community was removed from the bustle and noise, but still close enough that it wasn't a long trip for work or otherwise.

There were still several lots in the community for purchase, as far as Tom knew, but they were getting picked up fast. All in all, the community would hold thirty homes on a grandeur scale. One of the many benefits of having money.

Camilla perked up in the passenger seat of Tom's Mercedes. She peered out of the window as they passed one home with humongous marble stairs leading to an even grander entrance of a three-level home.

"Where are we?" Camilla asked.

"Cornerstone Park," Tom said. "An up and coming gated community inside Melrose. Anyone making less than a couple of million a year is not a good fit."

"Meaning they can't afford it?"

"Yeah."

"Are we visiting someone, or something?"

"Or something," he replied.

Camilla shot him a look, but Tom only winked in response. They continued driving until Tom came to the very last lot in the community. One that toted the rawest acreage at a total of four.

Tom pulled the car over. "Do you want to go for a walk with me?"

"To do what, Tom?"

"Look around, I guess."

"At what, *trees?*"

He laughed. "City brat."

"Hey, I did grow up in Newport, thanks."

"My bad."

"Mmhmm. And don't forget it."

Tom chuckled, and turned off the engine. "Get out of the damn car,

Cam."

He exited the vehicle, and rested his arms on the roof while Camilla peered around once she too was out of the car. She bent down to pick up a couple of wildflowers growing just beyond the newly poured sidewalk.

Tom used her momentary distraction to grab an item out of the back of the car. He palmed the large blue tube, and shifted it from one hand to the other as he rounded the car.

Camilla glanced over her shoulder at him, and spied the item. "Is that … blueprints?"

"Maybe. Care to look inside for me?"

Tom offered the two foot long tube to her. Camilla cocked a single brow high as she plucked the tube from his outstretched hand. She cracked the seal open on the one end, and tipped the tube over to pull out the brand new set of blueprints that had been safely stored inside. Keeping one curious eye on him, she quickly unraveled the blueprints.

He waited, silent and still, as Camilla looked over the document. Plans for a three-level monster of a home. One with marble pillars supporting an overly large entrance, over-sized rooms made for royalty, and a grandiose foyer with not one, but two spiraling staircases leading to the upper levels of the home. Ten bedrooms. Twelve bathrooms. A six-door garage, and an indoor pool.

"Wow," Camilla said. "This looks amazing, Tom."

"You think?"

"Yeah, for sure. I love it. When did you have these done up?"

"A couple of months ago."

After he spoke with her father at that business meeting, he grabbed up the last lot when his father brought the new community to his attention. He had put a rush on the building plans.

Tom wanted to show Camilla something tangible about their future, and that he wanted one with her.

Camilla turned around so that her back was facing Tom. She glanced between the spread out blueprints in her hands, and the raw land up ahead.

"Did you pick a spot for the house, yet?" she asked.

Tom strolled forward, and pulled another item from his inner jacket pocket. Keeping the small box hidden from Camilla's view as he joined her side, he gestured to the far side of the lot where a small stake was sticking up. It had been painted bright orange so it was easy to see.

"Over there, actually."

"Why there?"

"Because then our bedroom windows will face the rising sun in the morning. I know you like morning light when you're getting ready for the day, and whatnot."

Camilla turned to him with a question burning in her brown eyes, but

Tom was already kneeling to the ground. Her gaze darted fast between his grin, and the black velvet box he had popped open. Resting in the middle of his palm, the box held his mother's engagement ring. The three carat princess cut diamond rested on a crown of smaller diamonds on top of a white gold band.

"I know things are crazy sometimes, and we're busy a lot," Tom said.

Camilla sucked in a shaky breath. "A little bit, yeah."

"But I think you also know that changes nothing for me and you. Whether it's now, or ten years from now, I'm going to want the same thing for us."

"We always find a way, don't we?"

"We do."

Camila waved a single hand over her face. "Don't you dare make me cry, Tommaso."

"Not your style, huh?"

"Nope."

Except her eyes were welling with unshed tears, and she was damn close to letting them start falling down her cheeks.

"Marry me, Camilla. Be my wife. Give me forever."

"You didn't even have to pose it as a question. You already knew, Tom."

"Indulge me, Cam."

"Yes, I'll marry you," she whispered.

His lips were on hers before she had even finished her sentence. He made sure to quickly wipe the few tears that had escaped from her eyes away because like she said … crying just wasn't her style. Even if they were happy tears.

He could have done some grand show, or made a bigger speech out of the whole thing, but that wasn't *his* style. His love for Camilla wasn't for others to indulge their need for a happy ending, and this had been a long time coming.

Love didn't like to wait.

Their love had taught him that.

Six months later …

"It's a shame we couldn't have had the wedding in Chicago."

"Ma," Tom said, giving his mother a side-long look to quiet her.

Tommas chuckled as he passed his wife by in the church's private room. "Don't start with that old whine again today, Ella. It's the bride's day, and you know it. You will have your own brides to throw the biggest weddings for in Chicago someday."

Abriella clicked her tongue and rolled her eyes upward. "I was just saying. Then maybe more of our family could have been here for Tommaso."

"And then where would that have left Camilla's family?" his father asked.

"Well ..."

"Exactly," Tommas said when his wife couldn't come up with a suitable answer. "This is the young woman's last day living in New York— her last day of being able to wake up, and know her family is just a short drive away in any direction. I think bending to her one wish of having the wedding here is not such a big deal at the end of the day."

Tom's mother sighed, but still smiled. "No, I guess not."

"You're tying that wrong, Tommaso."

He grumbled under his breath at his father's correction. Tommas pretended like his son hadn't said a word as he came over to fix the knot on Tom's tie.

"It's not *wrong*," Tom said, "just crooked."

His father glanced at him curiously as he worked the light gray silk into a perfect, straight knot. "You know how to tie one of these."

He did.

He was just ...

Fumbling.

Jittery.

Stumbling.

Stuttering.

"Ah," his father said like he could read Tom's mind. "You know, on the morning I married your mother ..." Tommas trailed off, and placed his hands to his son's shoulders. "I put my shoes on the wrong feet twice. I also suddenly forgot how to tie my laces. Damian saved the day for me, and never spoke about it again."

"You never told me about that," Abriella said from the other side of the room.

Tommas never looked away from his son. "Abriella was the one thing I was most sure of in my life, and there I was on our wedding day ... fumbling like an idiot because of my nerves."

Tom laughed, and some of the edginess bled away. His father patted his cheek, and gave him a nod.

"I'm proud of you, son."

"Are you?" he asked.

"Of course. How could I not be?" Tommas chuckled, saying quickly, "Oh, sure, you made some things difficult for me these past couple of years, but you taught me important things, too. About being a good boss, and a good father. I love you, my boy. My blood, huh?"

Tom nodded. "Yeah, Dad."

Tommas let him go, and checked his watch. "Shit, Ella. We've got thirty minutes to make sure the girls are finished getting ready, and take our places."

"Oh, calm down. Not everything is a rush, Tommy." Abriella stopped at Tom's side to cup his jaw in her hand, and kiss his cheek. "I love you, Tommaso. You did well with her. You know that, don't you?"

"Of course, Ma."

Abriella winked, and patted his cheek harder than his father had. "And don't you forget it."

How could he?

Tom's whole life had been spent watching his parents together, and loving. An exceptionally strong man, and an equally strong woman who lived their love honestly, and openly. It had been them who taught him that the tough, difficult women were the ones most worth loving. They made life fun.

"Come on, Ella," his father said, waving at the now opened door.

"You're so impatient," Abriella muttered as she left her son's side.

"Yeah, yeah."

"And why didn't you tell me about our wedding day? Don't think I forgot just because five minutes passed, either."

"Oh, my God, Ella," his father groaned as the two headed into the hallway. "You don't need to know everything."

"Yes, I do, Tommy! Every little last *thing*."

"You're ridiculous. I hope you know that."

"Yes, and who made me this way?"

Tom shook his head, and walked over to close the door. It drowned out the bickering of his parents. Still, their pseudo argument comforted Tom, and reminded him of years gone by. It also helped to settle the last of his nerves.

He was back in front of the mirror to tuck in the matching pocket square, and straighten the cufflinks on his sleeves. It wouldn't be long before someone came to get him to help settle his over-excited sisters before they had to make their appearance down the aisle. Even though that's where his parents had been headed to deal with the girls, Sara and Rebeka likely wouldn't calm down until it was Tom talking to them, and explaining one more time why this day was so important for him.

A knock on the private room door took his attention away from the mirror momentarily. Seemed like he wasn't going to get any time alone, apparently.

"Just a minute," he called out.

Tom's gaze went back to the mirror. Whoever it was behind the door didn't want to wait, as they just opened it right up and slipped inside.

He froze as the most beautiful woman wearing the most amazing dress slid into the room. Camilla shot him a grin as she closed and locked the door behind her. His gaze traveled down over the ivory-colored, lace mermaid-style gown she wore.

It was the very first time he was seeing the dress she had picked for their day. It fit her like a glove—hugged every single one of her curves perfectly, and made his mouth dry at the sight. Capped sleeves, a modest bodice, and a *very* low-cut back.

She had lost the mermaid hair about a month ago, and went to a brown shade that she swore was as close to her natural color as she could remember. The wild, messy curls had been swept up in a high up-do for their day.

He wondered how long the brown would last.

Her makeup had been done up in that same edgy way, too, with crystals along the cut line of her brow, and dark kohl on her eyes. Today, though, she wore a lighter color lipstick.

Tom turned away from the mirror as he finally gained enough bearings to talk again. "What are you doing in here, Cam?"

She shrugged as she strolled across the room. "I finally got to sneak away from August for five minutes. She's a fucking tyrant."

"She's your Maid of Honor. It's her job to keep you, and everyone else, in line and on time today."

"Yeah, well, I've got maybe ten minutes before she figures out where I went. So, let's make this quick, Tom."

"Quick—what?"

She grabbed for him, and pulled him in for a kiss. The kind of kiss that made his dick hard, and a groan fighting its way out of his chest. It left no room for question about what she wanted. Hell, he could taste the promise of sex on his tongue.

"You didn't think I was going to wait forever to see you in your tux, and then wait until tonight to get you the fuck out of it, did you?"

Tom laughed. "I'm not surprised, no. You look …"

Camilla blinked up at him. "What, Tom?"

"So beautiful, babe."

Her smile bloomed wide and sinful. "Don't ruin my makeup, and make it quick but good, okay?"

"I'll take that challenge."

They were five minutes late for their wedding.

Her makeup was fine and they were still out of breath when they took their places. Laughter rumbled through the pews when someone said they were found together in an upstairs room.

It was worth it.

ACKNOWLEDGMENTS

So much love and thanks to the following people who got me through this book, and the processes that came after it:

The ladies who proofread. Eli, for editing. Jay, for the beautiful cover. Sasha for cheering me on, and Sunny for getting a copy just to get a copy and squeal about it.

Honestly, you ladies make this job worth doing most days.

To my lovely readers: I thought you might like something a little less heavy to break up the heavy that was the *Cross + Catherine* series and the upcoming *John + Siena* duet. Tom and Cam were certainly like a break, I think. Easy … effortless.

Hugs, love.

More is always coming soon.

Bethany-Kris

ABOUT THE AUTHOR

Bethany-Kris is a Canadian author, lover of much, and mother to four young sons, one cat, and three dogs. A small town in Eastern Canada where she was born and raised is where she has always called home. With her boys under her feet, a snuggling cat, barking dogs, and a spouse calling over his shoulder, she is nearly always writing something ... when she can find the time.

Find Bethany-Kris at:
Her website www.bethanykris.com or on Facebook at
www.facebook.com/bethanykriswrites on her blog at
http://www.bethanykris.com/blog or on Twitter - @BethanyKris.

Sign up to Bethany-Kris's New Release Newsletter here:
http://eepurl.com/bf9lzD.

OTHER BOOKS

Cross + Catherine

Always
Revere
Unruly

Guzzi Duet

Unraveled, Book One
Entangled, Book Two

DeLuca Duet

Waste of Worth: Part One
Worth of Waste: Part Two

Standalone Titles

Effortless
Inflict

Donati Bloodlines

Thin Lies
Thin Lines
Thin Lives
Behind the Bloodlines
The Complete Trilogy

EFFORTLESS

Filthy Marcellos

Antony
Lucian
Giovanni
Dante
Legacy
A Very Marcello Christmas
The Complete Collection

Seasons of Betrayal

Where the Sun Hides
Where the Snow Falls
Where the Wind Whispers

Gun Moll Trilogy

Gun Moll
Gangster Moll
Madame Moll

The Chicago War

Deathless & Divided
Reckless & Ruined
Scarless & Sacred
Breathless & Bloodstained
The Complete Series

The Russian Guns

The Arrangement
The Life
The Score
Demyan & Ana
Shattered
The Jersey Vignettes

Find more on Bethany-Kris's website at www.bethanykris.com.

www.ingramcontent.com/pod-product-compliance
Lightning Source LLC
Chambersburg PA
CBHW072354020726
47506CB00004B/1113